$\mathcal{V}$OICES OF THE $\mathcal{S}$OUTH

# THE LAST
# OF THE SOUTHERN GIRLS

# THE
# LAST
# OF THE

# SOUTHERN
# GIRLS

## by WILLIE MORRIS

LOUISIANA STATE UNIVERSITY PRESS    Baton Rouge

Copyright © 1973 by Willie Morris
Originally published by Alfred A. Knopf
LSU Press edition published 1994 by arrangement with the author
All rights reserved
Manufactured in the United States of America
11  10  09  08  07  06  05  04  03  02
10  9  8  7  6

Library of Congress Cataloging in Publication Data

Morris, Willie.
    The last of the Southern girls.

    I. Title.
PZ4.M8795Las  [PS3563.08745]  813'.5'4  72–11040
ISBN 0-8071-1956-3

The paper in this book meets the guidelines for permanence and durability
of the Committee on Production Guidelines for Book Longevity of the
Council on Library Resources. ∞

To Marian Weaks Morris

with gratitude and love

and to my friend Ed Yoder

There was nothing that was worth going far to get: all was lies. Every smile concealed a yawn of boredom, every joy a misery. Every pleasure brought its surfeit; and the loveliest kisses only left upon your lips a baffled longing for a more intense delight.

—*Madame Bovary*, GUSTAVE FLAUBERT

# AUTHOR'S NOTE

A writer's life, the totality of it, is at best bizarre, and at worst horrendous. There are human reasons for this. You live through each book, and each book in signal retrospect represents and evokes for you the particular period in which you wrote it, the especial tribulations and compulsions of, as the Nixon people said, that point in time.

That is why most writers choose, whenever possible, to forget the books they've written, because each takes a specific piece out of you, a big chunk of your own personal history. It is reported that William Faulkner, among others, always got the drunkest between books.

When I wrote *The Last of the Southern Girls,* mostly alone and in a drab and snowy wintertime in an old house near the Atlantic on eastern Long Island, I was severely discombobulated. A few of my trustworthy comrades thought me momentarily deranged. I had recently left my crowning ambition at the time, the editorship of a venerable national magazine, in a notable and embittered editorial dispute. My beloved black Lab, Ichabod H. Crane, whom I had kidnapped from my ex-wife in New York City, had just been run over by a truck, and I had had to bury him myself on the banks of a frozen inlet named Wainscot Pond, pronouncing at the grave in solitary bereavement the words from *The Episcopal Book of Common Prayer* (1928 version) on the Burial of a Child.

In addition, I was broke. I contracted with Robert Gottlieb, the head man at Knopf and one of the most talented editors in New York, famous as the editor of such books as *Catch-22,* to write a love story. The love tale itself, I must confess at this late date, had palpable antecedents. Not only had my dog died, my relationship with a beautiful, complex, Washington, D.C., celebrity whom I loved had culminated, too.

Some people who subsequently read the book said I had undergone some sort of odd psychic breakdown. Others observed that my words, which had apparently seldom failed me, had certainly done so now. As I recall, one of the few favorable reviews was by Jonathan Yardley in the *New Republic*, and some said he, too, had taken temporary leave of his inmost senses. Jon Yardley, I note, would later win a Pulitzer for his book reviewing, but one surmises he was callow then.

As such things happen in America, the book made more money by far than anything else I've ever written, before or since. It got me through alimony, child support, and the school bursar. There was a substantial Hollywood option, with a screenplay by Mart Crowley and Dominick Dunne, whom I met in a mansion in the Bahamas on profligate tinsel-land expenses to confer, and I was later told the Beverly Hills poobahs came within a breath of filming it, with Faye Dunaway in her bedazzled prime as the heroine.

As for me, I haven't reread the book since what was then called galley proofs. I still get occasional letters about the pages on the childhood and adolescence of Carol, later the Chi Omega at Ole Miss, in her Arkansas village, and on the textures of our nation's capital in that epoch, and on the hazards of headstrong love, and these letters are invariably kindly and exalting. I'm also brushed with dark ambivalent wisps of memory and emotion, about myself and the girl Carol, back when you could call a woman a girl and get away with it, and about Washington in the sixties and seventies, for any book has the writer's surreptitious scars on it in perpetuity. Unlike members of various modern-day professions, a writer more than most others must be left forever with what he did do, or didn't.

W. M.
Jackson, Mississippi
May, 1994.

# THE LAST
# OF THE SOUTHERN GIRLS

# 1

Her friends and enemies had been wondering what would become of her. She had lived in Washington for twelve years. They asked themselves if she intended to remain its *enfant terrible* for the rest of her days. Most of the women disliked her and were jealous of her, for good reason. Most of the men lusted for her but were somewhat obsequious before her, for better reason still. Washington in the age when American omnipotence had had its day was exceedingly contradictory, yet those who were mystified by it, or perhaps frightened by it, seldom recognized that its vast bureaucratic mazes and the tangled actualities of its institutional power disguised the most ingenuous simplicity. It had all the illusions of a large city, compounded by the sources and appurtenances of national authority which gave it its character. Yet strip off these layers and there, for any outsider to see, lay the quintessential American small town. It was one of the few capitals of the world that was not the most interesting place in its country, like Bern, perhaps, The Hague, Canberra, *Brasília!* There were many causes of this, the

Southern founders for a beginning, and the very act of compromise which brought it into being, but at the heart of it,
certainly, was its especial political nature and the dire transience of our politics. It was a large city but not a truly com-
munitied one, being as it was and always had been a kind of
national waystation, a least common denominator of a dis-
parate society; it was the capital of a great modern power
but the practitioners of that power, as they knew best of all,
were impermanent residents, susceptible to the arcane pre-
dilections of our people. So that in the best echelons of its
society the truly permanent citizens—the politicians who
managed to stay on year after year, the journalists and the
columnists and the television personalities, the lawyers and
businessmen with the most fruitful connections, the most
entrenched and powerful of the civil servants, the foreign
service officers, three or four dozen key foreigners, the retired
diplomats and statesmen and respectable hangers-on—were
not a very large group at all. Practically everyone in this community knew everyone else. The outsider also usually forgot
that, numerically, Washington was essentially a black city,
with narrowing white enclaves scattered throughout. With
the inexorable movement to the tranquillity of the outlands,
so expressive of what America had become in her day, the
old aspiring federal city outside these enclaves of modern
high-rises and the more settled places was a maw of bureaucracies and tenements. So in describing a fixed white
society in our most chameleon of American metropolises, one
must keep in mind a small threatened island.

Its political character and small town ambience gave an
unusual quality to the nature of its talk, exacerbated in the
1960's by an ill-tempered restiveness owing to the saddest of
our many wars. Its people seemed not to take language seriously. In this regard the political melted into the social in

ways that were childish and destructive. *They seemed not to understand the consequences of words.* They babbled away to anyone about anything, principally about each other. Words should have real weight for intelligent members of the species, who must perceive by now that they can evoke and titillate and inspire and damage and delude as effectively as actions, yet language in this locale seemed somehow off at the edges of perception. The most rapt confessionals between friends, the most desultory persiflage between confidants, entered the public domain swiftly, circling and gyrating and eventually returning home. One is not speaking here so much of conventional gossip but of the whole illusory, circuitous, and benighted trajectory of human talk when talk has little root or foundation. Not that Washington was not princely ground for the more mundane gossip, for indeed it was—unlike Manhattan Island in those years, which was too colossal and fragmented for gossip to have much more blood and ooze in it than the quip. But when words and their consequences meant nothing, and when everyone talked to everyone about everyone else, and when the dimensions of the permanent community within the larger metropolis remained relatively contained and homogeneous, one tended finally to become confused, perhaps, about truth and fantasy, about sympathy and malice, about friendship and enmity. And what, pray, must all of this have done to the nature of privacy? How could the privacy of the soul acquit itself against that most underestimated of human sins? For that sin, after all, was *calumny.*

THIS WAS THE MILIEU in which Carol Hollywell, née Templeton, a Southern debutante from the Mississippi River town of De Soto Point, Arkansas, had grown from girlhood into

maturity. They talked of her incessantly and she, being a
child of this most unusual city, talked also of them. In a
town, so Southern in character, where females were then
such appendages to ambitious husbands and where the more
independent seethed under this inferiority, where society
was ordered for males and the urges of their politics—a
place of powerful men, and women they married when they
were young, Mrs. Holmes said axiomatically, of hostile wives
whose men had vanished long before into the toils and
sweats and circumlocutions of their calling—she was both
unattached, being a divorcée for two years, and outspoken.
When she first met people, she talked with them as if she
had been familiar with them and their kin for a very long
time. Her eyes in such moments moved constantly, and so
did her lips; her whole being, indeed, hummed with motion.
She could be charming, fine-humored, and inexhaustibly
garrulous, but still she was a girl of immediate caprices:
swift to act, often perhaps a little too swift, and swifter yet
to anger. There was a large strain of design and crudeness in
her; chaos, commotion, and even emotional calamity often
followed in the wake of her tempestuous pride, and her life
unfolded from one crisis to the next, at first with a deft, his-
trionic aplomb, as if she could only survive on catharsis. But
all this coexisted with a loveliness and grace, for an aura of
romance and beauty surrounded her, there was a rare electricity to her movements, she seemed touched with gold, and people would stare at her in the streets or in the restaurants, not
just because of this radiance, but something more: the good
juices and spirits of life which encompassed her, her elegance and proud defiance. These strangers when touched by
this magnetism might sense that she was fully observant of
herself, and that she viewed herself with an unusual regard.
At an election party one year, for instance, where she fol-

lowed the men into a paneled library on Foxhall Road for brandy, leaving the women to dwell on her audacity, three United States Senators stood in a corner watching the election results on television. She was conversing quietly with the Secretary of Commerce, on whose right she had sat at the expensively catered dinner and who had been so entranced with her candid observations that his wife had watched him quizzically from across the room, when the three Senators burst into exuberant shouts. "What on earth is it?" she asked one of them. "*Claiborne's been re-elected!*" he replied, for Senators, as it is known to some, are all but maternal in their protectiveness of colleagues. "Claiborne!" she said. "He's the only liberal I know whose victory is a defeat for liberalism," causing all the men in the room, including His Honor the Secretary, to stare wordlessly at her before returning glumly to their cigars. Sitting one evening in the Presidential box at the ballet with her escort, an influential but somewhat prosaic adviser on domestic affairs, she noticed the thousand pairs of eyes on them from below, then quite precipitously she leaned across and kissed the man on his nose. It was well known that she had suddenly declared at a glum buffet in Kenwood that she hoped her black brethren would soon achieve home rule because the city needed not only soul but *pizang* (a word she had added to her repertoire, curiously enough, in her first year at the University of Mississippi) almost as bad as that particular buffet needed it. In a place where the best men, in the words of Carol Hollywell's ebullient Washington friend Jennie Grand, "fucked beneath themselves," she had had affairs with a United States Senator, a Yale man in the State Department, a Presidential adviser, and three mighty men of the media—and in the bright new spirit of the day had proven superior to them all. In a society where young women were expected to sit quietly at the table, she teemed with anecdotes and observations fully worthy of her heroine Alice Roosevelt Longworth. Hence she was much in demand among the younger political set, and though she considered herself a solid moderate-to-liberal Democrat, she crossed partisan lines with little difficulty and, in fact, considerable pleasure. There was a warrant officer who followed within a few yards of the President of the United States wherever he went, even sitting just outside his bedroom, or his bathroom when he had to go there, carrying a black briefcase with the day's special code for the nuclear deterrent. People talked about the time she suddenly embraced this man, kissing him on the cheek, and asking, "Is it a lucky number today?" Little wonder that most Washington matrons considered her an unfeminine parvenu, a willful bitch, and that in moods of sad introspection before she turned thirty-three she told herself she was wasting her life, and indeed had become little more than the court jester. In a city where dinner parties broke up at 11 p.m., when even the randy young men went home to their memoranda at that drastic stroke of the clock, she was known to entertain for perambulating homosexuals, New York novelists, professional football players, women reformers from the Midwest, with more than a few of these entertainments raging perilously toward dawn. All of Georgetown knew she occasionally rode a motorscooter in the shortest mini-skirt in Washington, and that she had once been serenaded from her front steps by four drunken Southern Congressmen wearing Scottish kilts.

All of Georgetown, for that matter, knew that she could give proper but gay dinners as well, for diplomats, civil servants, professors from the university, and foreigners spending their obligatory two days in the "capital of the world." They knew she was an exceptionally good cook in the American way who prepared her own food and served only the best wines, that she was an earthy but ingratiating hostess, and that her townhouse, which she had decorated by her own wits, was a dazzling place with its amusing bric-a-brac and its sharp joyous colors and its good comfortable old pieces of early American.

Just what did she want? they asked. With her trenchant tongue and her flamboyant Southern wit, they said, her hasty expressions and passionate imprecations, she could take over the leadership of the movement for the liberation of women just then sweeping the Grand Old Union. Quite obviously her mind was better than those curiously arch and emotionless girls who had become bywords in that revolution. Carol Hollywell did have flair, after all, and experience with conceiving and bearing and raising an actual human being. She was intrepid in her disdain of iron-maiden marriages, and indeed of all the formal circumscriptions; she believed in her inmost being that it was women who held American society together. But she had had her moments with the movement toward liberation and had found that the campfollowers and footsoldiers of it left an emptiness in her, as did all those Simón Bolívars of the clitoris against the forces of reaction behind the labia minora, majora, and the deeper but equally irrelevant extras. "I mean, hell," she stunned a cadre of anti-chauvinist liberationists one day by paraphrasing Mr. Mailer, "which is more impressive, the anchovy or the cucumber?" Then why did she not marry another wealthy man, a better breed of wealthy man this time, and seek power more tactfully than before? Because, she said, she had known wealth when she was merely twenty-six, and had found it restricting. Or transport herself to Manhattan and find a niche there in that citadel of trends and gestures? Because, she replied, she did not like the steam that came out of the sewers on its streets, and because Washington was her town and because she was bound to it with all her longings and hopes.

What, indeed, did she want? She herself did not know.

The truth is that Carol Hollywell, being a Southern girl, was American to the blood, and hence was both an irredeemable romantic and a fitful pragmatist. She might suffer along the way, as indeed she had, but she was going to do all right before it was over. It might take a while, but she was prepared to wait her time. Before her sudden fall from grace and power, hadn't the British Ambassador once removed, an imperious London intellectual, told her the night before he went home that she was the most promising young woman in Washington? Hadn't Dean Acheson kissed her on the cheek and said she had more vivacity than any lady he had ever known? Hadn't Mr. Buchwald, master of the droll and whimsical, deemed her the most jocose of raconteurs? And hadn't Joseph Alsop himself pronounced her the most beautiful creature in Georgetown and said that only she had the imagination to amalgamate the executive, the legislative, and the judiciary into a new form of governance, a little indigenous but largely Anglophilic?

SHE WAS TALL AND SLENDER, about five eight, with darkbrown hair and wisping curlicues that tumbled into her eyes, enough of it to set off a face with expressions so varied that she could seem a different person altogether from the one she had been five minutes before: a healthy American face with sturdy bloodlines. It could be an amusing face, and a mean and calculating one, and then straightforwardly and wholesomely beautiful, and mock serious in a way that fooled everyone, and in rare moments there would be a look around her mouth, an expectant look, at once tender and vulnerable. Her bright green eyes were touched with mischief. There was structure in the bones, and beauty that would likely last: and small breasts, and long slender legs that kept a summer's tan. She had an agreeable Southern voice, medium-pitched, with enough of the Deep South in it yet, and loud enthusiastic laughter that curdled the women and often frightened the men away. There was about her a slight suggestion of the Southern tomboy. She had never thought of herself as beautiful, yet she had heard it told her so often since her debutante days along the river that she had taken full advantage of the proposition, and it had spoiled her, making her a little headstrong and high-strung. Her wit could be as self-serving as it could be self-deprecatory, but fortunately for her the latter won the day. "I've had two rivers in my life," she would say, "the Mississippi and the Potomac. I'm fast, murky, and polluted." A likable girl? That was too plain a word for her, but those very few who knew her well saw character there, and impulsiveness and generosity, and the most curious disguised naiveté and innocence: a woman of the world, true, but beneath that the child who grew up in a time when the quiet streets of a small Southern town were the limits of that world, and all the streets and houses and pathways were where she remembered they belonged. She was, in fact, born at almost the last moment in time when it was possible to get, firsthand, a feel of what the older Southern life had been. The South was the root of her strength, though she did not know it yet, the irascibility of the South, that and her innate sense of the absurd, the one naturally following the other. Those who dwelled with their feelings were the ones who were drawn to her, and people hated her and people loved her, for she defied prediction, and she was not to be effaced.

. . .

S<small>HE HAD COME UP</small> to the Hill to work on the staff of a Congressman from Arkansas, a remote acquaintance of her
uncle. The Congressman's most recent campaign cards had
pronounced him "Against Every Ism But Americanism,"
helping him to re-election for a fifth term over a female
justice of the peace with one leg. She was twenty-one, recently out of Ole Miss with a degree in political science, and
considerable applied knowledge of the insane Mississippi
dances, three-day drinking sprees, and orgiastic roadtrips to
Memphis and New Orleans which gave the University of
Mississippi its unique distinction before the great American
academy. She had also left a 230-pound Johnnie Rebel linebacker who had been elected Colonel Rebel the year before
she was Miss Ole Miss and who, as a luminary in the Fellowship of Christian Athletes and president of Sigma Alpha
Epsilon fraternity, had obtained a sturdy foothold in the
Memphis real estate market, a chain of drive-in hardware
stores, and a partnership with the Chrysler–Plymouth
dealer. She had been the most "popular" girl on the campus,
a little too irreverent perhaps for her own good but not
excessively so, and she had read enough textbook politics to
get her by in Washington City while she learned what might
be wanted there of her. Washington City! That is what her
grandmother, the eighth daughter of a Confederate brevet-
colonel, had called it, and the name itself had been resonant
and mysterious and slightly alien to her all during her childhood. She had ordered a guide to her nation's capital, and in
her last days home she sat in one of her shaded childhood
haunts on Anderson's Ridge overlooking the river and traced
her way around the city with her fingers, absorbing there in
Arkansas all of L'Enfant's nostalgia for Versailles.

On a fine June morning in 1957 she stepped off the Crescent Limited in Union Station. On arriving in the vast echoing hall, she followed a porter pushing the cartful of new, polished leather luggage acquired in Memphis, walking gingerly on her toes, smiling for no reason at all at inessential strangers—and then, safely in a taxicab, admired the marbled certitude of Columbus out front, fresh to the New World on a ship's prow. She radiated warmth and foolishness and good will; she smiled when she read the inscription in stone on Union Station: *He who would bring home the wealth of the Indies must carry the wealth of the Indies with him.* An onlooker on that day would have become aware of the rush and flow of the blood through her, the robustness of her body, a robustness which seemed so extraordinarily vital because it was not in the least merely voluptuous, a young woman who was entirely resolute about her beauty. Even then she recognized somewhere down in the heart of her the restless gnaw of ambition. Because she was intelligent if not bookish, and resourceful in the ways of society, and heiress to a good Southern name with a United States Senator in its genealogy, and recipient of 750 dollars a month for life from her grandfather's estate, she harbored scant fears of intimidation or inferiority. And like the splendid Scarlett, whom she adored and envied for having lived during a magnificent calamity so commensurate with her gifts and whom she had secretly emulated at scores of weddings and balls down on the river, she hoped all the men on the Hill would soon beseech her to be allowed to fetch her barbecue. And she was not far wrong.

EVEN BEFORE she took her position with the Congressman she rented a small apartment near Wisconsin Avenue in

Georgetown, painting it herself in bright colors and furnishing it with the early American pieces she had bought at auctions in the countryside. How she loved the city! She loved to stand in high places on spring evenings and look down at the monuments and edifices and the broad boulevards bordered with their great shade trees to admire the vistas opening from one of L'Enfant's circles, to gaze across from the Lee House at Arlington in a hazy autumn light toward the nest of its bureaucracies, its parks and plazas, to walk the quiet backways of Georgetown and browse in the tiny shops, to tarry among the dogwoods and sweet covers of honeysuckle and wildcrab among the ravines and hillsides of Rock Creek Park, to hear the bells of Washington Cathedral on dark lonesome Sundays, to find out-of-the-way places in northern Virginia and to see the battlefields at Fredericksburg, Chancellorsville, Spotsylvania, Bull Run, and the Wilderness. She imagined Lincoln walking all over the city alone during the Civil War, and the levees at the old Willard, and Whitman on his rounds of the emergency hospitals, and Mrs. Madison's drawingroom, and the rhetoric thundering forth from the inaugurals in front of the Capitol. She adored the corridors of Old Treasury with its great eagles and pilasters, and the pigeons and starlings in the tree-shaded parks, and Rochambeau in bronze in Lafayette Square, and the surging crowds that emerged in late afternoons from the monumental gray buildings of the Triangle, and the wooded reaches of the Potomac leading down into the Chesapeake, and the passageways and enclaves of the Capitol: here, on Capitol Hill, down the Mall and Pennsylvania Avenue to the Treasury, was the clash and play of the intractable Continent. And she would be part of it!

Later, on the Hill, she would come to know many of the young people who were working as researchers and assistants. "The presence of power," one of the most promising of them said to her, a little mysteriously, "begets ambiguity," but she was immediately at home in those unrestrained environs, for unlike certain other parts of Washington it had a nimbus of her hometown to it, an easy buoyancy, a shared sense verging on fellowship of being commonly at the mercy of thistly electorates hundreds of miles removed. She would grow then to love the final nights of sessions when the House of Representatives whiled away the last hours waiting on a conference committee, or making perfunctory insertions in the *Record*, or enjoying the antics of the sugar lobbyists, and when the liquor flowed freely and the old horny House members, usually perpetual Southerners from the reddest hills or the blackest deltas, came uncertainly in pursuit of her. On one of these first closing nights she sat above the Mall with two or three young Congressmen and their assistants, drinking Scotch from paper cups in the twilight, watching the lights of the city come on and the sun on the marble and limestone all about her, feeling in a girlish glow the promise and variety of this new place she had chosen for herself.

Her first assignment for her Congressman was to investigate the complexities which might be lurking in a bill he intended to introduce in the new session. The bill, which had inspired considerable enthusiasm in her employer and various members of his staff, would replace the forty-eight American flags which encircled the Washington Monument with the flags of the forty-eight states.

"How should I research it, sir?" she asked him.

"Just get out and talk to people! Find out what the sentiment is. I'm sure everybody's for it. Everybody and his brother! Just think of all the different colors flappin' there in the breeze."

"Yessir."

She did not perform any pertinent formal investigations, but she thought about the prospective legislation on the way home, and the next afternoon she arranged to see her Congressman in his office.

"Well, what did you find out, pretty girl?"

"Congressman, it looks very controversial."

"*Controversial!* Who the hell thinks?"

"Everyone I talked to on the Hill—lawyers, economists, A.A.'s. They say you'll be accused of being the man who . . ."

"Accused of what?"

". . . the man who took down the American flag from the Washington Monument."

His broad open face was suddenly washed with sadness. For a time he said nothing, looking silently at his great gnarled hands and the stacks of paper on his desk and the signed photographs of Orval E. Faubus.

"By god, honey, you're right! That could get us into real trouble back home."

"Yessir."

"Now go get me Tommy!" he shouted. "It was *his* idea."

Naturally she was disillusioned when her second task for the Congressman was to read all of Winston Churchill's major speeches to prepare a memorandum for him on how he could best emulate Churchill's oratory in Arkansas. She was disappointed not because of Churchill, but because she did not wish this mission in any measure to juxtapose that marvelous old Tory with her Congressman. The Congressman saw himself as a descendant of the lordly Southern Bourbons, but in fact he was a small backcountry yeoman who had once raised cabbage and eggplants and soybeans: shrewd in the ways of the Hill but little more enlightened in her haughty opinion than the cows and livestock and country people who were his constituents, the first two generally outnumbering the last. "This man has no class," her uncle had told her. "Learn the Hill fast and then get something better."

"Well, little lady," the Congressman had said to her, "I think you've done a real good job on the Churchill memo."

"Thank you, Congressman."

"I even intend to take your advice on most of it, and I don't take advice from many men."

"I'm flattered."

"Yes ma'am, pretty girl, I intend to give that version you did of his Iron Curtain speech in Marked Tree next month, and I'm using a little of the speech he gave to the House of Commons in September 1941, in Paragould in August. Just the high points."

"Yessir, Congressman."

"Little lady, you're goin' a far way."

Not too far as it turned out, but just up the street to the Senate Office Building. She worked four months for the Congressman. Then quite unexpectedly one night she found an entrée into Georgetown society, and this event would rearrange her whole existence.

# 2

SHE WENT TO A DANCE that autumn with a young Democratic Congressman from Pennsylvania, a Rhodes Scholar as it turned out, whose impeccable intellectual credentials disguised for the nonce a mighty pomposity, but who nonetheless was in good stead with a number of the powerful, wealthy Democrats and diplomats who were waiting there for the dawn of the better day; he was, for the moment, a protégé of that liberal part of the city which shapes so much of its character. The dance was in one of those palatial Georgetown houses near Dumbarton Oaks with flowing tapestries and Victorian settees and high terraced lawns and rose gardens hidden by brick walls covered in ivy. The Congressman, whose name was Sidney Ricks and who had played squash and soccer at Princeton, told her in the taxi that it was his favorite house in Washington. And indeed she had walked by it many times on the way to the Georgetown library, had heard the sounds of music and the light play of many voices and seen the silvery chandeliers through the open windows. Her imagination in those early days fastened itself on certain of these Georgetown dwellings. As the first dying leaves of October swirled on the rusty brick sidewalks and streets and the lamplights flickered in the dusk, she walked down the hill from Rock Creek Park toward her own apartment, admiring those mansions and quaint old town-houses and the clapboards with coach lamps and gabled roofs and dormers and brightly colored doors which to her seemed touched, ever so fragilely, with age and influence. And the past suffused her in these moments, embraced her in a feel of lost moments, of powerful men and their ladies vanished forever now from the Great Republic.

The host that evening was a Georgetown eminence, Ambassador to Moscow, the Court of St. James, and Paris under various past administrations, a rich New Englander, born as some said with a silver railroad in his mouth, one of the most respected diplomats in America. "He is really quite charming," Congressman Ricks told her in the taxicab. "He's not the least bit egotistical, and after everything he's been through."

"Do you know him well?"

"Well enough. I met him when I was up at Oxford during his time in London. I spent some weekends with him and his wife in Cornwall. He talked me into going into politics."

"Do you like politics, Sidney?"

"Once you get over the crudeness. I've got a fairly safe district."

"And what's your ambition?"

"I want to be President of the United States."

Carol looked across at him and smiled. He took her by the hand. He was utterly serious.

"I'll bet if you ever git up there, you'll stick if you kin," she said.

"Beg pardon?"

"It's something Mark Twain once said. My uncle recited it to me when I was little and we were out in the river catfishing."

"I see."

"I wonder if the Ambassador is serving catfish tonight."

"I doubt it. They go in for French cooking. Their chef is from Paris."

She was beautiful that night in a white taffeta gown. Her brown hair was long and flowed to her shoulders. Her face and arms were still tan from the summer. With clothes she was tasteful and acquisitive. Unlike many of the dowdy young secretaries and assistants from the great hinterland on the Hill, she flashed with cashmeres of all the colors, and bizarre belts, and necklaces; in a mere half hour's browsing about Garfinckel's she could muster together a stylish ensemble worthy of a princess, and for all this she was grateful to her grandfather's inheritance, and to Eli Whitney, and to the humming black earth of De Soto County.

It was a massive, cream-colored brick house with severe lines, and under a pedimented portico they walked up the stairway leading to the entrance. She and Congressman Ricks stood in a corner, drank champagne, and watched the dancers, and she saw the reflections in the enormous Venetian chandelier and felt a sharp twinge of excitement, a giddy weightlessness almost sexual in its self-beholding. Her escort pointed out the luminaries: the Senators and Justices and diplomats and ranking old Chairmen from the House side and columnists and editors. Up until now she had gone only to entertainments given by young Congressmen or House assistants, or drunk beer with friends in the bars around the Hill. She knew that her own poor Congressman from Arkansas would not even be allowed to tend the bar for such an evening. The thought made her whimsical.

The orchestra was playing a medley of the more tortuous love songs of that day—"Tenderly" and "April Love" and "You Belong to Me"—which sometimes had seemed to her to have shaped the very essences of her adolescence and girlhood, that common poetry of the glands echoing gently from a dozen Southern country club verandas onto lonely sloping fairways.

"I'm having a pretty good time, Sidney."

"I'm glad to hear that."

"What are you frowning over, Mr. Congressman?"

"I was wondering if anyone ever asked you to marry."

"Oh, honey!" She could tell him, she supposed, about her handsome Ole Miss linebacker, who had come as close to raping a virgin as a virgin can be raped statutorily under the Constitution of 1890 of the sovereign state of Mississippi, in a ranch-style house borrowed for the weekend from the Chrysler–Plymouth dealer in Kosciusko. Who yanked the caps off beer bottles with his teeth. Who claimed even though she knew he lied that he once killed a Negro with a .38 pistol on a lonely road near Itta Bena because the Negro would not help him repair a flat tire. Who promised her two million dollars before she was thirty. Even if her 230-pound linebacker had been the best Ole Miss could offer, she thought it would be neither fitting nor politic to tell her histories to a varsity squash player from Princeton.

At that moment a tall, powerful gentleman of advanced middle age, a little unkempt in his tuxedo, broke in for a dance. "Hello, Senator," Sidney Ricks said. "This is Miss Carol Templeton."

"Ah, Miss Templeton, you're the most beautiful lady on this dance floor." The Senator beamed with good will. But his eyes were narrow slits.

"Senator," she said, tilting her head far back to catch his

gaze, "you're even more handsome than your photographs. I've watched you at work from the gallery, you know. I've been an admirer of yours since I was about *this* high. My uncle always said you're the most admirable Majority Leader in years. Better even than Oscar W. Underwood."

"Oscar Underwood!" the Senator laughed. "That was a long time ago."

"Yessir. Back in the 'twenties."

"And do you live in Washington, young lady?" His accent was heavy and touched with the earth.

"Yessir, I do. I work for you. By that I mean, I work on the Hill. For Congressman Purdy of Arkansas."

"Purdy!" The Senator looked down at her.

"Senator, don't be cruel. It would be like a big old cat playing with a tiny mouse."

"That it would." It was a whispered reply, crackling and unexpected, and she barely heard it. "Well you drop by and see me sometime later, or Mr. Brandt of our staff. Maybe we can find a good job for you on one of my . . ."

Someone else tapped the Senator on the shoulder. "Miss Templeton," the Senator said, "have you met our host?" He was a graying man of medium build, with pale blue eyes and the profile of a hawk. The Senator exuded raw blunt power. The Ambassador was merely dashing and restrained.

"Yessir," she said. "Briefly at the door."

"Hello, Miss Templeton. Are you enjoying yourself?"

"Mr. Ambassador, I'm having more fun than I ever had in my life. It's better than my graduation dance from high school. The people are much more attractive and almost as important."

"I believe Sidney tells me you work on the Hill. Do you like it?"

"I do, Mr. Ambassador, but I believe I prefer the diplomatic corps."

"Do you, now? And do you like Congressman Ricks?"

"Well, yessir."

"A little dull," the Ambassador whispered. "A well-meaning fellow, but he bears little resemblance to Cecil Rhodes. I wish he'd stop saying he's fighting the world's good fight. Still, he'll come out all right."

"He wants to be President."

"There's your next President, though no one believes me." He pointed to a junior Senator from the East, who was smoking a thin cigar and talking with Sidney Ricks.

"No sir. He's too ugly."

The Ambassador laughed, and after considerably more amiable banter he said, "Well, Miss Templeton, tell me about yourself."

She told him about De Soto Point, Arkansas, and the University of Mississippi, and that she was learning about Washington.

"And what is the most important lesson you've learned, my dear?"

"Mr. Ambassador, I can't tell you."

"You must."

"Well, sir, I've learned that it can all be so *accessible* if you love it and have a mind for it. And one other thing."

"Yes?"

"Mr. Roosevelt didn't appoint his Ambassador to Moscow on the basis of ability."

"No? On what then?"

"On virility and good looks! I've said it. Don't be angry."

"Hah!" He whirled her around the floor, waving gingerly every so often to his guests.

"So you work on the Hill? What do you do?"

"Sir, I'm talking out of school, but let me just tell you what happened to me recently." She told him about her Congressman and the flagpoles at the monument and Winston Churchill's speeches.

"Young lady, I can't bear this. Come have a glass of champagne and meet my wife." He led her into a drawing-room nearby, where a charming and rather pretty woman, tiny like a doll, was talking with a small circle of people. "May I present Miss Carol Templeton, from De Soto Point, Arkansas?"

"I'm delighted to see you, my dear." She introduced her to two Senators and a magazine correspondent.

"Now, Miss Templeton. Will you repeat that story about Winston Churchill?"

She did so with relish, adding a few rich embroideries of her own. She felt no guilt. She wanted to be as entertaining as she had ever been in her whole life. The appreciative laughter which followed told her she had succeeded.

"I believe De Soto Point is on the Mississippi," one of the Senators said. "Am I correct?"

"Yessir, it was the last I heard. But my uncle is a river engineer, and he claims that before the flood of 1927, De Soto Point was actually in the state of Mississippi, and then the river changed course and it was in Arkansas. Then Arkansas tried to give it back across the river to Mississippi but Senator Eastland said it would take up too much space on his plantation."

The Senators laughed, and one of them said, "Old Eastland would *say* that, too."

"Do you like it in Washington, Miss Templeton?" the Ambassador's wife asked.

"Oh yes ma'am, I do. This party's made me feel I want to live here forever!"

"Perhaps you will," the Ambassador said. "I think this town can use a little vitality right about now."

She danced again until her legs were weary, and just as she and the other guests were leaving, the Ambassador's wife caught her by the arm at the stairway. "Miss Templeton, we're giving a little buffet next Thursday for the British Ambassador, an old dear friend, and my husband and I were wondering . . ."

MANY YEARS LATER she would look back on the night with complicated hindsights. It had been a crucial moment in her life. She had just turned twenty-two. Was there a choice to make?

She had been supremely happy that night, dazzled with the splendor of her hosts and their guests and by the manner in which they accepted her. Her whole life, the grace and the ease and the good-natured badinage, seemed to have prepared her for it, sprang from the soil of her birth. It had been so easy. She had learned a very important secret: *they were starved for a beautiful irreverent woman.* She had no notion then—how could she?—that somewhere in this town there was a line, blurred and indefinable but no less real, beyond which one traveled only in wariness and travail. Nor did she know that even on that night, in the flush of her girlhood, hostile eyes had been upon her. She only knew that from the Georgetown palace, beyond it toward the monuments of the civilization we had made for ourselves, her imagination soared in fulfillment.

THERE WERE NIGHTS in the great Georgetown houses or the more modern palaces of McLean or Kalorama or Spring

Valley, sitting at the table next to a Senator or a member of the Cabinet or a foreign diplomat, when the host of the evening would say, "Now, Carol, please fill this group in on what you've been up to lately. We've been waiting." She became a giddy, accomplished master of the Washington monologue, as on one among many similar evenings in the home of a former Assistant Secretary of State:

"Well, sir, as you know I've gone to work for the senior Senator from Kentucky, with a debt of thanks to his friend Ambassador Fountain. The Senator has taught all of us to be solicitous to constituents who wander in off the streets. I believe he'd have us give the male constituents massages with baby oil in the bridal suite of the Hay-Adams if he thought he could get away with it. I'd do it too," she would say, with an eye toward one of the politicians at the table, "if I thought it would help with his foreign aid amendment right now. A constituent from Louisville came in a couple of weeks ago wanting the Senator to help impeach the Chief Justice. I sent him over to a girl I know who is one of the Chief Justice's secretaries, and she was so taken with him she introduced the man to the Chief Justice in the hallway waiting for an elevator. The man just wilted on the spot. My friend said, 'Mr. Chief Justice, Mr. So-and-So wants to impeach you,' and she said the man replied, 'No sir, I'm *reconsiderin'* it.' A portly gentleman came in last week and said he was an insurance executive from Frankfort and wanted three minutes of the Senator's time. I was working on a memo about the aid amendment and one of the girls brought him to me. He sounded so important I went and told the Senator's secretary he should see the gentleman for three or four minutes before he left for the Capitol and she managed it. The poor Senator must have gotten trapped, but after fifteen minutes he stormed out of his office and roared for all of us to hear: 'Get this son-of-a-bitch out of here. He's from Indiana and he's trying to sell me a home owner's policy!' The Senator is a genius, you know, when it comes to remembering names, but some of us were out helping him campaign last month and he confessed to us on the plane that he gets detailed memos on the people he'll probably see in each town and he reads them to refresh his memory, but for the life of him, he associates the faces with the towns because that's the way he memorizes them, so that if a face from Elkton turns up in Guthrie or a Paducah man meets him in Eddyville, he's in trouble. This happened the last time. We were in Drakesboro at ten in the morning and he saw this rich old farmer and said, 'Why Tom Nelson, how's your wife?' and he said, 'Thank you for rememberin', Senator. She's feelin' poorly and has been in the hospital for a week with some female disease and was runnin' a 102 fever at eight this mornin'.' Then that afternoon at six the same man turned up at Caneyville thirty miles down the road. The Senator didn't recognize him but said, 'Why hello, my friend, how's the wife?' and the farmer said, 'Well, Senator, there ain't been no change in her condition since eight a.m., thanks for rememberin'.' "

And when the laughter had subsided, she might continue: "Back during Truman when the Senator was a very young man he was up for his first re-election. He was in Maysville on the Ohio line in eastern Kentucky. It's a country he knows so well! During the Civil War even the families were divided, and there he was before a huge audience and someone interrupted him and shouted, '*What's your stand on the FEPC?*' He looked down at the faces and knew there were Unionists there and Yankees and Confederates and racists and Lord knows what else, and then he paused for a moment and finally said, 'I'm all right on the FEPC,' and then went right on with his speech. A few years ago the Senator went on a plane with the Southern Governors to spread good will in Latin America. They'd land at these airports at all hours of the day and night and speak to the people who'd gathered to hear them. The Governor of Mississippi was with them but he was indisposed the whole time and they wouldn't let him off the plane. But they knew they had to allow him *one* speech, so about midnight they landed at some small airport in Nicaragua, and there were about three hundred people there, and they gave the Governor of Mississippi some mouthwash and guided him off the plane onto the speaker's platform. It was the first time he'd been off the plane in two days. So he said to the crowd, 'I'm honored to say hello to all you folks. I send the warm greetings of the people of the sovereign state of Mississippi to all you fine citizens of . . .' Then he looked around and said: '*Cinzano Seco!*' "

And there were times she was more pointedly on public display. She accepted an invitation to give a speech of orientation to a group of recently arrived young ladies from the provinces who were starting to work on the Hill. She prepared diligently for this effort; seldom was she more rosy-cheeked and hearty than when the full bloom of attention was upon her. Already the word had got around that the pertinacious young beauty from the Kentucky Senator's staff was going to lecture to the new arrivals about the nation's capital, and a substantial audience was likely.

It was a lovely spring morning, Washington at its best, all green and cool from the rains, the air fragrant with the smell of growing things, the marbles and domes and columns gleaming in the sun, the little yellow buds glimmering in the oaks and elms of the plazas and squares. Soon the foliage would burst overnight into flaming springtime colors, first the forsythia and cherries and then the azaleas and dogwoods, and the promise of an early spring matched her mood, for she had never felt happier than on the drive up Pennsylvania Avenue, and in her bright red sweater and bronze necklace and flaring white skirt she herself was touched ineffably with the season.

Her talk, which was in one of the larger committee rooms of the Old Senate Office building, was, not surprisingly, a success, a tour de force, although when she discussed in graphic detail the exploits of such hellborn Washington heroines from the far past as Peggy Eaton and Kate Chase Sprague many of the young ladies, especially those from the Midwest, were unsure whether to be titillated or informed, or perhaps forewarned. She described her diverse tasks for her Senator. Versatility was the key to advancement on the Hill, she counseled. Once, for instance, she had received a telephone call when she was working in her office late at night from several drunk constituents in a bedraggled Mexican town across the Rio Grande from Texas. They had tarried too long in a bordello and had returned to the one-lane wooden bridge to find the gate closed. "We've been locked out of our country!" one of the constituents said. On the advice of the Senator's administrative assistant, she contacted the Embassy in Mexico City, and the victims were again within the hegemony of the good green passport in less than two hours. "Three of them," she complained, "supported our opponent in the last primary. Gratitude, like fame, is the least permanent of conditions, especially in this city. Prepare yourselves for that fact and you'll spare yourself some anguish."

"Go to the Capitol terrace at sunset," she said. "This is a beautiful city. The ground on which we stand was first explored by the best of the English stock, unlike the New England Puritans, who first fell on their knees and then on the aborigines. Walk through the Capitol Building when the tourists aren't there, not the well-known corridors and chambers but the hidden stairways and deserted rooms. These are rich in their own special chaos. Most of the people who live here are native to other soils, gathering and dispersing with great regularity, but remember that each year some of us stay here a little longer because we care so deeply for it.

"Never disregard the true value of our social life here, because it brings together all those different worlds of the executive, the legislative, the judiciary, the diplomatic, and the press, which are usually divided by the broadest chasms. And our generation is the beneficiary of a greater informality in manners. We're a long way from those days a generation or two ago when everything was prescribed by formal calls, by the most rigorous demands of protocol and seniority. Remember also," she continued, "some of the trivial little rules that should be followed. A guest of honor leaves a party first. Back in Arkansas he stays until the last dregs have evaporated. Here a husband goes before his wife down a receiving line. In Arkansas we don't do this, even on Saturday nights. Who knows? Perhaps if we follow the small rules we can break the big ones. Above all be patient. Be of good cheer. Honor your constituents, even when they ask for tours of the Government Printing Office or the Capitol Power Plant. Understand power! Some day one of us may be in the big white mansion down the avenue. I must warn you, however: *I have a year's head start.*"

After it was over, when she was leaving the room, she noticed a young Senator from a Midwestern state standing near the doorway. He came to greet her. He was handsome and well tailored, and the slightest bit guarded.

"I just stumbled in on that performance," he said. "Can I have a copy?"

"I'll type it out for you, Senator."

They were walking casually down the broad corridor and soon were standing in the marble rotunda.

"Any chance I can steal you for my office?" He laughed.

"I don't think so," she said. "I've learned so much about Kentucky I'd hate to have to throw it all away."

"But getting constituents across wooden bridges isn't my idea of power."

"I'm afraid I made that up." Her laughter wafted through the capacious hallway, and several passersby turned to look.

"Well, anyway, the least we can do is have dinner sometime." These words were pronounced in a suddenly hushed voice, as if he were avoiding echoes.

"You're *married*," she whispered back.

His expression changed unexpectedly. "Of course. I mean at my house. We have people in once a week."

"I'd like it," Carol said. "I've always admired you. I was in the gallery when you gave your speech last week on . . ."

"Price supports."

"You convinced me to support price supports with all my heart."

And there were times in that season of her triumphant maidenhood when an evening with her elders captured for her something of the subtlety and complexity of the city as it truly was.

Congressman Ricks, who soon was destined to vanish from her life, less as an act of choice or even of will but quite in the nature of things, as a quiet perfunctory tide recedes under a full moon and is forgotten, for Washington had forever been a place in which people were perpetually slipping out of other people's lives (he was to be defeated by a Negro activist with a harelip from south Philadelphia), escorted her to a dinner whose honor guest was a tenacious old

Senator from the deeper South. The party was in the home
of a lawyer from one of the less sedate firms that specialized
in representing big corporations before the government, a
New Dealer who long since had defected, not sheepishly but
indeed with a considerable degree of enthusiasm, to the
economic royalists who once were his enemies: an eminently
American metamorphosis. He lived in a dark-red block of
row houses, in one of those three-storied structures built
toward the end of the last century with a high basement and
an alcove above the entrance hall and a large Victorian
dining room that could easily seat, as it did on this night,
two dozen or so guests at three or four separate tables. Upon
arriving, she was momentarily entranced by the host, a
ruddy Irishman who entertained her before dinner with tales
of FDR, and Ickes, and Hopkins, and Henry Wallace, a wily
fox noted for dealing hard and swiftly in the subterranean
reaches of the agencies, who was seen in Congress only
slightly less regularly than the Speaker of the House, and
who at that moment was balancing a martini in one hand
and gesturing with the other.

"Don't you miss those exciting days, sir?" she asked him.

"Oh, my dear, I do. But I learned so much."

"What did you learn?"

"Why, to be *practical* in regard to all things. It sounds
quite easy, but believe me it wasn't."

"Should a young lady learn to be practical also?"

"In this town," he beamed, "everyone should be practical
except lame duck politicians and pretty girls. Leave that to
the incumbents and the lawyers. And just to prove it I'm
seating you next to our guest of honor. He's a quiet bachelor,
you know, who usually dines alone. I believe he's tired of his
own practicalities. He's been at it thirty years. And just
between you and me," he whispered, "he's a little, you
know—*senile*."

Later Congressman Ricks brought over a rather dour member of the Federal Communications Commission and introduced him.

"Mr. Commissioner," she said after a few pleasantries, "you've done so much to improve TV. When are you going to improve TV dinners?"

"Really, Carol," the Congressman said.

At the table, sipping wine from tall crystal goblets, she found herself in earnest discourse with a high-ranking veteran of the civil service; she had had some peripheral dealings with him in regard to her Senator's work, and she had nicknamed him The Inscrutable Humanoid. She listened now to his lengthy disquisition on the standardization of soybean allotments and the percentage of waste in gas seepage. Skillfully she guided him to a more intricate discussion of reciprocal tariffs with the countries of the North Atlantic Treaty Organization. He was immediately interested in the matter and, not to be diverted from it, broadened his assessments to include the Norwegian Ambassador's wife on the other side of him, giving Carol a means of withdrawal.

She turned to the Senator on her right. He had the head of a lion, with shaggy white hair and a rough weathered face lined with the deepest wrinkles she had ever seen, the face of a man who had forgone much, who had experienced many jeopardies and suffered more than one's share of fools. She had heard of him, of course, as a girl. She remembered he had once sought his party's Presidential nomination and to his surprise had failed badly, leaving him a little embittered, as if he had a stake now in losing and being alone. Over the years he had been consummate in the tactics of the cloakrooms, had indeed acquired much of his power and respect there; hidden thus from the public gaze he did not learn until too late that the American people, no matter that they had molded a system which depended on such secret arts, usually seek more pristine figures for their Presidency. His pale-blue eyes appraised her with absolute confidence, yet she sensed him to be a profoundly warm and complex being—a judgment which conflicted with her views of his politics, which she had always considered from afar to be much too narrow. She would encounter similar paradoxes in the future; the paradoxes would soon become part of her education.

"You remind me of a niece I once had," he said to her right away.

"I hope I do her justice, Senator."

"She came up and lived with me for a while after she graduated from school. Then she took sick in Paris, France. We buried her in the Protestant cemetery. That was a long time ago."

"And you've been here thirty years, I believe?"

"Four terms and one year to go on another."

"I imagine it's changed a lot."

"It has indeed. We all felt so deeply involved with the country. It was a fine old town. Very soft and proper. It charmed us all. Now there's a viciousness to it. It's hard to explain. Like the rest of the country it all got out of hand within a generation, within my lifetime. I worry about the lack of dignity and civility. But back then it was splendid. You could even walk on the streets when the sun went down. Relationships were humane. Now nobody cares. People have gotten too smart."

"Maybe we should move the capital to Germantown, Pennsylvania. That's where John Adams wanted it all along. He worried about malaria."

He chuckled, then shrugged. "The pride people used to feel about working in the government is gone too, you know. Hell, back home when a girl like you got a job working on the Hill for a United States Senator, and a good one at that, from a distinguished *border* state, they gave her a  barbecue and did everything but ring all the church bells."

"That would've been fun," she said. "At least the Elks Club bought me some luggage. I haven't used it since I got here."

"Because you love this town?"

"Yessir. That's it."

"I do too. Despite all I say. It belongs to the American people. People like me just come and go."

"Do you go home often?"

"Not as much as I used to. Talk about your changes. It used to be green and clean and it *looked* old. Something more, too. Something that's finally indescribable. Something you and young people from home your age may be the last to understand or remember. I mean white *and* colored. Now it's becoming big cities and suburbs like everywhere. I'm afraid someday it'll be paved over like New Jersey. Have you ever noticed all the New Jersey license plates whenever you go to a pretty spot? They allowed their own state to become a parking lot, and now they're trying to take over other people's vacant spaces. They're *jousters*. Hell, some parts of this country the only places where you can still take a walk on grass is in the cemeteries."

"On weekends in Georgetown you have to stand in line to go down the sidewalk."

"Every time I'm home and driving in the countryside, I look over the fields and see the deserted tenant houses. The chemicals chased them away—the weed killers and the machines. I have a preacher friend named Will Campbell— he wanders around preaching to the Ku Kluxers and the coloreds, and he says pretty soon nobody will need *nobody*. He claims he sees tractors driving around cotton fields without drivers. The poor souls who lived in those tenant houses are crowded away now in Chicago or Detroit or out here around Swann and Fifteenth, and don't you think they'd rather be back home sitting on the porch drinking cool water from a dipper and smelling all the smells of the earth and watching their children climbing a chinaberry or swinging in a tire roped to a tree? Brother Will says people have been fooled all to hell by the word *freedom*." He paused for a moment, looking down at her. "I suppose you're one of the liberated ones too."

"Well, when I see two pieces of inner tube tied to a half of shoe tongue and a wooden stock I call it a *slingshot*, although you can probably guess what I'm thinking, and when I go home I say, 'How's your Mamma-an-nem' and, 'Ain't it a bitch?' and things like that."

He laughed again, gazing remotely about the room, then after a time turned to her and whispered: "Sometimes, you know, I think I failed, that what with all the little things the big things passed me by. But my generation acted from blood and earth, and we never forgot. That's it, *we never forgot*. And I've learned that most Southerners go home sooner or later for good, even if it's in a coffin. You'll learn that too some day."

"Well, I hope the best of it lasts, sir."

"I have a secret," he said. "Sometimes I truly wonder if the whole country might not be better off if the South had won that war. Slavery! It was a curse and an abomination. But it would have gone. There would have been an accommodation. Maybe the whole country would be a little gentler, a little more genuinely tragic." He looked away and sighed: "*Sometimes I wonder.*"

Carol leaned toward him and spoke softly into his ear. "Don't tell anybody, Senator, but sometimes late at night when I'm alone I wonder too." They laughed quietly, like guilty conspirators.

"Tell me what you're looking for here," he said after a time.

"Oh, Senator! Maybe I'm seeking fame. Or maybe love."

Across the table, half obscured, fortunately, by a vase of red tulips, the robust wife of the Congressman from Michigan, fortified perhaps by Beaujolais, or disappointed for having been ignored until now by the Senator, proclaimed for the entire company to hear: "Love? What outmoded notions you have. Can one talk of love today?"

"Now and through the generations, madame," he replied. "Beware of the rhetoric you hear these days. I'm an authority on rhetoric."

He had been pointing slightly with his hand, and he accidently overturned the decanter of wine, a little of which spilled on Carol's dress.

"I'm so sorry," he said.

"You're just sorry we've lost half a bottle," Carol replied.

The Congressman's wife, unvanquished even in retreat, said heatedly: "How do you dare speak to the Senator that way?"

He leaned far across the table, catching the woman's gaze with his pale-blue eyes. "Because she is an ally and knows that I don't mind at all."

Later, as they were leaving the table, Carol turned to him. "Sir, thank you for defending me."

"It gave me great pleasure, just as you did. Come on down to my place and see me, you hear? Would you believe it? Sometimes I'm afraid I get lonesome."

"Senator," she said, "you're in good company even when you're by yourself."

After he had left, indicating the others should go also, she thought: I should give a little dinner for him. Two weeks later she picked up the *Post,* and there on the front page she saw that he had died, a heart attack while he was alone in his apartment, and his death made her strangely sad.

There were times, also, when she was serious and quiet, listening to someone expressing his frustrations over conference committees or re-election difficulties or diplomacy in Latin America. But mostly they expected her to sparkle, to scintillate with her extravagant anecdotes or raillery. For large parties she often helped the wives with recipes and with the service, and more than a few of them, lacking in urbanity but desiring it badly, asked her help in choosing clothes or furniture or important gifts. Always she encouraged them to be unconventional. When the wife of a young Republican Senator asked her to help serve at a large cocktail party for a ponderous gathering of Republican campaign organizers and their wives, she turned out in a tight black satin dress with lace stockings and high heels. One of the men from a remote Midwestern neighborhood was heard to remark: "I think those radical employment agencies have gone too far this time." Later that night in the flow of liquor and champagne she stood by the pianist at the baby grand and began to dance to the tunes of the 'forties, swaying her hips in the generous undulations of sex and singing in an exaggerated nightclub voice; men and women alike were subdued in the powerful web of her, and the same man was heard again to observe, "I'm movin' to the left pretty fast."

And then there were times, also, when her telephone rang late at night.

"Carol?"

"Yes."

"This is _____."

"Hello, Mr. Secretary."

"I wish you'd come by for a couple of drinks."

"It's pretty late. Does your wife want to stay up for a while?"

"Well, she and the children are back home for a couple of weeks."

"Oh."

She did not go, but that would come in time.

SHE MADE TWO CLOSE FRIENDS in those months of initiation, friendships which served her well, perhaps, for a time, for the three of them were young and new to the city, and had lessons and warnings to share, and an occasional disgruntlement.

Elaine Rossiter was four or five years Carol's elder. She was a Manhattan girl, the daughter of a rich Jewish lawyer, a prodigy at Dalton and a Phi Beta Kappa at Barnard, knowledgeable in the theater and the arts and indeed in most aspects of that Manhattan culture so accessible from their earliest days to bright young children who grow up there. She was a small, dark-complexioned girl, petite almost, with a rich bass voice that could be raucous in anger, which always surprised the stranger expecting a light feminine tenor along with her miniature proportions. She had enjoyed a certain success quite early, for her precocity in New York constantly sought new outlets, and it was perfectly natural that she have a fling at politics just as she had at painting, music, and drama, not to mention psychoanalysis and the ballet. At Barnard she began writing sharp brittle pieces for the *Village Voice* on reform organizations, and later an occasional contribution to *The Reporter* and *The New Republic*. By the time she had turned twenty-three, still innocent in the true ways of politics, thoroughly ideo-

logical in the Upper West Side manner, she decided (as
Carol herself had decided, but in Elaine Rossiter's case with
a larger sense of mission, in substance *intellectual*) to make
her career in Washington.

She got a good job with one of the liberal magazines based
in New York, and a curious but by no means unprecedented
thing happened to her once she had settled into the life of
the city. Unlike Jennie Grand, who would soon become
Carol's closest friend, a young woman who became satiated
with the political fare and sought other and wider interests,
Elaine was drawn to Washington politics like fine iron filings
to a magnet. She lived, talked, and absorbed the minutiae of
politics in a condition bordering on the euphoric. Art, reli-
gion, literature, men, the temperature, fashion became mere
impedimenta to her. On occasional trips to New York her
talk—delivered in a deep but otherwise nondescript mono-
tone about conference committees, the hidden prospects in
forthcoming national elections, the hazards of political polls,
the conversation the Secretary of the Interior had had with an
Assistant Secretary of State on the previous Tuesday, some
revealing thread of cocktail chatter about SEATO overheard
at a Georgetown party on the day before yesterday—never
failed to astonish her former Manhattan friends. "What
happened to Elaine Rossiter?" they asked themselves. If
some old Manhattan acquaintance from Columbia brought
up the New York Philharmonic, she countered with a de-
scription of what the junior Senator from Illinois told her
about home rule during a summer evening's conversation at
Watergate. If another dared discuss the latest trends in New
York publishing, she retorted with a compliment to the daily
miracle of getting out the *Congressional Record*. If an acute
and only vaguely calvinistic column by Mr. Reston writing
from the heart of the cornbelt in the *Times* were evoked, she

rebutted that the Washington *Post* was infinitely livelier than the unfortunate old gray lady. Her New York friends, somewhat alien to Washington as most Manhattan intellectuals were, a little bored by it, and, in truth, frightened by its very presence, did not understand that they were witnessing in Elaine the sudden flourishing of a Washington phenomenon, old as the city itself. For people like Elaine, with rather narrow imaginations, often fall so easily under the sway of the town's "number one industry," that most pervasive of Washington clichés, that they begin to appropriate all the official nuances and institutionalized formalities of the place as if these had somehow belonged to them all along. She would grow one day into a woman of feeling, but as for now her magazine pieces were hard going because they seldom confronted life, they almost never dealt with the engorged emotions behind even the most straightforward politics. Little matter. She was good at her calling. There was a market for her insights in the liberal magazines.

One might think it strange that Carol and Elaine became friends for life: the beautiful Southern belle born of the womb and depth of Arkansas, with an eye for the romantic happenstance, and the delicately scornful New York prodigy. If Carol existed by her whims, Elaine thrived in the essential rootlessness of her adopted place. She lived by the political *moment;* that is, what was happening that week in Washington, be it committee hearings on Congressional pay raises or Presidential talks with British ministers or Senate amendments to an aid bill, was important to a degree that precluded all else, including Gettysburg on the afternoon of July 3, 1863, Tennessee Williams' latest Broadway endeavor, Ingmar Bergman's newest film, or the ramifications through recorded American time of President Monroe's Doctrine.

Yet there is an electricity between white Southerners and

Eastern Jews, for despite the most manifest disparities they have emerged from two similar cultures, buttressed by old traditions of anguish and the promise of justice. They sense this in each other; in the happiest of circumstances they exist to one another somewhat like parallel lines. They bemuse one another. For if the Jews are the carriers of culture, taking it with them wherever they go, from Warsaw to Scarsdale, the Southerners themselves are the oldest of the Americans, adventurers, dreamers of dreams, high-tempered and stubborn, playful even in the direst times, the classic founders of states and indeed of our nation.

"Buy yourself a new dress, for God's sake," Carol would say. "Get a boyfriend. Come drink with us in the Congressional."

"I can't," Elaine would reply. "I have a deadline on the Senate hearings."

"Then tell me about the hearings. What are they about? Who does what to who? I just want the key words."

Then Elaine Rossiter would outline in detail the significance of the issues which had engrossed her. And Carol, listening with an eye arrogantly cocked while slicing squash and baking casseroles, would be more than adequately briefed for the next evening's dinner at the home of the *Post*'s editor.

Once Carol got Elaine a date to a dance at the Shoreham with an economist in Health, Education and Welfare.

"What did you think of him?" Carol asked her the next day at the Sans Souci where they occasionally lunched.

"He's conservative. We argued the whole time."

"Hell."

"He believes the South will solve the racial dilemma before the rest of America does." Elaine shrugged and groaned.

"So do I," Carol said with a laugh.

"It's nonsense. This is the year 1958. Really, Carol, you're too naive. Don't you read the papers? Why did you ever come here?"

"Do you want to see him again?"

"I'm going to his office tomorrow to do some research on the education bill."

"What's in that bill? Does it stand a chance? Just give me the broad view."

But Elaine Rossiter, writing her next piece in her mind's eye, described the legislation at such length, lingering heavily on the cloakroom maneuvering and the likelihood of all the small and tawdry floor amendments, that only over the coffee was she able to record her summations. That night, at the buffet at her Kentucky Senator's, Mrs. Oveta Culp Hobby offered Carol a job.

Her other new friend was a buxom young woman from the Great Northwest, vital as a dairy maid and twice as strong, who was wife and helpmate to an ambitious Congressman only recently arrived in the city. Her name was Ruth Ann Pennebaker, and since her husband's office was next door to Carol's Arkansas Congressman in the New House Office Building, they had met quite early on the Hill. Ruth Ann knew nothing of artistry. Like Carol she had come to Washington to learn all there was to know, but unlike her she would cease to learn at some imprecise point which Carol assumed to be the starting line. She forever bubbled with good cheer, and she undisguisedly adored her new friend, whose beauty, grooming, and lighthearted sophistication captivated her loyal heart. Ruth Ann was not the first Washington lady Carol taught to plan entertainments and to shop for inexpensive clothes, but the recipient of these instructions was by far the most gratified by them, and hence the most appreciative.

Ruth Ann Pennebaker's heroine was Eleanor Roosevelt,

and in her own ingenuous way she considered herself one of the new Washington women. On afternoons when the work was slow she and Carol slipped into the cafeteria for coffee. Here she told Carol how difficult it was to have to run two houses in two far removed parts of the country. The constant telephone calls. The unpredictable mealtimes. The drudgeries she and her husband had to perform to gain office. The problems of putting their children in new schools. She and her husband had no money, and she worked every day in his office. She answered mail, dealt with the telephone, took constituents on tours, watched the House from the gallery, planned her husband's speaking schedules and press releases, and wrote a column twice a month for several newspapers in the home district. In the midst of all this she also raised two small children. She was as uncomplaining as a waterfall, balancing the official and the private with a guileless virtuosity all her own.

Carol admired her, found in her some secret strength not entirely unlike her own, and for a time this undissembling Congressman's wife from the West was the closest confidante she had ever had. Perhaps this is what Washington really is, she once thought to herself: hard undramatic work, dedication, loyalty, and decency before all the beleaguered ideals of the Great Republic. But Ruth Ann Pennebaker also baffled her, even threatened her a little, causing her at times to wonder about herself.

One weekday in early spring, before the onslaught of the tourists, the two of them took the afternoon off and drove out to Mount Vernon. They roamed through the house and through the serene gardens, they went down to the grave, and later they sat on a bench in the sunshine, hearing the chatter of birds and watching the boats far out on the Potomac.

"Well, I just joined the Democratic Congressional Wives Forum," Ruth Ann said with a sigh.

For the first time since they had met Carol gazed at her with suspicion. "Why do you work so hard?" she said.

"What do you mean?"

"I mean, you're at that office every day, you organize everything under the sun for him. You should run for Congress yourself."

"I guess so."

"Why do you do it?"

"Do you really want to know?"

"Yes."

"Well, I love him."

"And so?"

Carol's friend blushed deeply. "I like to be fucked."

"*What?*"

"Yes. I made a decision a long time ago that I'd work completely with him. He wants to make the Senate, you know. He's working all the time. It's the only way I can see him. I save him a salary on the payroll. That way he gets to come home a little earlier. He can spend a little more time with the kids."

"And . . . more time to make love?"

"I was wild. I slept with everybody in college. I still feel wild. It frightens me. But he steadies me, you see. He knows how to love. Sometimes when we're working late at night we lock the door of the office. I need him." Once again she blushed.

Carol looked at the ground. "What does he do to you?"

"All the best things. You know."

"Yes."

"Carol! I believe you're a virgin."

"Oh, no."

Later, driving toward the city in Carol's car, just as they
caught sight of the Monument from the parkway, Carol
said:

"So that's the answer. You like to make love?"

"Well, I believe in being a good liberal. But that's second."

Then they laughed uproariously, like schoolgirls.


THE YEARS PASSED, three of them; she became known there as
one of the most unusual young women in the city. She continued as an assistant for the senior Senator from Kentucky.
She wrote drafts of speeches for the Senate, conferring at
length with other assistants and with friends like Elaine
Rossiter before she set about her work. Sometimes she
supervised the office secretaries, or oversaw the correspondence with powerful constituents. She became on occasion
an ornament of the idle rich, with their predisposition to
accumulate fine spirits just as they would stocks, or real
estate, or race horses, or exquisite backgammon sets. There
were weekends in the hunt country of Virginia, or sometimes
at beachside mansions in the Caribbean; the perquisites of
unchallenged wealth came easy to her, for she reveled in their
comfort, in the taste of delicate truffles, in excellent champagne by moonlight, in the sight of placid inlets at morning
from perfect terraces. On visits home to Arkansas or Mississippi she entertained her contemporaries, who were spawn-
ing babies and immersing themselves in the country club
society, with tales of the life she had made for herself. She
found they were losing the vivacity which had once been
theirs, her old comrades and Southern belles, that they were
growing the slightest bit narrow and smug and afraid of
their husbands, while they toward her seemed merely envi-
ous when not straightforwardly in awe; for good reason she

thought, for their contrast gave her sustenance. She took a larger and more expensive apartment in Georgetown, and when her uncle came to see her from home she impressed him with an elegant buffet dinner in his honor with guests including two Senators, two White House assistants, four national columnists, and a drunk emigré poet from Poland.

One afternoon one of the Presidential assistants escorted her to a formal tea at the White House, where she met for the first time a President and his Lady. She had always been fascinated by the way power unfolded in her city, not so much through its established institutions—her brain was never an ideologue's—but by the manner in which it manifested itself in personal, human terms. The give-and-take of advisers, the scrambling for higher station, the envies and aspirations at the core of things had beguiled her imagination ever since she had read the standard histories as a college girl. So that in her first social visit to the White House that day, a little stunned by all its trappings of influence, she was nonetheless unable to associate her pleasant surroundings with all the mighty happenings which had taken place there; the midnight conferences, the fireside chats so indelible to her childhood, the crisis meetings of cabinets, the notes and the telephone calls that had gone out from there, the Presidents in their angers and jubilations—all these in the presence of the elderly couple who mingled unaffectedly with their two or three dozen guests seemed rather mythic. She sat in the Green Room on a sofa once owned by Daniel Webster, near a portrait of Ben Franklin over the mantel, and she strolled out into the main corridor, the silence overpowering the chatter of many voices, and through the window she saw the greensward of the White House grounds with the Monument far out in the distance. She felt pleased with herself. In a hush she turned back toward the corridor and looked for a long time all around her. To be alone and unobserved now in such a place! She was almost tempted to laugh. Then, a little pridefully, she pursed her lips, tossed her hair from her eyes, and rejoined the group in the room.

It was a year or so before the change in administrations that she met Jennie Grand. Jennie was a rather plain, willowy brunette from the West, the wife of a television executive who specialized in the politics of Washington. If Carol soared, Jennie was earthbound: at twenty-nine, solid, independent, exceedingly intelligent. She had lived long enough to know that she was not invulnerable nor invincible nor any of the things that the more misty-eyed, such as Carol Templeton, believed themselves to be. Once she had been trusting and expectant, living as she had in a climate of the sure, the safe, and the kind. She had only recently survived, with the help of a Bethesda psychotherapist, a confused and badly understood love affair. Now she believed she had an understanding, only lately assumed, of the ways of the world, of the plots, the tricks, the skepticisms available to those who cared to use them, and since she was growing older and approaching the sharp divide of thirty, she had become cynical in the ways of her city. She was thus a counterpoise to Carol, and because they had so little in common they became the closest of friends. "No one in Washington has much of a sense of irony about himself," she told Carol. "This is a town full of interesting women who've been drained of their vitality. The really ambitious ones grow masculine, and the gentle ones grow sorry for themselves." Another time she would say "I'm absolutely convinced a *staggering* number of men here don't sleep with their wives. Maybe that's why so many ladies in the northwest neighborhoods are paranoid about rape," suggesting, she supposed, that politics takes the place not only of romance, but sex too. Carol adored her and trusted her, too much perhaps, while Jennie Grand considered her new friend irredeemably innocent, but viewed her nonetheless with wonder and the merest touch of envy, and felt in her something uncanny.

Jennie spent considerable time in New York, where she was conversant with the writers and painters and the community of the theater and the musical comedy, and although she enjoyed these forays, more indeed than she ever admitted, she came back from them saying, "No one really cares about anyone else any more." Her townhouse in Georgetown was lately a place where the intellectuals and reformers came together. She cared not a whit for glitter and display. She and her husband had been around Washington long enough to know, as she told Carol, "to leave ninety-five percent of the Senators and Congressmen alone because they never listen to you; instead they wait their next cue. They get that glazed, faraway look in their eyes when you're talking to them, and you can tell they've just remembered another story." If Carol's failing, then, seemed scarcely more complicated than a young woman's ingratiating self-regard, Jennie Grand's was less common. Ever since she was a girl in California, the daughter of a rich businessman who dabbled a bit in politics and scholarship and the arts, she had been surrounded by worldly people. She took her fellow beings for granted. "Never follow a loser," became her favorite watchword. She was sometimes terribly wrong about others. She did not intend to be, for there was little abject narrowness in her nature, but it was as if her whole experience had prepared her to be skeptical, skepticism for her being a first line of defense, as well as a manner of survival. She had lost something of her sense of wonder, she was unable to see consistently in terms of character and accomplishment, and because of all this she saw everyone in much the same light, without much subtlety or nuance. Washington compounded her ennui.

For Jennie in truth was a skater on parquet, never the queen but perpetually the lady-in-waiting: she charmed, she entertained, she informed, a role as old as formal society. Early in life plain women of high intelligence learn of themselves that they must succeed on personality, and the best of them like Jennie discover after a while that personality conscientiously pursued is indeed quite often as efficacious as beauty itself. Her conversation was piquant. She could not, for instance, approach a well-known politician and say, "What do you think of Mr. Fulbright's speech?" Rather she would say, "What on earth do you think of so-and-so putting his foot in his mouth about Mr. Fulbright's speech?" She was like the bee going from blossom to blossom, picking up something organic at every flower and carrying it on to the next, and for Jennie this was not just an art form but also a news service and, finally, a method of quality reportage. Conversation with Jennie was like giving secret portfolios to Reuters. In the same communicative tradition of Marconi and Morse, of Gutenberg and Xerox, she interrogated her acquaintances on the *vitae* of hapless newcomers; swift as the most artistic basketball pass she forthwith began to accumulate her dossiers. She was seldom especially malicious, and in this regard she was on a plane considerably above the less talented of her Washington colleagues; malice would evaporate her sources. Playing all sides, she was not as subtle as she conceived herself to be. She was only ever so slightly poisonous, not in the spirit of manipulation, or of the machinations she felt she newly understood, but to inspire in the larger interests of truth. *"I wouldn't tell you this if I felt you shouldn't know,"* she would say, "but _____ has been saying about you . . ."

Jennie saw and reported all the passions and despairs of others as if these were expressions of a fanciful swirl. She saw the torments of hearts less as events in the great human comedy than as other items to be distributed in fellowship and largesse. It was, almost classically, the point of view of the observer. Unlike her predecessors among equally indigenous Americans who prospered in giving ammunition to the Red Indians, her conscience never bothered her, and indeed why should it at all? For she existed in living vicariously, and in enjoying vicariously the fruits of her own inestimable vicariousness.

They pooled their resources. Jennie, the preeminent conversationalist in this city of unencumbered talkers, knew everyone, and she invested Carol with her private intelligences and set out to make matches. "Be yourself," she would say. "I was talking with a Congressman's wife the other day and she said, 'Nobody knows my name.'" For a time she tried to persuade Carol to ignore her two companions from the earlier days, Elaine Rossiter and Ruth Ann Pennebaker, for she considered them much too typical of those very qualities which made Washington mundane. Carol made her shrimp and pork and chicken dishes for Jennie's parties, rivaling the occasional Senator who came to them with talk of her own, and it was at Jennie's, when she was twenty-three, that she was introduced to the attractive Yale bachelor in the State Department and had the first serious affair of her life, and at Jennie's also that she later met the writer for one of the mighty newsweeklies and had the second. What were her affairs? A ceaseless parade of parties at the embassies, and the hotel balls and the Disease Dances, and the Georgetown dinners, and innocent lovemaking in her apartment or theirs, in motels in Maryland, and cottages on the shore. It may have worried her at first that love was inessential and of little consequence, without sensation or pleasure beyond the enjoyment of being held and pampered. She was becoming aware of a certain vague interior need, but she gave little thought to these curious stirrings, for she did not truly perceive them. She dismissed the small awareness of her fragilities. She was having fun! And in both instances, she could tell with a satisfaction which amused her more than it disturbed her, the Yale man in State and the writer for the mighty newsweekly began by being deeply in love with her, and proud of her, and then became wholly intimidated by her. Sometimes her comments at parties embarrassed them; the raw earthy South in her became entirely too much for them. Both affairs ended acrimoniously. Since competitiveness was so deeply ingrained in her being, even in the rush of love there were things to be seriously reckoned with. The tongues of a dozen women who had suffered her artistries in silence, who had witnessed their husbands attending her fawningly in the presence of others, began finally to assail her. Her period of grace was not over. Neither was it destined to last forever.

The talk of her grew; in dozens of matronly conclaves and afternoon teas she was dissected and found excessive, such as the one among many that Jennie Grand reported to her:

"She's a vulgar prattler," Jennie's friend who was a Senator's wife would say. "Nothing but pure ambition."

"She's a flirtatious little nymph," the wife of a civil servant would add. "Did you see her last night lifting the trousers of that Congressman and asking him why he wore garters?"

"She's just a free spirit," Jennie would say. "She's young and uninhibited and full of life. Don't fault her for that."

"She won't be young forever," one of the wives said.

"I think she has a horrible streak of insecurity," the other said.

And Jennie: "Some day she's going to be a truly great woman."

"How do you know?"

"She's brave and she's so alive."

"Pure vulgarity!"


JIM HOLLYWELL. She met him finally at a dinner party given by her Senator. At thirty-five he was ten years older than she, a darkly handsome young man, tall and angular, who had inherited thirty million dollars and dealt leisurely in the market. He was a generous contributor to partisan causes, a New England Yankee from Hartford who had spent most of his adult years in Washington, and one of the most eligible bachelors now in the city's *haute* society. And no tweedy Ivy Leaguer like the men from State and the newsweekly: on the contrary, he had studied finance at the University of Virginia, though she later learned he had managed to fail the Harvard Graduate School of Business, preserving that fact in the fine oils of discretion.

She had noticed him gazing in admiration at her from across the table at her Senator's. She had been at her best that night, first boisterous and amusing before the assembled company and then, when she and her Senator began discussing for all to hear the approaching change in administrations, she had spoken of Washington politics and the American past with a passion that astonished even her. The nation goes on, she said, for we are the oldest surviving democracy; and furthermore we were forged in blood, in the suffering and dying of hundreds of thousands of boys. Did the Ambassador from Argentina know how many of these boys Grant lost at Old Cold Harbor in fifteen minutes? The deaths at Antietam in one day? Her great-grandfather had almost died of wounds at Petersburg, she said, and when he returned to Arkansas he told his wife and daughters, "I'm *whupped,* and with the Union to stay." All this left her a little breathless, and she reached for her glass of wine. Yet she truly *felt* those generations. And how she had learned Washington in four years! Her girlish debutante good looks had deepened, there were stronger dimensions in them, a maturing radiance that only the most naturally beautiful attain at the approach of thirty, and she was surer of herself now than ever in her life. A brief silence followed her soliloquy. Most of the women at the table looked down at their napkins, but the men watched her affectionately as she drank her wine. Finally her Senator said, "Well then, Carol, a toast to your Grand Old Union, with all its faults and virtues," to which the Argentine Ambassador added, "Hear, hear!" and she was in no measure astonished when the bachelor Hollywell asked her to dinner for the following night.

Jennie Grand had been criticizing her recently because she had been going out with a succession of journalists and television correspondents and making light of them all. "Why are you on that line, Carol?"

"Well, they're casual lays," she replied. She had begun to speak that way, in lighthearted obscenities that belied a certain want of the sensual, a paradox she was not wholly able to acknowledge.

"Do you tell them you love them? Or even like them?"

"Only when I have to."

"Get yourself a doctor or a lawyer or a businessman," Jennie said. "Or maybe a psychiatrist. Don't get trapped with the mass media." She was delighted to hear about Hollywell. "I've met him once or twice. Very handsome and quiet. And my God rich! Haven't you always liked money?"

Indeed she had. She had liked it more than she had

heretofore admitted. Fortunes in Washington, she had noticed, could go a very long way. They had the ring of versatility.

Hollywell was determined. At their dinner that night, in an exquisite new French restaurant on M Street, he had spoken for her before the first course arrived. "You're the most unusual woman I've ever known," he said. "I want you to marry me. I'm not going to let you go." He proved true to his word. He sent her flowers and telegrams. He bought her jewelry. He invited her and several of her friends to sail on his boat among the coves and islands off Maine. He showed her his house in the hunt country. Driving down H Street one day he said, with a slight gesture of his wrist, "I own the next three blocks." Perhaps she had grown a little querulous after all of her journalists and television men, their deadlines and bickerings and insoluble problems of alimony.

But at first she was not interested. Except that he loved her and adored her and would give her everything she had ever wanted, he had very little else to say on any subject that might enchant her. But what was a purposeful and aspiring Southern girl, scioness of a vanished and gentried wealth, to do? What indeed? One soft April night during cherry blossom time, on a boat drifting down the Potomac with a dance ensemble playing her favorite tunes, he asked her for the tenth time to marry him, and she accepted. They kissed tentatively in the moonlight. The engagement ring was fourteen carats.

They went down to De Soto Point, Arkansas, for the wedding. Born as she was to her fancies and exhibitionisms, she gloried in the incredulous attentions of her townspeople toward their entourage, so that for five days she barely noticed the landmarks and inheritances of her upbringing—
. the flat fields and the ridge sweeping toward the river and

the flowering trees along the streets—nor for that matter did she pay much mind to her own people; her garrulous father and her ardent mother and even her robust Uncle Tolbert seemed quaintly redundant and out of place in the midst of this imported glamour, as did all the hearty souls she had grown up among a quarter of a century before. The friends of her girlhood thought him the most handsome and distinguished man they had ever seen, and his eight groomsmen shipped by private plane from Washington were the most urbane gentlemen who had ever walked down her street called Boulevard. "My God, Carol!" one of them said. "How did you come from *this* place?" The wedding got a full society page in the Memphis *Commercial Appeal* and the Arkansas *Gazette*, and almost that in the Washington *Post* and the *Evening Star*. At the reception dance at the De Soto Country Club, Carol Hollywell, giddy with champagne, with the simple avidity of those who are still young enough to be unaware of themselves, thought this place had lost her forever, had become even now a mere dying memento. The river of her childhood, the immense and eternal old River, flowed on in the darkness. It took her six months to know she did not care for him, and never would.

HE BOUGHT her a house in Cleveland Park, not far from the old summer residence of President Cleveland—the chintz and brains section, said the perspicacious Mr. Baker of the *Times*—a rambling Victorian house in the Southern style with three stories and a gallery on its front and sides and ten fireplaces, a livingroom large enough to have a dance in, and the biggest kitchen she had ever seen. There were two acres of land, and a tapering front lawn bordered with willows and oaks, and all this set back from a narrow winding street echoing with the sounds of children at play. Her neighbors were Cabinet members and corporation lawyers and businessmen who strolled with their families at dusk on weathered brick sidewalks and shouted pleasantries across clipped green hedges on Saturdays in autumn: a neighborhood touched with a tender fellowship and bipartisan civility far removed from the city's conflicts and agitations.

Within a year she had a child, a son named Templeton Hollywell. Her marriage lasted six years, less by dint of effort than by her ultimate pursuit, as before, of her own separate wants. As the months passed she grew to believe that her husband's extraordinary silences, which more than a few persons admired precisely because they were not altogether habitual in Washington society, sheltered a banality of imperial proportions. She scourged herself. Why had she not discovered this during her courtship? Had she been too engaged in her own dramas to assess him by her own God-given intelligence? He was accomplished enough when it came to the more casual pleasantries, but beyond that she saw a witless vacuity, an absence of life and curiosity so profound that his dark good looks became to her merely deceitful. In his placid stolidity nothing involved him. She thought him a stranger to dreams, emotions, passions, laughter. He could not talk with her; she tried and failed, tried again and gave up. "For Christ's sake, *say* something. Say anything! Do you agree or disagree?" He looked at her with the baffled tremulous eyes of a very large dog who does not quite comprehend his master's commands but would make the effort if only he grasped the motives behind them. He was gentle and solicitous and deeply in love with her, but this only fed her scoffing impatience. Subordinates ran his businesses, and he had all the leisure in the world at his office to telephone her six or eight times a day, and every evening he read the newspaper straight through, including the classifieds, the horoscopes, and the grocery advertisements, but she never heard him advance an opinion on anything more notable than the horrendous sufferings of the Washington Senators baseball club. Once she believed she saw him reading a book, an Arthur Hailey novel which he chose not to finish, and their guests would try to draw him into conversation until they, too, sensed the wastage involved; they seemed to shrug inwardly before they turned to her, leaving him to himself: as a desolate piece of wreckage drifts in the wake of a merry oceanliner.

One evening the junior Senator from Ohio was discussing the complexities of the new Administration and turned to him.

"Do you think the inaugural speech held out too many promises?"

"Too many promises?" Hollywell repeated.

"Yes. Too much rhetoric maybe?"

"Well, I haven't thought too much that way."

"I think it did," the Senator said.

"Well, every man has an opinion on this. I'll analyze it."

Or a pedantic little Teuton from the Library of Congress would ask:

"And, Jim, do you admire Hemingway also?"

To divert her embarrassment, Carol took the man's glass. "Can I sweeten it up?" she asked.

"I never studied him," Hollywell said. "He killed himself with a shotgun. I read it was a twelve gauge."

"I think he's overrated."

"He found the key to the gun closet. He used his toes."

She noticed people exchanging sly glances about him. To her discredit she would needle him in front of others, cruel pinpricks expressive of a nearly venomous disregard. Almost as a rational act of her own will, he ceased after a time to be a presence for her. She did not regard him seriously. Poor man! He was decent and kindly; she was harsh and self-deceiving. He was not the insensitive dullard she wished him to be. She thwarted his charitable heart. Someday he might surprise her. But he did not know what he had gotten into.

AND STILL, she thought, Hollywell seemed to believe he was making her happy.

One morning he came into breakfast with the day's mail and showed her a surprise. They were sitting in the big sunny kitchen in the house in Cleveland Park, the kind of kitchen she had always wanted, opulent in its modern gadgetry, large enough for a table for eight, and she was staring vacantly out the window at the lawn. Her son was digging in a sandbox, and on the rusty brick wall by the creek a tomcat was arching his back and absorbing the warm morning's sun. From far down the hill she heard the sound of chimes, and children's voices next door from the dense branches of an oak tree.

Her husband leaned down and kissed her on the cheek. "What are you thinking?" he asked.

"About trees."

"Trees?"

"The trees I climbed when I was a little girl. And the chimes we had in the church."

"Do you want to go home for a few days?"

"Not now. Maybe I'll take the boy for Christmas."

"What are you planning for today?"

She sighed. "I don't know. I guess I'll go shopping. I may climb a tree." She laughed to herself, a sad inward laugh. There was nothing she wanted to do.

"Well, look at my surprise."

He handed her a large card. She saw the gold seal of the United States, and she read the invitation to the formal dinner at the White House.

"For Monsieur and Madame Malraux," she read aloud.

"He's a writer from France," Hollywell said.

"I know perfectly well who he is," Carol replied. "*Man's Fate* got as far as Ole Miss."

"A week from Thursday," he said.

The evening was perhaps historic, for it may have been the first time a marriage almost dissolved under the North Portico. Her husband had recently acquired, at the cost of eight or nine thousand dollars, a handsome black 1938 Packard, which he used on only the most formal occasions. After showing their invitation at the gate, they entered the White House drive, and it was at this point that the motor died.

"Oh hell!" she snapped. "You couldn't have planned it better."

"I'll get it going." It was an idle promise. People in the cars behind them got out to investigate the trouble. A Senator of their acquaintance asked if they needed a push. Someone blew a horn. A man in a mustache began laughing. She later discovered he was Tennessee Williams.

"Next time get a Volkswagen," she whispered to her husband. Her usual flair in absurd moments always somehow eluded her in his presence. She was embarrassed.

"It has a guarantee," he said.

A group of Marines came down from the portico and ceremoniously began pushing the car. They found a place to park, and when Hollywell got out he asked a sergeant, "Do you suppose I can leave it here overnight?"

"We'll try to get it fixed for you," he said.

"I once had a car fall apart in a graveyard," Carol said to the Marine. "Nothing so grand as this." Then, to Hollywell, "It's me or the antique."

She composed herself with smiles, and looked around at the famous gentlemen and ladies from literature and the theater, with the smattering of wealthy loyalists and the few politicians and their wives. They stood in line and soon were announced as they entered the foyer. Then they were greeted by their host and hostess.

"That's what you get for buying a Packard," the host said.

"Oh no!" she replied.

"The Senator told me."

A number of small tables were set in the State Dining Room. The splendor of the moment caused Carol to pause before the scene with delight, the magnificent chandelier catching the glow of the dozens of candles, the oak walls done in white, the immense golden curtains, and a somber Abe Lincoln over the fireplace. From somewhere came the sound of soft music. She began greeting others among the guests. Her legs felt strangely light, and as she sipped her champagne she thought to herself: "I'll have to get used to this."

"You're one of the two prettiest girls in the room," her dinner partner, a famous best-selling novelist, vaguely middle-aged, who may have been ever so slightly drunk, said to her.

"Who's the other?" she said.

"The girl at the main table."

"Who would have thought?" she replied. She looked briefly at the hostess. For the first time in a long while she felt a twinge of feline jealousy.

But she succumbed to delicacy and elegance, to the perfection of twinkling crystal and gold-trimmed china and light spring wine. From across the way she caught a glimpse of her husband, quite austere between a female playwright and a stately actress. What in the world would he be saying to them? The thought made her playful.

"This is a long way from the Dew Drop Inn in De Soto Point, Arkansas," she said to the novelist.

"It's a long way from the school cafeteria in Terre Haute, Indiana," he said.

"Is that where you're from?"

"Yes. But I met Malraux in Paris, not in Terre Haute."

"Have you ever written about Washington?"

"No. Everybody's too native to somewhere else."

"Northerners consider it Southern and Southerners think it Northern."

"That's why it's here."

"Well, I'm a native, and I really liked your last book."

"Can I come see you?"

"No. That's my husband over there." She pointed to him.

"Why's he so glum?"

"Because he hasn't seen a play in ten years. Also he's *consigliere* for a major Mafia family."

"No kidding?"

"How do you think I got invited?"

"I don't believe I like Washington," the novelist said, making a dour face full of contempt.

"Well, you see," she replied, "we're like the Confederate Army in the winter of 1863, always fighting among ourselves. But when the New Yorkers and the others come at us and make light of our ways, we always close ranks. Grant learned that lesson, and I hope you do too." She lifted her glass to him and smiled.

"I don't even like the layout of the place," the novelist said. "Everyone else seems to go into convulsions about how wonderful L'Enfant was and what a shame they finally made him stop, but the way this city spreads out and arches around and goes hysterical on diagonals and tunnels under circles and insane boulevards like wheel spokes horrifies me somehow. It frightens me. I'm always getting hopelessly lost, and when I'm driving my car down a street named for some obscure letter in the alphabet I have the most terrible feeling I'm in an elevator. You should've done what the visionaries did in Salt Lake City. They were so obsessed with crosses they laid it out in a plain old grid."

Carol looked at the roguish figure beside her. She smiled again coquettishly. "Don't be too harsh on us. Maybe you should stick to writing about wars."

"This town is too artificial and imposed and planned, like the capitals of dictatorships. It's downright un-American! Who wanted another Versailles in the swamp bottoms?"

"Well, we had to start from nothing."

"And why the hell is it all its politicians have such thin lips, as if they're constantly anticipating dental surgery? Why can't some of them have those sensuous fish-lips the dictators have—Mussolini, Batista, Franco, Perón, Papa Doc Duvalier? And the politicians' wives! You talk with them in a rational European way about things that matter, or you ask a perfectly intelligent question or two about their lives, and right away they get *suspicious*. They're very well trained, you see, like geishas. Something about them reminds me of what I've heard about the discipline in the Sultan's harem in the Seraglio when Constantinople was in bloom. And I'd imagine their husbands fornicate when they're out on the road as if they expected it by divine right."

"They surround themselves with worshipful admirers," she said. "It's their solemn duty to get carried away. It's not so much the nature of their glands as the nature of their calling."

"And while I've got you—listen, I may be getting jaded, but I've been living abroad for a long time, and when I came home this trip something hit me hard. The way people of a certain set in this town, supposedly intelligent and civilized people, talk about each other is stunning. It's even worse than the 'thirties—hell, worse than the 'thirties because now it's so gratuitous."

"Maybe it's true everywhere."

"Maybe so."

"Here, have some more wine," she said.

"I'll remember this conversation," her companion said, looking across at her with a faraway but no less affectionate gaze, his agitation diminished now, then adding in afterthought, a little wistfully: "And still, I suppose, we should all try and get to know Washington. It's a kind of responsibility."

"We'll give you a special escort back to Europe, where everything is chaos and democracy," she said. And with this she gently squeezed his hand.

"Cheers to that, my lovely."

Soon the host stood to make the toast. Silence descended. All eyes were upon him.

"This will be the first speech about relations between France and the United States that does not include a tribute to Lafayette," he said. "It seems that almost every Frenchman who comes to the United States feels that Lafayette was a rather confused sort of ineffectual, elderly figure, hovering over French politics, and is astonished to find that we regard him as a golden, young, romantic figure—next to George Washington, our most distinguished citizen. Therefore he will not be mentioned, but instead I will mention a predecessor of mine, who was our first President to live in the White House. John Adams asked that on his gravestone be written, 'He kept the peace with France.'"

Everyone laughed appropriately. There was a scattering of applause. As the host continued his deft remarks, Carol for the second time that night experienced a sharp stab of emotion, a melodramatic discontent, as if with one false turn she had irrevocably committed herself to inessential things. She not only felt incomplete and strangely insecure, she sensed even more the wreckage of her girlish hopes and desires. In the surroundings of the evening she should have been lighthearted and fulfilled, but the happy mood, the trappings of power and sophistication, the subtle commingling of the moment with this mansion's past, rushed by her like the ghosts in dreams. *Should I have sought greatness in a husband?* she silently wondered, but this was merely the surface of her sudden bitter anguish, for in her heart she conceded, wordlessly, with the swift wisdom of released emotion, that she may have ignored and failed, defied and abandoned her own dreams of herself.

The guests retired now to the foyer for champagne and a brief performance by a string ensemble. She felt a tug at her elbow. Turning, she saw her friend Ruth Ann Pennebaker.

"Where have you been, Carol? I haven't seen you in three months." She whispered in excitement, "Do you know we're the only Congressman here? Isn't it glorious?"

"It's the pinnacle of my existence," Carol said.

"Mine too! Do you know who I sat next to? Let me tell you what he said . . ."

For the first time since her childhood she yielded to unusual rages. After the evening with the junior Senator from Ohio she took a carving knife and pried the heels off all her husband's thirty pairs of shoes. One morning as he was leaving for his office she taped a slip of paper on the back of his coat which said: NOTHING INSIDE. She cut the buttons off his five tuxedos. On Thanksgiving Day she burned the turkey and threw it out the window by a leg. At *Gone with the Wind* she hit him on the head a half dozen times with her purse when he yawned during the rape of Atlanta. One spring afternoon in the 1960's she invited two or three dozen anti-war demonstrators into her house, where she shampooed hair and clipped locks and gave them buttermilk-soaked fried chicken and Carta Blanca beer, shocking her husband and angering her serenely liberal neighbors with the pungent smell of pot which wafted over her hedges and mimosas.

No one could encompass the variety of these moods. One day she was to meet her husband on the ground floor of the West Corridor of the Capitol and join some friends in a nearby restaurant for lunch. That morning she went to the House to hear an important debate. Already at the early hour the galleries were nearly filled. She took a seat in the top row and gazed down at the scene before her, that familiar tableau which she had grown so well to know as a young girl, and which now was touched with the subtle animation that always hovers over that chamber when its denizens know they are being, to a degree, noticed. The debate had to do with a critical issue of the day, one of those issues which had come to symbolize the extraordinary tensions then wracking the nation. She sat there alone and listened to the speeches for a long time, and she was about to get up and slip away when Ruth Ann Pennebaker's husband, whom she had seldom taken very seriously, if indeed she thought of him at all, stood to be recognized.

To her surprise he was impressive. He was tall and dignified, and he spoke in distinguished phrases, with moments of eloquence. She remembered him as an awkward young Congressman who dressed in shapeless suits and asked embarrassing questions and was a fool for simple drudgery. Now, unmistakably, she saw how much he had grown. What in the world had happened? Had she herself been standing still all these years? Then, when she looked down to the first row of the gallery and saw his wife, Ruth Ann, beaming with contentment, the sight of her suddenly made her angry. She barely heard his concluding plea for a more rational temper: "All this ignores the diversity, darkness, and nobility of the country, and threatens severe damage to our living together with reason." Almost as if she were running away, she got up and left.

She walked outside the gallery to meet Hollywell. She wandered about the corridors and staircases, looking in her distraction at the statues and paintings. She tapped the toe of her shoe on the floor in rhythm with her disconsonant thoughts. She could not begin to fathom the roots of her grievance; she only knew there was a necessity to it, something true in her heart's fear of failure and humiliation. Amidst all the Brumidi frescoes and Latrobe's unlikely cornstalks and tobacco plants she felt as if she were a leaf that had drifted in through an open passageway. Everything about her reminded her not of achievement, but of catafalques and mourning.

She looked down the corridor and saw her husband approaching. As she would so frequently, she fastened her sourceless discontent upon him. When he reached her he embraced her lightly, then stepped back: "Well?"

"It wasn't very good. Only Ruth Ann's husband."

"Maybe Ruth Ann writes his speeches."

They were walking side by side. They stopped for a moment in the Hall of Columns, among the statues of long-vanished state luminaries, all sweetly contrived when Washington was a struggling country town. They were standing between James P. Clarke, Governor of Arkansas, by Pompeo

Coppini, and J. L. L. Curry, Alabama educator. She chose her words.

"You know as little about greatness as these Italians. Look what they worked with."

"Is something wrong?"

She walked ahead, up the stairway into Statuary Hall, pausing dramatically to stroke an old notable under the chin. For a moment she thought he was gone, but he joined her again.

"Is something wrong?" he repeated.

Now they were in front of Dr. John Garrie of Florida, inventor of the artificial ice machine.

"You're artificial ice," she said.

A large group of tourists came by, with accents and twangs that were coast-to-coast in their eclectic sweep. They drifted across the room to eavesdrop on the young couple standing exposed among the statues. Their timing was perfect. Carol reached into her purse and threw a tube of lipstick at her husband. It zoomed over his left shoulder and struck the outstretched palm of Governor Zebulon Vance of North Carolina.

"Get control of yourself."

A flying compact hit Hollywell on the elbow, caroming then off the midriff of Doctor Florence Rena Sabin of Colorado. By this time the spectators were talking among themselves.

"I think it's some kind of act," a rotund Midwestern lady said.

"They told me we'd see this sort of thing," a companion in red sneakers and bermuda shorts said.

"She's certainly pretty, whoever she is."

"She's a she-wolf."

These judgments were lost on her. She retreated through

the crowd and hurried down the stairway. Her husband departed in the opposite direction.

The tourists followed her. She was standing to get her bearings under WESTWARD THE COURSE OF EMPIRE TAKES ITS WAY. The tourists stood to the side of her, watching her with curiosity and respect. Grimly she returned their stares; when she walked briefly toward them, several of the more timid began backing slowly away, their eyes registering her slightest movement. Then, just before she left, she raised both her arms, and shouted, in a voice which reverberated down the West Grand Stairway toward the farthest reaches of the Rotunda: "*Get out of here!*"

THE LOVE SHE BORE in stolid aggrievement. Where were the ecstasy and rapture the manuals had prescribed for her, the bliss that was the birthright of all liberated American females, ill-fated or illustrious? Every week or so she sensed him trailing her about the house. "Oh holy Jesus!" she whispered. It would be brief and spasmic, the mating of sparrows. When he had given her something she wanted, she generously pretended.

Since she was at heart a Southern girl of her day, instilled with the final guilt about adultery and divorce, she was determined to remain true, in a word, to endure. She remembered a little boy from her childhood. They were both twelve years old, and for days in the classroom he made knots in his hair with quivering fingers and would not respond when the teacher asked him a question, moping there all by himself. And then she found out why. His father had been caught by a woman neighbor in a hotel room in Helena with a nurse from the hospital. His mother had told him everything, and how his parents were getting divorced. She would never forget the look in his eyes. No, she would find her fulfillment in the joy and station that money could bring. She even began to suspect she had married for this very reason. She hurled herself after the good things. She went to the best stores in New York, and the chic shops in Georgetown, making all the Washington rosters of the very best dressed; her photographs in the latest and most daring fashions were in the society pages, and her name appeared with greater frequency than ever in the more urbane of the gossip columns.

"The great thing about a do at the Shivas," wrote the incomparable Suzy of a Manhattan buffet, "is the mixed bag of people they manage to bring together—everybody from Truman Capote to Senator and Mrs. Javits, from Countess Suni Rattazzi to Bo Polk, from Kitty Hawks to George Plimpton, from Minnie Fosburgh to Ahmet Ertegun, from Elizabeth Oxenberg to Salvador Dali, from Prince Rupert Lowenstein to D.C.'s Carol Hollywell—but you get the picture." She became an arbiter of the high society, she helped organize the balls in the Shoreham and the Statler, and she and her husband were one of the most sought after of young Washington couples on Embassy Row, so much so that she unwittingly gained ten pounds on spun sugar and frozen molds before she took respite in bicycling daily through Rock Creek Park. On her twenty-eighth birthday he gave her an elaborate costume party to which three hundred guests turned out, including practically every notable person in town. The President's press secretary, a notorious wag, was asked at the daily press briefing: "Is the President planning to attend Mrs. Carol Hollywell's birthday party?" The secretary replied: "We're sending the Vice President."

Fortunately for her the early years of her marriage were a good time to be there, the adventuresome days of a new generation seeking what it thought to be, speaking much of it, a larger destiny. She went to the parties with their mixture of the newly powerful people and the younger ones on their way up. They were so devastatingly funny, and they would never grow old! There were evenings then at the French Embassy when all the proper souls departed at eleven, and as if on signal the Ambassador's wife would disarrange her hair a bit and perhaps pull down a strap of her dress three or four inches, and out of nowhere an orchestra would appear and the young people would gyrate into the small hours to the twist.

Her own house was one of the places for the joyous liberators of Camelot to attend. In late afternoon she had Administration wives to tea and served Sangría and Mexican hors d'oeuvres, and twice a week she gave her delightful dinners and served the dishes from the South: barbecue and biscuits and fried chicken and smoked ham with the pungent sauces from her childhood and acorn squash and corn-on-the-cob and cheese grits and bell peppers and richly bodied wines that flowed everlastingly. She threw herself into these smaller passions as fully as she might some grander calling. Her pictures were now occasionally in the newsweeklies, accompanied with the adjectives *dynamic, explosive, charismatic, irresistible;* the University of Mississippi named her its Alumna of the Year, and Chi Omega sorority gave her the cover of its national magazine. Occasionally, in rare moments of solitude, she looked about her and saw, beneath the veneer of felicity and accomplishment, the troubled people and broken lives, the grievous marriages spawned at the apex of our last American revolution. Was something lost in her as well?

She was becoming a little crude and voluptuous and, in moments, rather destructive. She began to make cruel obser-

vations about everyone around her. Her friendships with
Elaine Rossiter and Ruth Ann Pennebaker ended for the
moment in acrimony. Her girlish charm had become peev-
ish. She felt there was nothing else to learn or feel. She was
overly proud of herself, and she thought herself very unhappy.

"Something's wrong with me," she said to Jennie Grand.

"Perhaps you're tired of Washington. As the French say,
the more it changes the more it's the same."

"I have a confession to make. It hurts me to make it."

"What is it?"

"I've never loved a man."

"Consider yourself lucky. It doesn't last these days. It's the
price of the freedom."

"I should start throwing more things."

"Well, divorce him," Jennie Grand said. They were
lunching at the Four Seasons on one of their frequent buying
trips to New York when she often stayed for days, with no
complaints from her husband.

"It's not him. I don't want to divorce him. I just feel unsettled."

"Why not get analyzed?"

"You can't get in for the television people. Analysts are
scared to death of Southerners. There aren't five psycho-
analysts in the State of Arkansas."

"That's because there aren't enough people worth saving
in Arkansas."

"That's because there aren't five Jewish intellectuals."

"Then go back to work for your Senator."

"I got bored with that long before I left it."

"You have a rotten marriage but you don't want to leave
it. You think you have an insipid husband and I disagree
with you but you like the life. Have an affair! For every

twenty vain bastards in that town there's got to be at least one that's worth your while. I can introduce you to two or three right today in New York. Maybe you need to get seduced. Pretty girls sometimes do, despite what they teach in Arkansas."

"No, it's not that . . ."

But later on in her marriage it was. Why not? she thought. It was little more complicated than that. One night a month later when her husband was out of town she got the kind of telephone call she knew so well from her early years. The young Senator from the Midwest who had heard her talk before the young ladies on the Hill during her second year in town and whom she'd danced the frug with at the Kuwait Embassy last week wanted to come by for a drink.

"Where's Louise?" she asked.

"She's down in Williamsburg."

For a moment she said nothing. Then: "Well, come on over in half an hour."

This lasted five months. They met in motels. They flew separately to New York and Chicago and Miami. Once she stayed with him in his best friend's house in the capital city of his state. They even parked in cars. One day they met to talk in the aquarium in the basement of the Commerce Building. In front of two albino trout, bathed in an eerie green glow, they decided she would join him for two days in Greenwich Village that weekend. He departed first, and as she was leaving she suddenly saw Elaine Rossiter, who, notebook in hand, was on her way to the elevators.

"I didn't know you'd recognize me," Elaine said. "I read about you now and again."

"How are you, Elaine?"

"I'd forgotten the Senator is interested in game and fisheries."

"I bumped into him. He says he comes to learn from the baby sharks."

"I see."

"I've got to run."

"Well, run along."

For a brief time she believed she might be able then to care. There was little nonsense about him; he was intelligent and controlled and he knew what he wanted, and his ambition, which was very direct and professional, momentarily made her admire and cherish something enduring in him. "I want to sell out," he might laugh, "but I don't know how in hell you go about it." But he pleaded too often and too forcefully for discretion. In love as in politics his watchword was caution. Walking past the Palm Court of the Plaza one night he was recognized by a photographer, who snapped his picture. It appeared the next day in one of the New York tabloids. Part of her was next to him in the photograph, and although she was unrecognizable, it had been a nervous brush with the Midwestern fates. He called an end to it. He was close to the White House and the polls showed him marginal back home. She was left a little numb. With surprisingly little anguish she dismissed him from her thoughts.

She and her husband took a vacation in France. She stood in Chartres Cathedral at dusk one gray November afternoon. Tomorrow they would hear of the Assassination and return home to their disastrous and riven country, but on this day the stained glass shone darkly with the dying light. From the gloomy corners and chapels came echoes like sighs, muted footsteps and whispers. The organist was playing Bach, and the chords overpowered her, touched some secret place inside her; for the first time in a long while she pondered the mindless riddle of who she was, wondered what true course her destinies had taken since her night long ago in the mansion in Georgetown. She felt now, standing alone in a shadowy recess near the altar, the languor of sanctified places that always had evoked in her the drowsiest rememberings. She leaned against a wall and felt in Bach's strains the dreamy presence of the river of her childhood, as if this moment in Chartres and all she was living through were driving her back toward the old and abiding things she had put away.

# 3

Soocho-mucho-wahoo-zimblat-squashbean! *Lumbo-teebo-wahoo-zimblat-turnipgreen!* That was how Buddy Carr sang to the catfish in his big rowboat named *Cindy Lou.* She had written it down one day to remember, but it never worked for her. The river had been a little too much for her, but not for Buddy Carr, though still it was its timeless presence that had dominated their childhood, just as it must have every child of that day who grew up on its shores. They knew it had taken the bones of Indians, Spaniards, Portuguese, Frenchmen, British, and Yankees, not to mention all the Mississippi and Arkansas children it had claimed without regard to color within their own young memory.

*De Soto Point:* Black alluvial earth surrounded it, earth that buzzed and hummed and made grand noises and swarmed with small things in the nighttime and was broken only by the long narrow ridge which began in Missouri 150 miles away and ended at the river, an old uneroded strip between two ancient channels of the Mississippi, wild in the steamy hot summers with Virginia creepers and patches of flowers. Mark Twain was their poet, but they did not need him then. For then it was enough to sit on the bluffs of Anderson's Ridge and look down on the river and the sandbars and the cypress swamps beyond, and to count the endless procession there before them: the sternwheelers and dredge boats and snag boats and government dredges and snub-nosed survey boats and lighthouse boats and towboats behind the great barges drifting south to New Orleans. The packet boats had vanished, and the mechanical monsters and the deaf-and-dumb diesels were taking over, but the river of her childhood haunted her then with its power. All along the banks on both sides were the twisting cypresses and willows with their boughs drooping into the waters, and the tin doghouses of the shanty-dwellers, and the long white cranes perched on the snags. On the sun-baked wharf she visited with the black roustabouts who worked in pairs with iron tongs loading the cotton bales, who later would retire to the shacks on stilts beyond Main Street under the levee to play coon-can and drink rotgut whiskey. Down along Levee Street were the stark, worn houses once echoing with revelry and laughter. She was caught as a little girl at the juncture between cultures, at some almost precise point where change comes, though she was the last to know it; but enough of the old life remained for her there, so that she would be one of the last who lived, if she cared to remember, to remember what it was.

"De Soto Point is too beautiful to burn," Grant had said. It was a graceful town despite its river rawness, with a heavily arched romanesque courthouse, and an Episcopal church with a hand on its spire pointing skyward to the Lord and chandeliers from the stateroom of the *Natchez* inside, and long rows of business houses overshadowed by the levee which by the time of her childhood had been under water so often they had the faint musty coloring of mildew. Rising above the county courthouse was a clock tower and a cupola, and under the clock a belfry where bells had chimed every quarter hour for five generations, duplicating the Westminster chimes, sending forth each hour the song to which some long-ago Episcopal organist had made the words:

> *Lord through this hour*
> *Be thou our Guide*
> *So by thy power*
> *No foot shall slide.*

Her great-grandfather's house on Boulevard, a wide street with frame colonial houses and screened galleries and climbing roses and water oaks in sweeping green lawns, had a hole in the façade made by a cannonball; her great-grandfather, the brevet-colonel, took a dare in 1868 and climbed to the roof of St. Paul's Cathedral in London and carved the initials D.R.T. followed by C.S.A. for David R. Templeton, Confederate States of America. And her grandmother, his eighth daughter and mother of the United States Senator after Reconstruction, had told her when she was a girl, *you're just like him because nobody can do anything with you, and I doubt if they ever can because they never could with him, bless his memory.*

One day they would rip out the big trees and tear down the houses for service stations and parking lots and shopping centers designed in Milwaukee or Cincinnati, duplicating every last Yankee excess and ravage, but she would not be there to suffer it. Then it was an unhurried place with its wide avenues and forests of crape myrtle and the old houses faintly ruined. Widow ladies and spinsters, pale gossamers of the past, sat on the galleries of the dark houses in summer twilights cooling themselves with paper fans from the funeral home. She and her uncle on aimless walks when she was a child, strolling on the way to the cemetery past Judge Lamb's home and the old Lester house, greeted each lady by turn, and they by turn heard the childlike voices in response, everything imbued with the shadows and the oversweet fragrance of lovevines and earth fecund with the dead leaves of the vanished autumns. And then back to her own house, the family homeplace nearly a century old, a little disordered now, the one-story gray frame with its steep gabled roof and the gallery with iron balustrades and the ancient firebell in the front yard.

On a grassy eminence around the corner near the courthouse was an immense four-sided monument which she had loved as a child, the memorial to Southern ladies, which she read in awe and puzzlement. It was carved in rough-hewn Arkansas granite, shaded by magnolias whose summer fragrance caused the senses to reel with delight, a not inappropriate accompaniment to the sentiments it proclaimed. *"Our Mothers:* to the women of the Confederacy whose pious ministrations to our wounded soldiers soothed the last hours of those who died far from the objects of their tenderest love . . ." *"Our daughters:* they kept the mounds of loved ones sweet with flowers . . ." *"Our wives:* they loved their land because it was their own and scorned to seek another reason why. Calamity was their touchstone and in the ordeal of fire they never wilted." *"Our sisters:* when the Dragon of War closed its fangs of poison and death they like Guardian Angels entwined their hands in the hands of their brothers . . ." One day she asked Buddy Carr's colored cook Victoria what that meant. "Oh, mercy, girl. It remembers the *white* girls."

Farther down Forrest toward town, almost hidden from

view by elms and pecans, was the small colonial that had
belonged to her mother's grandfather. It also had long since
been sold, and was soon to be leveled for a parking lot for
the new Jitney Jungle across the way. On rainy afternoons in wintertime she would climb sometimes to the attic
of her house and thumb the yellowed manuscripts of his
unpublished novels. He had been the editor of the newspaper, and the motivations of his life, as her mother would
often describe him, were steady Episcopalianism, truth, hon-
esty, decency, respect for womanhood, and the Democratic
Party as the final extension of the Southern ideal. Money was
not important, a young man of his age and background was
bound to apply himself to any situation with earnestness and
diligence, but the system took care of his needs. There was
always a family business or a farm to run, or a newspaper to
edit, and for many of his contemporaries the professions that
could be embarked upon with little more training than a
respectable Southern education. He labored over his books,
writing them out in copper-plate longhand, and they were
always tales of virtuous Southern ladies without emotion,
and gentlemanly men who when they fell from their lofty
ideals were suitably punished. And yet even then, as she
might later read for herself on those rainy winter afternoons,
his innocent dithyrambic mishaps might suddenly be punctuated with beautiful prose descriptions done with vividness
and emotion: the river during a snowstorm, Vicksburg in the
depths of the siege, the wounded federal soldiers in the
Templeton house, the coming of autumn in the great cypress
woods.

She and her Uncle Tolbert Templeton and her uncle's
friends, the river engineers and firemen and farmers and
erstwhile loafers from the Dew Drop Inn, poets and
schemers and practical men, went out in motor launches to

catch the yellow catfish and the buffalo and to torment the gars and to pay calls on sick shanty-dwellers and to watch the boat revivals where country charlatans from far back in the cypress brakes talked in the tongues of ancient Israel and Samaria. Bend after bend they would wind their way in the boat to landings on the plantations for barbecues and country baseball games and hunts: squirrels and muskrats and coons and deer and possum. *Huntin's no place for a girl,* her father said, too often to remember. *Huntin's the best place for a girl if the huntin's good,* her Uncle Tolbert replied, so that by the time she was twelve she could handle a .22 and by fifteen when she gave it up she even was doing tolerably well with a sturdy old .10-.10 automatic. Once Tolbert took her thirty miles downriver to a Civil War fort, a decaying apparition of stockades and lopsided huts which Sam Grant himself, it was said, visited before the Vicksburg siege, and there were plantation houses along here with punkahs from Calcutta bought right off the boats when the river flourished a century before. She and her contemporaries, boys and girls alike, explored the creeks and rivers and bayous which emptied into the river and wound out from the fields and woods, learning to treat respectfully its permanent residents, the rattlers and moccasins and lizards and large hairy swamp spiders, and one day a shanty-dweller showed them a hunting dog of eclectic ancestry who could actually climb a tree. This had been the land of the Mound Dwellers and later of the Indians, the river itself was the River of the Indians, and she had a veritable museum of arrowheads and pottery and unidentifiable bones bleached stark white. "These are the bones of an Indian princess named Tishominga," she told Buddy Carr and Lena Teasbury in her museum in the garage, and Buddy Carr said, "Then that's the only princess I ever saw who was shaped

like a possum." Sometimes in high water someone would
suddenly yell, *Things are comin'!* and people would dash to
the wharf to see tables, chairs, doors, fences, and clothes
floating crazily down river in endless variety. One day in
1944 a garrulous old veterinarian from Memphis floated into
De Soto Point from Memphis, 125 miles away, in a washtub
built on automobile tires, and she took him home and scram-
bled him six eggs and gave him a bottle of her father's best
Bourbon to celebrate. There were nights when the fog
drifted up from the river to the very streets of the town
itself, and days when they caught the tail of a hurricane
sweeping northward from the Gulf and the water surged in
and out in immense gray tides and the willows on the banks
were bent in anguished shapes. And there were evenings in
the wild Arkansas spring when the flickering of a river light
far out on the Mississippi side and the echo of a boat's horn,
two long, one short, filled the girl's heart with yearnings she
did not understand.

Her mind gloried in the fabled De Soto, for legend had it
that he crossed the river and landed on its west bank on a
spring day in 1541 half a mile north of town. She read everything about him in the library and embroidered the most
fanciful stories, which everyone under the age of nine and a
few residents over twenty-one more or less believed. She had
to do something with her small girl's imagination, and the
more resourceful the better. Lifting, for instance, an entry
from the encyclopedia when she was thirteen, she shaped it
to her own devices and gave this report to the third grade at
the Negro school during Hernando De Soto Week:

Mr. De Soto's army contained the noblest sons of Spain and
Portugal. The great, clumsy European war machine, complete with knights of armor, cannon, hogs on the hoof, pick-

up trucks, tanks, and jeeps, sloshed through the swamps just across the river outside of our town swatting mosquitoes, dodging arrows, hunger, and disease. He radioed back to Spain for help and found the radio didn't work because it got waterlogged. He kept on going. Soon he discovered the Mississippi River. He tramped up to the river bank close to where Mr. Ames Terrell's plantation is now on the Mississippi side and with pomp and ceremony, surrounded by knights on prancing chargers and gaily bedecked Injuns and Negroes, fired a bazooka, had a high mass, and planted a cross on the spot, and Mr. Ames Terrell's relatives fed the noble soldiers chicken and french fries and R. C. Cola. Part of the cross is in my museum on Boulevard. The public is welcome. Later De Soto died of polio and was put in a hollow log tied down with stones and placed in the river. The stones broke loose and the log floated to shore about three miles down the river on the Arkansas side. Last spring Buddy Carr and I spotted a hollow log about three miles down the river. Looking inside we saw these bones and some wet books written in Spanish. We returned the bones in a wheelbarrow to my house and discovered they were the bones of De Soto. We knew from the history book in the library that De Soto had six teeth missing and a broken big toe, and so did these bones. The Indians called him the Child of the Sun, but he doesn't look like much now. Although the bones when left in the open air in my garage shrunk to the size of a possum, you can view them in my house every Saturday afternoon. . . .

She was raised an only child, daughter of an uncertain and ill-tempered father who owned a bank and whose principal interests were money and debentures and Bourbon, and who seldom talked except when he had been into the corn gourd and then largely about the coloreds, and an enervated and kindly mother who remained in shadows and picked up pieces. Quite unexpectedly one day, shortly before her daughter departed for college, she read aloud to her from Monsieur Flaubert, on which she was preparing a report for her reading circle: "A man, at any rate, is free. He can explore the passions and the continents, surmount obstacles, reach out for the most distant joys. Whereas a woman is constantly thwarted. At once inert and pliant, she has to contend with both physical weakness and legal subordination. Always there is a desire that impels and a convention that restrains."

"That's not me, Mama," Carol said haughtily.

"Well, it's me," her mother shrugged. "And most of the women in this town."

"It won't ever be me."

It was her Uncle Tolbert who possessed the spirit of his grandfather the brevet-colonel. He was tall and lean, a hunter and fisherman, country in his heart and attuned to its rhythms, an iconoclast by nature and a bachelor by calling, a reader of books and a teller of tales. During Hernando De Soto Week when she was a child, four hundred years to the day after his crossing, the Memphis *Commercial Appeal* asked him to describe the philosophy of De Soto Point for its pages and he wrote:

A small-town people with a historic heritage, we have known a little of both victory and defeat. We know how to remember. Many of us have a mental background of furrowed hot fields and a hope for rain. We De Soto Point folk both white and colored live together and love one another. We are both dependent on and modified by the sporadic blessings of forces that we cannot control. We are bosomed by the earth that conditions us, touched by the river that has ever threatened and liberated us. We think as our land thinks, and those who understand our psychology and accept our way as being complete rather than clever find us tolerant but not susceptible, easy to amuse but hard to convince, able in the use of words but wary of deceivers. Our faith is in God, the river, next year's crops, the strange benevolence of nature, and the Democratic Party.

He was a river engineer. He had been a Phi Beta Kappa at the state university in Fayetteville and had decided to come home where he thought he belonged. She went often to his office opposite the courthouse where there was a large gray map on the wall charting all the changes along the river: filling channels which might require a dredge near Helena, or a sandbar forming under water close to Cypress Bend. Sometimes he would go out with a crew and several boats from Memphis or Greenville during the rains to slice straight through one of the loops in the river. It was the floodtimes which were the most difficult for him, and he still talked about the Great Flood of '27 which inundated a good portion of the town. Now during the lesser floods he would not sleep for days. He would supervise the sandbagging and the mudboxing on top of the levees, or organize the levee guard, or rescue people from roofs and trees, or feed the refugees. Two or three times at least he had almost drowned, and one afternoon during the spring rains of 1939 he was washed out of his boat and it took three firemen from town who were out with him half an hour to rope him in from the currents. "We were workin' a cave-in around the mouth of the Arkansas in thirty-one," he told her, "and about three tons of wet dirt fell all around our heads into the boat, and then about two hundred rattlers and moccasins started fallin' out of the willow trees, all wrapped up together and buzzin'. I never danced any better in my life that time. And the water was off in town when I got back, so I couldn't wash the dirt off for four days. I went to work the next day smellin' like the swamp." She was proud of him. "When you get scared of something," he would tell her, "just keep in mind that the next man is probably as scared as you." One night when she was nine years old, he had gone out in a boat with some rousters to rescue a family whose house had washed down three miles away. He was gone all night. The next morning before school she went down to the wharf. A crowd had gathered at the docks, and she saw Tolbert's boat as it approached the landing. He walked slowly down the gangplank with a dead child wrapped in a soggy blanket in his arms. The crowd was silent, for they were bringing out more corpses on stretchers. He saw her standing there with the others, a skinny tow-headed little girl in a blue cotton dress, and for a long time she would remember the look he gave her and the way he moved his head: "Get the hell out of here and go to school!" And then, ashamed perhaps of his vehemence, he handed the blanket to one of the firemen and walked over to her. There was mud on his khakis and his face was seared with weariness. He took her hand and said, "I'm sorry, honey, but this is no place for a little girl. Go on, now," and she ran all the way to school.

On Sunday afternoons on various errands they drove out to places named Luna Landing, Yancopin, Little De Soto, Eudora, Lake Village, and Hushpeckena. Sometimes they drove through the plantation country, and in still twilights she would look out at the black fields and the standing water and the remnants of the old woods at their farthest edge and, far from the road, a farmhouse lost to the entangling vines and thorns, falling into its last decay. She saw the giant cypresses in the bayous and lakes, their knees rising grotesquely out of the water thirty feet or more from the trunks, and the bayous which ran like veins through the flat moist country, their banks shaded by the willows and water oaks. In spring the earth would be ridged with the young planted cotton, and there would be a profusion of dogwood, redbud, and crabapple, and four o'clocks, and cape jasmine, and blue larkspur in empty lots. And then the Arkansas autumn: the smell of woodsmoke, the echoings of dogs barking far away, the dull thud of an axe on wood, the flight of mallards circling downward into a swamp.

She loved most of all to meet Tolbert when his boat landed at the wharf after a week's surveying and dredging, and to discover what treasures he had brought back with him this time. Sometimes there would be a skeleton they had found in the swamps, or a tomahawk, or a handful of Spanish doubloons, or a pair of buffalo horns, or a rusty cannonball, or a bell off a wrecked boat that had run aground on a sandbar. On afternoons when he returned, she sat in the coffee place on Main Street, with its sawdust floors and two separate counters where the whites sat on one side and the Negroes on the other, face to face forever, the Dew Drop Inn, and listened to the other engineers who had come down from Helena or Memphis, and the towboat men from St. Louis or Galena or Dubuque, and the lightboat crew from New Orleans. They were pranksters and storytellers and historians of violent mysteries, and the way they weaved the language filtered deep into her consciousness and made her feel she was one of them, while outside down by the wharf the rousters sang:

> *Vicksburg, Miss'ippi was a hilly town*
> *Til the Yankees come and cut it down.*

She was only five in the days at the tail end of the Depression. The drifters from the river and the tramps from the Missouri & Pacific railroad crossing came to the back of her house begging food. Her mother always had great quantities of cornbread and fatback and buttermilk in the kitchen for them. Once a whole Mexican family from Texas, a couple and six children, turned up at the back screen door, claiming they had not eaten in three days. "There's no end to it," her mother said. "The niggers and the shanty-dwellers know how to catch catfish. These poor souls can't do anything." She sat in the shade of the oaks in the back yard and absorbed the tales of the lost wanderers. One of them from New York told her the rats in the subways were four feet long and ate children and that the Empire State Building was three miles high. A farmer from Virginia said he and his friends had just recently torn down part of the Capitol building in Washington for kindling, and an Okie who had gone to California said he gave up on it and was riding the rails as far away from the West as they could go, to a place called *The Nantucket Island* if he could only get there. A wrinkled old man in tattered khakis reported that he had ridden with N. B. Forrest and taught niggers during the Reconstruction before becoming a professor at "the schoolhouse at Harvard" until the school shut down because it ran out of money. He taught her how to whittle a piece of wood with his jackknife, and that night, sitting under the stars, he showed her all the constellations and said, "Pretty little girl, don't never ignore them ol' stars. People live on 'em who are gettin' smarter than us in Arkansas all the time. They got little antennas stickin' from their heads. They can pick up our shortwave radio broadcasts. They can get WWL from New Orleans on a clear night. They don't have to eat. They just breathe in the air. They sleep under big ol' rocks. They learned the

English tongue before Columbus did." Then he gave her a brief lecture on "Niggers as a unit of measure"—"a carload of niggers went by," "a beerjoint full of niggers," "a houseful of niggers," "a truckful of nigger cottonpickers." She and the Harvard professor sat in the night for a long time eating cornbread and looking at the luminous inhabited stars. A clown from a defunct circus became sick in the yard one day, coughing up blood and wheezing like the engine to a derelict train. They carried him to the hospital and her father paid the bill, and then the clown showed his appreciation by putting on a show at the school. Two days later he got drunk down by the wharf and was last seen staggering up the road toward Helena. His name was Jeff the Clown, and he was from Cairo, Illinois.

The faces of the farmers on Main Street on Saturday afternoons were sour, and the cypress cutters in their cowboy hats had lost their exuberance. The children from the country in her school never bought the fifteen-cent lunches, but paid a nickel for a candy bar at the grocery store across the street; some of them did not wear shoes. Negroes brought catfish or buffalo or squirrel to her house in exchange for flour or money, and her Uncle Tolbert found half-starved families in his trips on the river, and he would say, "They've just give up on livin'."

*You're rich,* the children in school told her, for her family had more than enough to eat, and lived in one of the biggest and oldest houses in town on Boulevard. She and her family sat out on the balustraded porch on the hot nights and watched their neighbors stroll by on their evening's walk. If the fire truck came past, they all got in their cars to follow it. The houses were set out in a line under the soft green trees; the lawns would be wet with a summer's dew. Everything was heavy with sweet leafy smells, and the lightning bugs glowed and vanished as far as you could see. And for her when she was six the best of all was the great parade of humanity, without beginning or end, which stopped off there in its chartless migrations. Once they brought in a large crew of convicts to work on the levees and her Uncle Tolbert gave them supper in his garage. She remembered their striped uniforms and the bottle they kept passing around the tables and the men with guns who stood nearby, and when she peered inside the garage one of them saw her and shouted, "Come in, little lady, and sing us a song!" She stood on a wooden box and sang "Dixie" to the accompaniment of a dozen harmonicas, and then all the hymns she knew, from "Jesus Loves Me" to "Onward Christian Soldiers." They applauded with enthusiasm and one of them, who was crying in large whimpering sobs, fell out of his chair. She turned wide-eyed to her uncle for an explanation. He shrugged and said, "It wasn't the singin', sweetheart. It was something a lot less sweet and a lot more powerful."

HER UNCLE TOLBERT promised to take her on a day's trip down the river to survey a sandbar. It was the summer of 1944; she was eight years old. They met two other engineers and some rousters at the wharf and departed in a snub-nosed little boat from Memphis. On this day the river was low, but the tawny waters swirled and eddied, the gars splashed in crazy arcs, and the occasional tin doghouse bobbed gently as their boat came past. A tall white boy, naked to the waist, stood at the bow casting the lead and shouted the markings on his line in a high warbling chant. "See that doghouse over there?" one of the engineers said. "That fellow DeWitt has got fifty pictures of Jesus Christ hangin' inside. One Jesus glows in the dark." At the bow of the shanty the man De-

Witt was willow-weaving, making a chair or a footrest to take into De Soto Point or Lake Village or Greenville to sell for a quarter or fifty cents, and in the cotton fields on both sides of the river Negroes in clusters of fifteen or twenty chopped cotton and then stopped, frozen silhouettes gazing out toward the boat as it came into sight. A barge coming up river sounded its horn, and as they steered closer to the west bank a moccasin slithered under a snag. "Don't ever fool with one of them if you can help it," Tolbert said. "They worship their *privacy*," pronouncing it with a short "i," the way they do in England. They drifted by the country of the lakes which had the horseshoe shape of the old river bends, bordered now by the bright-green willows and russet-brown cypress. Tolbert said, "Marquette and Joliet tried to settle somewhere along in here. All those fellows thought Arkansas was made out of silver and gold. Even Tom Jefferson sent a man in here after the Louisiana Purchase to browse around and he came back as poor as all the rest."

"Your people come here a long time ago, didn't they, Tolbert?"

"This little girl's great-great-grandparents came down from Virginia and settled this country. They cleared it for the plantations. Our weaker relatives founded Little Rock."

About twenty miles or so down the river they sighted the sandbar. Her uncle and the others scurried about the boat and worked around the bar, while she sat in a willow chair with her feet propped under her, looking lazily toward the next wide bend in the river. The river turned in and out on itself as far as the eye could see; she watched the hot summer's sun play tricks with its changing surfaces. The heat made her sleepy, and she barely heard the subdued voices all around her. She would go out many times with them after that, but drowsing now in the sun she was captain of the whole river, and the whole river and all its wonderful things belonged only to her.

Later, on the way back, the water was more serene now, the strands of the sunset from the Arkansas side touched the surface in a listless orange, and the murmur of the first katydids and the noise of the night birds awakened her from her reverie. She felt her uncle tugging at her arms. "See that spot over there, honey? See that clearing just beyond those willows and two big chimneys?"

"It looks spooky," she said.

"It should. Your grandfather Templeton told me when I was your age about the house that used to be there. Once before the Civil War they had a wedding in that house and there were fifty house guests and five hundred people came just for the wedding. They all had their maids and valets and everybody came by steamboat from New Orleans. They got a famous chef who came with his whole staff a week before the wedding to make the food, and there were lights in all those big oaks down yonder, and they danced for two or three days. They had so much to eat they invited the boatmen in. Then they invited the slaves, too. They had *French* food. They called it *cuisine.*"

"Gracious!" she whispered. "Don't you wish that party was goin' on right now so we could go dance and eat that French . . ."

"Cuisine. But tonight we have pork chops and beans."

They tied up on a cypress while the men cooked supper. On the other side of the boat the rousters talked among themselves, shouting and laughing and rolling dice and singing their songs, and she and the engineers and Tolbert sat around the bow and ate under the bright quarter moon.

"The ancient Chinamen said words are boats on the river of thought," her uncle said, apropos of nothing as far as she could tell, but then that was his wont after two or three swallows of Bourbon from his tin cup.

"Tolbert," one of the men said, "what was the worst that happened to you in twenty-seven?"

"I'll tell you what it was, and honey you listen to this. It wasn't anything particular, it was mainly the *thinkin'*. I never saw the river take everything away with it that way. It was worse around here than anywhere I heard since. There was more land under water than the whole states of Rhode Island and Connecticut put together. I was thinkin' it would wash everybody and everything into the Gulf from twenty miles around. I didn't see an end to it. The worst was the thinkin'."

"Up around Helena," his friend said, "I saw a three-story house take off downstream with about fifteen people on top, including a preacher I knew from Sputtswood. There was a cow and about twenty moccasins on top of the house with them, and the preacher was conductin' some singin'. I was on the wharf at Helena and that house went by about forty miles an hour. I didn't know whether to wave or to pray."

"I tell you," Tolbert said, "I thought I knew this river pretty good until twenty-seven. Some of us met Mr. Hoover's people in Memphis for a *conference*. I told one of Hoover's assistants, some fellow from Washington dressed in a suit and tie with a bowler hat, after he'd told us we weren't doin' a good enough job, I said, '*Mister, this river in the last few days has been takin' a lot more out of everybody than it's been givin' back.*'"

The men laughed, and sipped on their whiskey from the tin cups. She moved up next to her uncle's chair. "Tolbert," she whispered. "I don't understand."

"Well, Carol," he said, patting her on the shoulder, "to tell you God's honest truth, I didn't either."

.    .    .

ONE NIGHT IN WASHINGTON she met a friend, Lena Teasbury,
from her hometown. They were in a bar of the Mayflower
and Lena Teasbury, who lived in Richmond, was halfway
through a third martini when she said, all of a sudden, "Do
you know who I miss the most?"

"Who?"

"Buddy Carr."

For a long moment Carol said nothing. She felt the sting
of an old muted emotion. Then she whispered: "*Buddy Carr.
Oh my God. Such a long long time.*"

Her friendship with Buddy Carr was rooted in that Southern river childhood, and she had known him so long she
could not even recall when she first laid eyes upon him, for
this was at last beyond memory. His father was a lawyer and
also the mayor, who sometimes directed traffic on Main
Street on Saturday nights, and Buddy Carr lived in a big
brick house shaded with pecan and elm and walnut trees
two blocks down the street. They were born three days
apart, and about the first thing she remembered him ever
saying in any seriousness was that long-ago afternoon Buddy
saw her killing ants on the sidewalk with a hammer and said,
"The Lord ain't gonna like that much." In the Episcopal
Christmas pageant when they were six, Buddy Carr was the
innkeeper, she was the Virgin Mary nine months pregnant,
and Joe Bob Luckett, son of the bookkeeper, was Joseph.
When Joseph knocked on the door the innkeeper was supposed to shout, "*No room in the inn!*" Instead Buddy Carr
said, "*Joe Bob, we run out of space.*" They listened to the
afternoon serials on the radio, they were quarantined for
days together during the polio scares, they collected coat-
hangers for the war effort and saw Spy Smasher films free,

they sold black-market bubble gum from Memphis, they collaborated on V-mail letters to two hometown Army boys in France, they scanned the skies for Nazi aircraft, and they saw *Guadalcanal Diary* three times. They saw *Gone with the Wind* at the Pic Theater when they were nine.

"Do you think them Yankees were really that mean?" Buddy asked.

"My grandmother said a lot of them were mean, but some weren't at all. They'd come to her house for food after the battle in Helena."

"They didn't put any of the good ones in the movie," Buddy said. "I don't trust a single one."

One day they were riding their bicycles out to the plantations and were eating sandwiches on a cypress stump near Oktebeha Creek. "All this used to be the bottom of the ocean," Buddy said. "So was the whole town."

"I think this was deeper, though," Carol said.

"I bet them Indians spent a lot of time down here. I hear them Indians were giants. They ate bugs. De Soto's men got scared to death of them Indians."

"Well, the soldiers didn't like it too much around here. A lot of his men got sick and died. De Soto had an upset stomach the whole time. He got homesick and a lot of the time he didn't know where he was."

"They didn't even have roads. The river was their *high-way*."

"Buddy, do you think any more Indians still live out here?"

"No. But they sure could hide back down here about five miles and nobody'd ever know. I guess the mosquitoes would get 'em by now though. The 'skeeters down in the bottoms are too thick to see through."

"My daddy says most of the Indians died of some strange

disease, but that old man Philpot sees their ghosts once a year around Thanksgiving."

"Say, Carol, *listen!*"

"What?"

"I hear somethin'."

"Whereabouts?"

"Over yonder, behind the trees."

"Where?"

"Eeeeaaahhhh! There's two giant Indians!"

Buddy Carr leapt from the tree stump. Carol was in such a hurry to get up she fell backward into the mud. She looked around; her blue jeans were soaking wet. Buddy laughed.

"I'll get you back, you rat."

She never could get Buddy Carr back. He always got the best of her. He was short and wiry, with rusty hair done in a crewcut, and his ambition was to play football for either the Arkansas Razorbacks or the Tennessee Volunteers. They decided they would go to college at the same place, where Buddy would be the fullback and she would lead the cheers.

"You put the thing in the girl, and then this stuff squirts out in their stomach. That's what makes the babies," Buddy said one day. They were throwing rocks at turtles on the logs and snags. They were ten years old.

"I know. I thought you had to get married, but Millard Filmore's sister told me you didn't."

"Did you see Millard's sister? Her belly's stickin' out like she swallowed a watermelon seed and *she* ain't married."

"Well, for a long time, see, I thought God put a seed in their bellies right when the preacher says they're married. When I was little I went to a wedding in the Methodist Church and kept lookin' for that seed to come down, but it didn't."

"It don't work that way," Buddy said.

"I know."

Buddy exerted an unusual private magic on the catfish. They fought vicious battles among themselves to get on his fish hook. Buddy's colored cook Victoria would fry them in a heavy batter and make hush-puppies and then they would feast under the walnut tree in Buddy's back yard.

"You know why they call 'em bullheads?" Buddy said in the rowboat. "You get him on the hook and sometimes he stands on his head and pulls down for some drift."

"I'm no good at it."

"*Soocho-mucho-wahoo-zimblat-squashbean! Lumbo-teebo-wahoo-zimblat-turnipgreen!*"

"What's that for?" Carol asked.

"I'm talkin' to the cats."

"Catfish don't understand words."

"Oh yeah?" Momentarily the line of Buddy's fishing pole was taut, and after a brief skirmish he had another. That made five in an hour.

"How do you do that?"

They were drifting slowly under some willows. Moss hung from the drooping boughs of the trees. Out in the middle of the river a towboat behind its long barges churned past, its twin smokestacks bellowing clouds of smoke high into the sky. The day before they and their friends had come to the river to see a famous lighthouse boat, one of the few side-wheelers left, and it had looked like a floating fortress on the water. Today there would be no such spectacle. They sat sleepily in the rowboat, absorbing all the Indian summer gold, and watched the great variety of tiny boats float by toward the last bend before town. They heard the afternoon whistle from the sawmill; a faint haze of early autumn clung to the green bluffs that were Anderson's Ridge. Then Buddy Carr was talking again:

"Did you know a nigger once killed another nigger in a boat in the middle of the river right down here a way? They took the dead body to the Mississippi side but they wouldn't take it, so they brought it back to the Arkansas side but the sheriff wouldn't take it either. That boat kept goin' back and forth for two days. They ended up flippin' a coin."

"Half the time I don't believe anything you say."

A flock of geese flew overhead. "See that first one?" Buddy said. "They elected him their leader. But if he goes to sleep on the job they put him in the back of the line."

Carol looked over at Buddy and started giggling.

"What's the matter?"

"You're just plain crazy."

A look of great panic suddenly came on Buddy Carr's face. "Carol! Don't move a muscle! *Be still!*"

"What is it?"

"There's a eight-foot moccasin's got in the boat. It's about six inches from your left foot."

She bolted from her seat and almost turned them over. She looked behind her. Nothing was there. Buddy Carr bent double laughing.

"I'll get you back, Buddy Carr!"

Later she and Buddy and Lena Teasbury from down the street sat at the big round table in the kitchen and drank Cokes while Victoria fried the catfish.

"Where's yours from, Lena?" Buddy asked.

She looked at the bottom of the bottle. "Jonesboro, Arkansas."

"Mine's from Texarkana, Arkansas," Buddy said.

"Mine's from Smackover, Arkansas," Victoria said.

Carol said: "Mine's from Poplar Bluff, Missouri. I get a wish."

"Make a wish and tell us what it is!" Buddy said.

Carol thought for a moment. "Okay."

"Well, what is it?"

"You really want to know?"

"Sure!"

"I want to be rich and beautiful and the wife of the most famous man in the United States!"

"Clark Gable?" Lena asked.

"No."

"Eisenhower?" Victoria suggested, moving back from the crackling skillet with her hands on her hips.

"No."

"Who then?"

"The wife of the *President!*"

"No!" Buddy said. "He's already married and crippled."

"I mean somebody *my* age someday, dummy."

"I'll be Governor of Arkansas," Buddy said. "I'll invite you and Lena to the mansion in Little Rock and Victoria will wear an evenin' dress and cook fried steak for everybody."

"Buddy!" Victoria cried. "You didn't clean these fish right. They *stink!*"

"That's when they're best," Buddy said. "They been way down to the bottom to eat the little fish that hide under rocks."

Buddy Carr was a good old boy, and good old boys never let you down: Buddy Carr who at age twelve could rifle a football straight through the hole in his garage twenty yards away from under the chinaberry tree, who had a black bicycle with *Buddy C.* written in white enamel on the back fender and who roared down Boulevard into the yard with it at all hours faster than the speed of sound, old Buddy C. and football were mutual and synonymous. Buddy C., who went right through World War II with her, who swapped war bubblegum cards every glorious wartime morning—Colin

Kelly diving headlong into the little Japs' big ship, Jonathan
Wainwright, Roger Young, Jimmy Doolittle, Corregidor,
Bataan, Iwo Jima, Normandy, the Bulge!—Buddy C.
wounded severely on the deaf-and-dumb grounds by a Jap
mortar, writhing in agony, *write my mama, nurse;* Buddy C.,
the first Yank in Tokyo, who on V-J Day after Truman spoke
ripped down Boulevard on his black bicycle yelling, *"We
whopped 'em! We whopped them ol' Japs!"*

Always there seemed to be the faint presence of smoke
everywhere, and the dogs barking from far away, and in the
afternoons of their childhood Saturdays they and their
friends, boys and girls alike, would sit on her front porch
and listen to the radio broadcasts: Ted Husing doing the
Black Knights of the Hudson and the Fighting Irish of Notre
Dame, Bill Stern at the Buckeyes of Ohio State versus the
Hoosiers of Indiana, Red Smith and his grand continental
roundups, Harry Wismer making poetry of the Golden
Gophers of Minnesota and the Boilermakers of Purdue, the
graceful romps of Shortie McWilliams for the Maroons of
Mississippi State, the feats of Charlie Conerly and Barney
Poole and Farley Salmon of the Johnnie Rebels of Ole Miss,
of Y. A. Tittle and Skinny Hall of the Bayou Bengals of
L.S.U., and Clyde "Smackover" Scott and Leon Campbell
and Alton Baldwin of the inestimable Arkansas Razorbacks.
Sometimes her uncle took her and Buddy Carr to the big
games in Memphis where they sat wide-eyed and shivering
in Crump Stadium and surrendered their beings to the
magic of towering punts and broken-field gallops in the cold
Tennessee sunshine, and later had milk-fed chicken in the
Gayosa or fried steak in the Chisca and applauded the
exuberant toasts of the Arkansas partisans.

By nine o'clock on a typical summer's day for her she
would be out of bed and on the move. First she made some

Kool-Aid in a red pitcher, gathered some Spy Smasher comic books, and put a card table under a pecan tree in her front yard. She made a sign in large block letters which said FUNNY BOOKS, 3 CENTS, KOOL-AID, 2 CENTS A GLASS. She might get two or three sales by noon, but that did not especially matter. To pass the time between sales she killed flies with a fly swatter, pretending they were Japanese Zeros. After a while she just sat in the shade of the tree and watched the morning go by: the red water truck sprinkling the street, the horse-drawn wagons going into town, a group of dogs all bunched together going to the town dump. People would pass in cars every so often and honk their horns and wave at her. At noon it was time for a glass of Kool-Aid and a ham sandwich, and then to drift into town to see the latest war movie at the Pic, walking along the sidewalks and avoiding all the cracks and finally taking a short cut down Ram-Cat Alley, where all the colored maids lived. A washerwoman would walk by with laundry balanced on her head, and occasionally she saw one of them she knew and shouted hello.

That day's movie was *First Yank in Tokyo.* After it was over, along about the middle of the afternoon, she was standing on Forrest and Main and sighted a quarter at the bottom of a sewer. She went to the alley behind the post office and found a long stick and then stuck the wad of gum she was chewing on the end. After several minutes she speared the quarter with the stick. Then she walked down to the Dew Drop Inn and had a cherry Coke and a piece of apple pie and gossiped with some of the country people about crops and weather and the weevils. Next she went to her Uncle Tolbert's and played for a while with his type-writer, then to the cotton center for the auction of the first bale, then to the Confederate monument to watch the old men whittle sticks and spit tobacco, then to the Armenian's to watch him make bread, and to the Italian's to watch him make coffee, and to North's Funeral Home to watch a funeral procession get started, and to the courthouse to watch part of a trial, and to the Catholic Church to look in the windows and get scared, even though no human sacrifices were taking place inside it that day. And then to the wharf to greet the rousters and eavesdrop on voodoo talk, and to No-Nigger Lane to watch the Negroes go by. Finally, on the way home, jumping over all the cracks in the sidewalk again, she stopped at Buddy Carr's, who by now was back from weighing cotton at Craw Ferris' Panther's Walk, and she and Buddy and Victoria baked a chocolate cake for Miss Mag Sibley, who was dying in her big house down the street.

AND THEN THE JANUARY when they were fourteen, long after the leaves were gone from the oaks and locusts and pecans and the river was full again with the cold rains, Carol's mother found her in the back yard one bitter Sunday morning before church and said, "Buddy Carr's lost in the swamp." Carol had been shooting baskets at the goal over the garage. She stopped dead still. The ball bounced forlornly into the bushes.

"How do you know?"

"His mother just called. He was out hunting squirrels yesterday morning with Craw Ferris and Joe Bob Luckett. They got separated and couldn't find him. They spent the night and just got back into town."

"What will they do?"

"Buddy's daddy's organizing a search party. I wish your daddy was here. They're meeting at Buddy's house."

She went into her room and changed into heavy khakis and boots.

"Where do you think you're going?" her mother asked from the doorway.

"To help find Buddy."

"No you're not!"

"*Yes I am!*" By now she was out the front door and down the steps.

"No you're not either!"

"Yes I am!" and ran down the street.

She met the men, about thirty of them, on Buddy Carr's front porch. She saw Joe Bob Luckett and Craw Ferris sitting on the steps.

"Where's Buddy?" she asked.

"We don't know," Craw Ferris said. "We went *way* back into Panther Creek, further than I've ever been. We got lost from him around the middle of the afternoon and haven't seen him since."

"He's okay," Joe Bob Luckett said. "He had some matches. He knows what to do."

At the far end of the porch she saw her Uncle Tolbert talking with the sheriff's deputies. She walked slowly over to him and stood at his side. "I'm going with you, Tolbert."

"No you're not either."

"I certainly am."

"Does your mother know?"

"She said I could go."

"All right," her uncle said. "But you stay right with me. We may be gone for a while, and it's no place for a girl."

"I can take care of myself."

They got in the trucks and went to the bottoms, along narrow gravel roads rutted with treacherous ridges and potholes. The sheriff organized them in small groups and plotted the search: broad circling movements aiming gradually for the farthest reaches of the swamp.

The temperature fell to sixteen before noon. All through the afternoon they searched. The bogs were icy now under their boots; the swamp in the stunning cold was eerie and silent. She and Tolbert and three firemen from town had entered woods so impenetrable they had to fight a path with their hands. Twice they built small fires to warm themselves before starting again, and one of the firemen squatting there said, "I ain't never been back here and I ain't never been this cold." They made careful tracks with scraps of newspapers and sawdust, and from far out in the distance they could hear the muffled voices of other groups, making their slow concentric circles one around the other.

She was tired and covered with scratches, and the cold now made her groggy and a little mindless. She looked at her watch. It was almost five o'clock and the sun was going down. Her compass fell out of her hand and she put it back around her neck. She sat for a moment in a small clearing and watched her uncle searching the ground for tracks near a big water oak. Then she saw Mr. Owen LeRoy, one of the firemen, rustling through the growth in their direction. He walked right past her and motioned to her uncle. Mr. Owen LeRoy was talking in a low voice, but she heard the words.

*"Tolbert. I found the boy."*

*"Where is he?"*

*"Back about fifty yards. He's dead."*

She sat quiet as could be. Mr. Owen LeRoy blew five notes on his hunting horn, and then three more. He did this again for several minutes. The sound whistled through the cold leaves and echoed back. She would remember the sound of it for the rest of her life.

"Come on, Tolbert," Mr. Owen LeRoy said.

She followed them through the brush, fighting the limbs and vines with her arms. Tolbert and the fireman stopped abruptly about twenty yards ahead of her. She remained where she was, half-hidden in the brush. Then she looked. She saw Buddy Carr extended against a tree, his head toward the sky, his arms rigid and his knuckles clenched tight.

ON THE DAY after her fifteenth birthday her schoolmates in De Soto Point High School elected her to highest honors. She was named Most Beautiful, Most Popular, and Best Dressed, only barely missing the coveted Most Versatile, which she would get the following year. That afternoon she walked home alone from the school across the streets of the town. The cotton bolls from the trucks going for ginning lined the edges of the curbs like fallen snow, and she looked into the trees on Boulevard and saw the brightly colored leaves and the gray squirrels leaping in the branches and thought: *the days are getting shorter again.* She was happy, but it was a bittersweet happiness, touched with the wistfulness of that sad and lovely time. She heard the soft rush of the river three blocks away down Main and across Ram-Cat Alley, the bell from a boat far in the distance, and the chimes on the courthouse sounding another quarter hour. All around her were the landmarks of her childhood, and the still autumn light reflected itself on the same fences and houses and trees rooted forever now in her sensibility. She could count the houses all along the street where people had died in her fifteen years, and she associated each house or each lawn or the whole back-yard world of gardens and barns and hideaways with words that had been said between her and others, or with things that had happened to her, or that she had done. When she was seven in this yard next to an oak tree she had found a dead sparrow and taken it home and given it a funeral. On the front porch of the house next door she had thrown a brickbat on a .22 bullet and it had exploded and almost hit her ankle. Two doors away was Miss Mag Sibley's, she dead for four years, who wore flowing black dresses and jasmine in her hair and celebrated Jeff Davis' birthday by playing the flute in her front yard, and they frightened her one night with croker sacks over their heads, and deposited dead rats and squirrels in her mailbox. Next door to Miss Mag's when she was nine and the war ended, she and Lena Teasbury set up a Kool-Aid stand and gave away free drinks and Guess-Whats they had bought in Memphis, and waved the American flag and danced down the middle of the street rattling tin cans on a string. She walked past Buddy Carr's, where in the walnut tree over the garage they had once built a trapeze and a birdhouse. Victoria was picking pecans in front. *"Hello, Victoria." "Hello, Carol honey." "How are you, Victoria?" "I'm fine, dumplins. Don't see enough of you no more."* All along here in the warm summer nights they had played hide-and-seek and kick-the-can and told stories on grass wet and shiny with dew. Out of a summer gloaming would drift a voice down the way: *"Buddy C-a-a-a-r." "Wh-a-a-t?"* Far away in the gathering dark: *"Come ho-o-me. Mama wants to spank you."* And she felt once more the sadness that always replaces some long and lingering grief, the quiet sadness that works its way into the bones even when you are young and becomes part of what you are.

At the far corner when she was ten she had seen Joe Bob Luckett's birddog named Napoleon Beauregard run over by a truck, and near the same place when she was eight she watched three boys from the sawmill whip a little colored boy with switches from a willow tree until he cried and begged to go home, and she threw rocks at them and called them bullies and took the little boy back with her for hot chocolate and Hershey bars, and under the locust tree behind Mrs. Claudia Miller's when she was twelve she was kissed for the first time by Mrs. Claudia's grandson from Shreveport, Louisiana. Now she was walking past her great-grandfather's birthplace at the corner of Boulevard and Hickory, a disheveled antebellum house with front galleries on the first and second floor and an elaborate Ionic portico, and roofs sloping gently on each side from the second-story window. In the side yard there was the solitary grave which had haunted her when she was a child, the Confederate soldier who had somehow wandered here from the Battle of Helena in 1863 and died on the front gallery in her great-grandmother's arms, and etched in a gray round stone: LIEUT. MARMADUKE, TENNESSEE. A Northern colonel had used it as headquarters in the Civil War, and the family had sold it in 1870, and she lingered in front of it now as she had since she was a child; she longed to hear its lost voices. Three houses on she saw Sonny Warren and the Warrens' colored yardman Perkins, who had been reprieved from the state prison in Varner into their care. They were raking leaves into piles and burning them and she smelled the pungent smoke which had always told her ever since she could remember that autumn was again on the land. Sonny Warren had graduated from high school four years before and already was a major league baseball player in St. Louis and a hero to everybody in town; once he had kissed her on the cheek and said he would wait for her to grow up, and she liked it because she had heard that line in war movies. *"Hello, Perkins." "Hello, Carol." "Hello, Sonny Warren." "Hello, Carol. I can't keep my eyes off you." "Can I have your autograph, Sonny?" "It'll cost you five dollars, honey."*

"What'd you bat this summer?" ".268 and seventeen homers." "Come see us, Sonny, you hear?" Farther down Boulevard she saw her own house with the long porch, the willow and pecan trees bordering the lawn and the pecans even now rustling through the branches toward the earth. Her father and mother and her Uncle Tolbert were sitting there. She surmised they were talking about her, and she was right. "My well-dressed, popular, beautiful niece," Tolbert said, standing up to his full height and bowing with an exaggerated flourish.

Often when she awakened in the morning before school she would hear them from the next room talking about her. Tolbert would drop by for a cup of coffee on his way to work, and she would listen to him and her father arguing, and the three of them would lapse into a long silence and then one of them would bring up her.

"She hasn't been to church in three Sundays," her mother said one morning.

"I haven't been in three years," her father replied.

"Let her alone," Tolbert said. "She's all right."

"She made a B in mathematics," her mother persisted. "She got a B in typing, too."

"You can use two fingers like me," Tolbert said.

"I don't like all these football games she tears around to," her father said.

Her mother agreed. "Where in heaven is the girl going to college?"

"She's got two more years before that," Tolbert argued.

"Maybe she ought to go to one of those finishing schools," her father said. "There's one in Missouri that caters to girls from good Southern families."

"That Ledbetter gal went to Stephens and came back saying the State of Arkansas was going to be in the hands of the Soviet Communists in ten years," Tolbert said.

"Maybe it will," her father replied.

"If I had my way I'd let 'em have Arkansas and throw in Mississippi too. They'd give up after six months."

"Well," her father said, "the principal tells me she could get into one of those good girls' schools in the North. He says she's got the brains. He says she's the finest girl this school's had in years. He says he'd recommend her to Vas-*sar*."

"Oh hell, send her to Fayetteville or Ole Miss. Up there they'd have her where she wouldn't know whether she was comin' or goin'."

She stretched good-naturedly in the bed. It was better than the radio. She could imagine her father's red bleary eyes and Tolbert sitting with his skinny legs on the coffee table, and the long narrow room with the fireplace and the oriental rugs and the antique what-nots and the stuffed antique furniture. She got up and took off her pajamas and admired her body in the full-length mirror, her small breasts with enormous pink nipples, her skin still brown from the three weeks on the beach at Biloxi, her hair long with a pony-tail in back. She looked on the wall at her picture in the Memphis paper. She was so wholesome that she might have posed for one of the Coca-Cola advertisements then in vogue, where unimaginably contented young men and women gathered at the counters of neighborhood drugstores and discussed dances and school spirit. She yawned and then glanced outside her window at the neighbor's birddog, who had something trapped in the elm tree. "Just let her alone," Tolbert was saying again. "She's doin' all right." She was more or less inclined to agree.

And why not? She was beloved of her teachers because, unique among her contemporaries, she sometimes read books; lionized by her schoolmates because she had a "good personality" and was generous to all and gave presents and parties; accepted cheerfully and even a little deferentially by her elders because she was an Arkansas Templeton. So she could look back perhaps on her teenage years as among the best she would ever get from the Lord's good earth.

She noticed that her father and mother never touched each other. They never embraced. They seldom even talked. There were uncontrollable outbursts in the night, and hot shouted recriminations. Sometimes he returned from a football weekend in Memphis and had to be bedded down drunk for twenty-four hours, and sometimes longer. Violence and madness lurked in the Templeton genes, as her grandmother had told her, and her father had likely absorbed more than his due inheritance. One night when she came home late from a dance he was waiting for her; he slapped her across the face and pushed her into a mahogany table. She went into the kitchen and sneaked up on him later in his study, dousing him with hot coffee and throwing a frying pan at him, which bounced off the side of his head and broke a family mirror. He was reaching for his grandfather's sword, the one which had been through Corinth and Shiloh and God knows what other crossroads skirmishes and nightmares, when her mother came in and shouted them into submission. *"What in mercy's name am I to do?* My own husband and daughter tryin' to murder each other! Go off to bed or I'll call Tolbert to come with his twelve gauge!"

For Carol too had something of the wildness that could burst forth on a moment's whim, a headstrong extravagance that she recognized even at fifteen she must somehow learn to subdue. The boys her age adored her and feared her, but most of them—Joe Bob Luckett and Craw Ferris and Jimmy Teebo and Weed North and Mole Dancey and the other luminaries on the De Soto Point football River Cats—were as fearless as she, engaging her fully in their camaraderie. Once when Joe Bob Luckett pinched her shapely posterior, she bit him so hard on the shoulder he carried the mark of it a whole year, showing it proudly to anyone who asked. She was the favorite of the ceaseless rounds of Coke Parties, where the young ladies sat around parlors in a circle nibbling on hot chicken casserole and cheese straws, and where every salad was garnished with mountains of fruit, so that she was destined never to get a good tossed salad until she went north. She led the cheers at the hometown field and at the games in Helena and Bald Knob and Pine Bluff and El Dorado, whirling and somersaulting to the River Cat Ramble in a pleated red skirt and a white woolen sweater with the yellow initials D.P. She marched in front of the band through the streets of the town on Friday afternoons before football games. They paraded in their flashy red and yellow uniforms from the wharf up Main Street and along Boulevard to the school; two or three dozen Negroes and an equal number of hound dogs from down by the river followed along behind them, making as much noise as the horn section. She traveled around the countryside with the boys, and with the daughters of boondocks hardnoses and cypress cutters as well as the other white lilies of Arkansas culture: the belles of the town gentry and of the plantations behind the levees. Aristocrat, middle class, yeoman, they imbibed the tumultuous Southern democracy.

She got drunk for the first time, insanely and with unusual suffering, when she was fifteen, and she had the dry heaves and promised herself she would never get them again. The staple of those years was the washtub of schoolboy punch—100-proof gin laced with fruit juices and orange and lemon peels and sometimes wood alcohol—placed strategically in the trunk of one of the boys' old cars. One Friday night in 1951 after the River Cats had savagely disposed of Pine Bluff, she and two dozen of her friends transported a washtub of schoolboy to the levee at Cypress Bend, and as a result of that celebration a fullback from the swampbottoms named Leon Ivy had to marry his girlfriend Pansy Silver, moving then to Memphis and seldom heard from since. Carol's mother had studied home economics at Fayetteville and taught her how to cook and all about clothes, taking her to Memphis to buy the latest fashions, the best casuals as seen in *Vogue* and *Harper's Bazaar* and tantalizing evening dresses for the debutante parties and the school dances. At the country club there and in a dozen hamlets and towns in Arkansas and the Mississippi delta they did the Memphis Shuffle and embraced closely and swayed to the strains of Nat King Cole

> *They tried to tell us we're too young,*
> *Too young to really be in love . . .*

lyrics which caused more premature pregnancies in those times in the Old Confederate states than the young passion itself; she danced more closely to the boys than any other girl and felt as no other proper girl dared, at least in public, the tense hardening of their bodies; on the verandas fronting the fairways she kissed them teasingly but never let them touch her very much; in parked cars along the river or in the vacant fields of Anderson's Ridge she *only went so far,* so that years afterward in Washington when a popularizing sociologist from New York interviewing her for a men's magazine asked if she had *ever petted them to climax,* she would say *indeed not, it wasn't the time or place,* lying only a little.

Lying only a little because when she was sixteen and a senior she took Craw Ferris' class ring and they went steady after the fashion: Craw Ferris, whose father owned a thousand-acre plantation named Panther's Walk, who played quarterback and lifted weights and was student-body president and Mr. DP High when she was Miss DP High (and was serenaded by four hundred voices to the finest tune of the Sigma Chis) who took her to dances across the river in Greenville and Clarksdale and as far as Indianola and Yazoo City and Greenwood where she met the soft-skinned double-named tripled-tongued Mississippi delta belles who later ran not only Chi O Sorority but the whole of Ole Miss—and for that matter the entire Sovereign State of Mississippi as well—Craw Ferris with the blond crewcut who coaxed and intimidated until she had to do *something* for the overconfident young son of Arkansas, which she did one Saturday morning in the summer two weeks before he departed virtually forever to Fayetteville and she to Oxford, Mississippi.

He drove her out to Panther's Walk that morning to the plantation house, empty on that warm August day because his family had gone to Memphis. They lay on his parents' bed with all the curtains drawn on the deep-set windows. The room was dark with shadows and they had only been there a brief time when they heard rustling movements outside.

"Anybody home?"

It was his grandmother called Mee-Maw, who had come from her house down the road and was trying all the doors. "Thank God I locked 'em," Craw Ferris whispered. Then his grandmother tried to look through the curtains. "Anybody in there?" she said. "I hear *somethin'!*" They lay quiet as could be. She started to giggle, but he put his hand over her mouth and gave her a warning look. Her hair was tied in a pink ribbon in the back and her light green eyes were soft and moist; she wore bermuda shorts and a gray sweater and brown and white saddle oxfords and Craw Ferris' class ring on her index finger with a little cotton under it to make it fit, and when she told him his grandmother had gone away it was in an accent so small-town deep Southern that an outsider would have had to listen very attentively to understand. How could she know how completely she was the child of the place and the moment? Some day later, perhaps, out across the green flat fields to the town and far beyond the river she would know. But not now.

"Yeah, she's gone," he said finally. "She's an old busybody. Once she caught my cousin with a nigger."

"If she comes back let's lock her in the smokehouse."

He put on a record and came back and lay next to her. He held her lightly and she gently kissed him on the neck.

*The evening breeze caressed the trees tenderly . . .*
*The trembling leaves caressed the breeze tenderly . . .*

"That's my favorite song," she said.

"Mine too."

He kissed her on the lips, and she put her arms around his shoulders and kissed him back. "I think I'll miss you, ol' Craw." They pressed close, and she rubbed her body up and down against him where he wanted her to. In a few moments for the first time she was naked with him. They touched and kissed, and they looked all over one another and then he reached near the bed and she saw the prophylactic.

"*No!*" she said.

"Please. You're so damned beautiful."

"No."

"Oh goddamn it! I got the stone-aches. *Please.*"

"I'll do this." She touched him again. Soon he groaned and sighed, his body shuddered in her arms, and she felt on her thighs what Buddy Carr had told her about all along.

As with all the fateful junctures in her life, the day before she left for college she climbed alone to the crest of Anderson's Ridge and sat in the sun and looked down upon the River. On this late summer's day of 1953, all the boats of her childhood seemed to drift there before her. She had brought *Alice in Wonderland*, the copy her uncle had given her on her eighth birthday, and thoughtlessly she read again from it now.

> *A boat beneath a sunny sky,*
> *Lingering onward dreamily*
> *In an evening of July—*
>
> *Children three that nestle near,*
> *Eager eye and willing ear,*
> *Pleased a simple tale to hear.*
>
> *In a Wonderland they lie,*
> *Dreaming as the days go by*
> *Dreaming as the summers die.*
>
> *Ever drifting down the stream—*
> *Lingering in the golden gleam—*
> *Life, what is it but a dream?*

She lay back ever so drowsily, feeling immense waves of sleep falling upon her. "*Carol.*" She yawned and closed her eyes, and from afar she sensed voices, the deep-sun warmth of summer, and then the sound of organ music echoing through vast chambers.

# 4

SIR, I danced with you quite a few years ago at a party."
"Of course I remember. How could I forget?" He wrinkled
his broad rough features, searching that endless procession
of faces and names which must have drifted like wisps
across his past. "Well, get yourself a drink and come join
us."

She turned to her friend, the White House assistant.
"Jesus, I'm nervous," she whispered.

"Don't be. This time of day he wants to relax. He likes
new faces."

There were ten or twelve people in the elongated corridor
of a room. She recognized most of them: four Southern
Senators and their wives, a columnist and an editor, a lawyer
who had been an adviser since the New Deal. She and her
husband chose a sofa on the fringes of the group. The conversation was aimless. Their host told a story about his early
days in Washington. He was just a boy then, he said, all wet
behind the ears but fast as a mustang. He rushed into Mr.
Roosevelt's office for an appointment concerning a dam in

his district and the first thing he said was, "Water water everywhere, Mr. President, but not a drop for my poor people to drink!" Everyone laughed. There was more talk now about legislation before the Congress, and then an awkward silence.

"Sir," the White House assistant said. "Mrs. Hollywell has been doing some yeoman work in the East Wing on the women's side of the campaign. They can't do without her." He gestured then in her direction.

"I'm not surprised to hear that. I'm all in favor of a little more glamour. Someone over there told me she's fixing up all the ladies with new wardrobes. That campaign train south could end up looking like one of those *discotheques*."

"No sir," she said. "We're going to be very dignified. But I learned a long time ago from my people in Arkansas that folks in the South want their leaders in Washington to look prosperous."

"That's true. Of course they expect their Senators and Congressmen to look seedy."

"And with present company excepted, don't you think they get their wish?"

"I don't know about that. The Senate's got some pretty gay blades these days." He gave her a quizzical wink.

"Yessir."

"You and your husband sit next to me at dinner. You can tell me how they spend their time over in the East Wing and I'll tell you all I know about Arkansas."

"Yessir. We'd consider it an honor."

After dinner that night, her friend the White House assistant took the two of them to see the Oval Room. She was gripped by its silence; its quiet isolation cast a spell, almost dreamlike, upon her. She looked at the large white telephone on the desk with its long rows of buttons. She examined the holes in the floor made by Mr. Eisenhower's golf shoes, and she admired Stuart's Washington over the fireplace.

They sat down. The assistant crossed his legs and lit a cigar. "Sometimes this room gives me the chills," he said.

"I like it," Hollywell said.

"I like it too," he said. "I'm getting used to it all the time."

He was not much taller than she, but he was taut and solid, wary in the edges of the eyes, feline in his movements. He was in his middle forties but he looked younger, with a deceptive boyish innocence peculiar to American males from the empty spaces. There was a presence to him of a man who had taken long draughts of mortification and had weathered them whole, who at some moments in the past might have felt confused but not ashamed by the full measure of his own subservience. He was now at the pinnacle of his life, and he seemed to take considerable satisfaction in the fact that others knew it. He had a wife and two children and he had made a small fortune in land and investments in his native state before he was summoned to the higher mission. He knew better than most the rules of survival.

The buzzer on the desk gave three sharp rings. He bolted from the sofa and walked briskly toward it.

"Yessir? . . . I'll bring it with me at seven. I'm showing Mr. and Mrs. Hollywell the office. Just a moment." He cradled the receiver and motioned to Hollywell. "He wants to speak with you." Hollywell walked toward the desk and the assistant sat down. He looked at Carol and shrugged.

"Whatever could he want?" she asked.

"Don't ask me. You've got the best-looking legs I ever saw."

Hollywell put down the telephone. "What did he say, honey?" she asked.

"He invited me to go swimming here tomorrow. He told

me to bring my own trunks." Carol and the assistant laughed, and after a while her husband did too.


FROM STUFFING ENVELOPES and suggesting clothes, she began advising the Lady and her assistants on entertainments. For the more gala occasions she volunteered as a hostess. She helped with the state dinners. She traveled with the ladies to distant cities. She guided them to the best hair stylists. Soon she was receiving chatty notes of appreciation from the Lady herself, who several times came to tea at Carol's house with a full retinue from the Secret Service, causing the traffic to stop outside so that on later visits they roped off the entire block. She frequently went to the casual family dinners at the mansion and joined in the friendly banter, leaving her husband with the evening papers; she sailed with them on nocturnal cruises down the Potomac; and three or four times she traveled in a helicopter to the weekend retreat in the mountains. At first she was a lady-in-waiting, but they knew she enjoyed a rare constituency all her own in the city, and with her looks and her enthusiasms she became a felicitous counselor to them of the good life, a loyal retainer from the vanished Camelot. Her new portfolio was rich in ingratiating little acts of fealty: gifts from Tiffany's and Cartier's and Lord & Taylor's and Neiman-Marcus, amusing notes about matters known only to them, expensive trinkets and bric-a-brac and souvenirs and mementos. The plainer ones in the entourage, she knew, were beginning now to talk. What did it matter? In four months she had become the court favorite.

"What does your little boy do when you're over here for dinner?" he asked one night at the table.

"Well, sir, he just watches television."

"I'll get that boy on the phone." He reached for the large white console telephone at his feet. "What's the boy's name?"

"Templeton Hollywell. Sometimes I call him The Temps."

*"Hello, is this the Temps? Did they tell you who I am? Well, young man, your mother's sitting over here in our house right now advising us on this election and I want you to know how much we appreciate you letting us have her. Be sure and watch the press conference on television to-night, boy. Someday you might be sitting in my chair and I think . . ."*

Or the night in the boat on the Potomac when, sur-rounded by five or six of the most powerful men in Washing-ton, he turned to her and said: "Let's ask Carol there. Honey, do *you* think I'm right on this little bill?"

"Sir, I have precious little doubt you're doing right. You always do. I got a letter from my uncle today and he said you'll carry Arkansas even if you come to Little Rock and read the Emancipation Proclamation out loud on television."

"You see?" he shrugged. "I ought to be listening to this pretty girl instead of all your racket." The men laughed, but it was empty laughter, and she noticed they exchanged quiet glances.


"You're spending a lot of time with them," her husband said. "Won't you wear out your welcome?"

"If so I'll be the first to know it," she replied.

They were having dinner in Trader Vic's. It was their sixth anniversary. Carol looked disconsolately at her spiced lobster, then across at Hollywell. "Besides, I really think they need me. You always said you believed in universal conscription."

The silence to which she had grown accustomed fell again

between them. Occasionally she saw someone she knew, a diplomat, a politician. She would wave them to the table.

"Carol, sweetheart," a columnist greeted her. "Are you going to New Orleans with us next week?"

"I wouldn't miss it. I'm flying down early to help with things. I'll even meet everybody at the train."

"Do you have any news? You know."

"Surely you don't expect gossip from a retainer," she replied.

"Well, I'll buy you one of those tall pink drinks at Pat O'Brien's."

And when he had departed Hollywell said: "What about New Orleans?"

"A big function. I'll only be gone two days."

"We don't see enough of each other," he blurted, almost as if he had rehearsed the lines.

"Well . . ." When she looked at him again she saw an expression of travail cross his features that she had never seen before. For a brief instant she was touched with something not unlike pity.

"I always thought we had a pretty good marriage," he said. "Lately I see I'm not at all what you expected. I've tried to give you what you wanted."

"You've been a good husband." But the turn of conversation disturbed her, made her a little contemptuous. She had never heard him speak this way.

"I don't think you spend enough time with the boy. I hope all this is worth it."

"Are you feeling all right?" she asked.

"Sometimes I feel I married you and became your mistress."

"My God! Are you being analyzed?"

"Here comes another friend," he said.

"I'm sorry."

"Carol! Are you coming with the party to New Orleans?"

"Hello, Congressman," she smiled, standing now from her chair. "Come have a drink. I wouldn't miss it for the world."

A LIAISON with the assistant was perhaps preordained. He was her sponsor, her lord advocate in the proper places and moments. But there had been one scandal in the press, only recently forgotten. She was being foolhardy. He was courting danger.

Whenever she was with them he was there, shuffling documents, taking calls, whispering commands to others. It was almost as if they were in complicity: he the broker for the imperial will, she the entertainer of the imperial whim. They had never so much as touched, yet she felt him a knowing collaborator. He was brisk and unruffled. She was beguiling and full of laughter. Once at the retreat in the mountains she tiptoed from the dining room and found him sifting papers in a tiny office.

"He wants the Prime Minister of Great Britain on the telephone," she said.

He leaned back in his chair, lighting a cigarette. "That's the second time today. Even I don't know what it's about."

"Can I listen on the other end?"

"Over my dead body."

"I used to do that when I was a girl. We had a party line, and in the middle of some serious conversation between lovers I'd start barking like a dog. Or I'd say something like, 'Both of you are lying,' or 'Now it's time to go to the bathroom.'"

"I wouldn't recommend that tonight." He picked up the telephone. She returned to the dining room and came back to him a few moments later.

"I asked him if I could listen in and he said yes."

"He didn't."

"He *did!* I was just joking but he told me to come tell you."

"If you're lying I'll have you guillotined. When this light flashes you pick up the telephone."

"Did you call collect?"

"We get it free."

"He says after this call he wants you to get the Governor of North Carolina. I can listen to that too."

"You're getting uppity."

"And then after that he wants to talk to my uncle in Arkansas and then my maid Josephine Wilkes."

"Christ!"

Later that night the two of them strolled onto the lawn. The air was cool, and blue lights twinkled far below. The communications trucks were parked under the towering pines, and she heard the rattling sounds of static and the rustling of men in the bushes.

"They carry guns, don't they?"

"Indeed they do. They'd carry bazookas and hand grenades if we'd let them. After all that's happened they'd have him travel in a tank."

"What if he decided to drop the Bomb on Moscow this very night?"

"Don't even talk about that. I guess I'd go in and try to persuade him not to and bring you along for help."

"No, really. I'm curious."

He did not answer. Instead he took a deep breath of the mountain air and looked down into the dark valley below. "You know," he said. "I'm about the happiest I've ever been in my life. Sometimes I say to myself, who would've thought?"

"Me too. But I wouldn't expect you to say it."

"I'll tell you something else. I wish I could take you off somewhere for a couple of weeks. Nassau maybe."

"Well, don't," she said.

"Why not?"

"Shhhh!" she said. "Someone's coming. Well, Lord!"

"*Hello sir!* Come get some of this good clean air."

The next evening she was helping serve coffee on the lawn to a group of guests who had come in by helicopters from town. He gave her another message and she walked down the hall to the small office. She heard a woman's voice, one of the assistants she knew from the native state.

"I tell you I don't trust her. You listen to me! I don't trust her. She talks too much. She's in with that whole other crowd."

"She's not any more. She's good for everybody. I've watched her."

"And the way she carries on. She has the men eating from her hand."

"Honey, I do think you're jealous."

She walked into the room. "Excuse me."

"That's all right," he said.

"He wants the Governor of New York, the Secretary of Commerce, and the Commissioner of Baseball, in that order."

"Very well. Come sit down." The woman left.

"She doesn't like me. I can't help being the way I am."

"Don't worry. You have to expect these things." He picked up the telephone.

"*Can I listen in?*"

He met her for lunch one day at the Sans Souci with his secretary. The secretary left the table to make a call. "I have to take you to bed, you know," he said.

"Do you?"

"Often."

"Well, I don't know about that."

"I've given a lot of thought to it."

"I'll bet."

"I have."

"What about your likeness on that cover last week?"

"It can be managed."

"I have a family, of course."

"So does everybody."

"And your wife?"

"It wouldn't be the first time."

"I'd guess not."

"I'll pick you up at the corner of M and 31st tonight at eight. On the northeast side. I'll be driving a new black Plymouth."

"You bastard! Next thing you'll give me the number of the license."

They both laughed. He said, "It's D.C. 873–106."

In the days after the whole town dropped her like an errant chambermaid and her marriage was broken apart, she believed some embarrassing disclosure at the penultimate source was the cause of it, but she was wrong. It was not the affair itself, for the security measures for this one made the discretions with her young Senator simple in comparison. No one was to ever find them out. The reason, although she would never know it, was nothing more subtle than his unreasoning cowardice, for in his fear it was he who negotiated that she never come near him and those he served again.

But since she did not know this, she would later ask herself, in great hurt and puzzlement, why she had gone to him in the first place. She had acquired much of what she always wanted; she had learned much about the treacherous ground on which power resides. Had she been attracted to the man? Not so very, although something in his nature had startled her, leaving her slightly equivocal. No: she would never confess to herself until long afterward the more tangible possibility. Was she wishing to make secure that which she had attained? Not knowing the true circumstances of what would make her overnight an outcast, from Georgetown to the Mansion to the Hill, from Chevy Chase to Cleveland Park to McLean, she was robbed of a lesson about her fellow beings, and of the desperate milieu in which she had trusted her fates.

In that illusory town where modern emperors had been made, and lesser men broken and thrown away, she too had reached the highest she would go. People turned to look at her in public. Politicians courted her favors. The powerless and the aspiring valued her invitations. Television and the newspapers sought her barbs and quips. She moved now with an almost theatrical elegance. Seldom had she esteemed herself so highly. She was almost thirty-three, and she was blind to her own vanity.

They were in the restaurant of a secluded inn in the Pennsylvania Dutch country, on a cold dry Saturday night in the autumn.

"Would you like his job?" she asked him.

"Lord no. I see what he endures. I'm with him when he suffers. When this is over I'm going home to make money and go to football games."

A stricken look crossed his face, an expression of such unbearable horror that she thought he had become ill.

"My God, what is it?"

"We're being followed."

"No."

"That man over there. I'm sure I've seen him two or three times before."

"It's got to be your imagination."

"Finish your dinner." They drove back to Washington in silence. He dropped her at a taxi stand. After half a year of preordained, purposeful, consummately arranged, and expertly logistical adultery, she never saw nor heard from him again.

"IT'S AN AXIOM of my life," Jennie Grand told her. "The bad things always come in streaks. Somebody's reminding us of our weaknesses." Carol should have seen it coming.

A week or so before she saw the last of her assistant, she had been at a fund-raising dinner in one of the large hotels. One of the assistant's colleagues, an earnest young man of considerable brilliance whom she had known since their days together on the Hill—a "straight-shooter," everyone called him, who had gone from the piney woods to the highest councils with his grace and dignity intact—hailed her from across the room and walked in her direction.

"You won't be hurt if I tell you something I shouldn't?" he said.

"Of course not."

"Watch yourself."

"What do you mean?"

"Some of our ladies are out for you."

"I know the ones who don't like me. They didn't from the start."

"This time it's different. This time they're motivated. That damned newspaper interview. Even *he's* mad."

"All I said was he eats steak sometimes with his fingers."

"That hits him where he lives."

"I'm sorry. I thought it was rather charming."

"Hah!"

The Monday after the weekend in Pennsylvania, her private pass to the Mansion was canceled. So was her luncheon with the ladies there on Tuesday. She was not needed to serve tea at a reception on Wednesday. The charming hand-written notes of gratitude ceased just as suddenly. So did the invitations to all the appropriate parties. The Georgetown eminences turned their backs on her in the street. The politicians and their wives who had sought her attentions vanished from her life. All this came with a swiftness and a concert so unceremonious that it left her disbelieving.

But the most unexpected blow of all came from her husband Hollywell. He had fallen in love, he told her one night with an almost courtly gentleness, with a young secretary in one of the embassies. They had been badly matched from the beginning, he said, and he had become lonely and unhappy. He wanted to try again with someone who respected him, as she never had and never would. He was tired of the high society; he had become jaded with her ambitions; her absences had made him bitter.

"Why didn't you ever tell me?" she asked. Her hands trembled. She felt beaten.

"I don't think you would've listened." Their son would remain with her. Of course he would support them both until she remarried.

*Hollywell!* Who would have known? Were her own perceptions of others so uncomprehending? In the bitterness of her defeat she told him she would try to do better. For the first time in their years together she felt a respect for him.

"No," he said. "For me it's too late. I may not keep up with your friends, but I have to think well of myself. It's about time I did."

She took a small house in Georgetown. She considered moving away somewhere for a time—to England or France, perhaps, or Mexico. She was more wretched than she had been in her whole life, the agent, she knew, of her own suffering. Since despair was new to her, she did not know quite how to confront it. She lived for a time on pills. She spent endless hours in bed watching old movies on television. For days she saw no one but Jennie Grand: Jennie and her maid Josephine who hovered over her and looked after her—and the journalists. "The journalists!" she told Jennie. "They'll string along with any old body." She went to Rock Creek Cemetery and sat on a bench pondering that curious statue they called "Grief," obsessed with that frightening hooded figure who seemed removed from all happiness or pain, and she thought of the poor suicide Mrs. Henry Adams who lay there beneath it. She promised whatever Being it was she envisioned up there above her that if he got her out of this misery and humiliation, she would not traffic with her own ambitions again. Her years there had bridged the faltering time of Cold War, the aftermath of McCarthy, the struggles for civil rights, the dark time of assassinations, and Asia, yet as she had grown older it would seem she had been curiously apart from them, remote and unheeding as if the city itself had come to lose for her the meanings of her girlhood. On the night of Dr. King's death she stood on the top floor of her house and watched the smoke rising everywhere about her from the fires of the city, gray spirals raging in the distance, mirroring now her own drastic mood: was her town being devastated before her eyes? Was the nation itself weighted with destruction? Were they somehow bound together—her own intractable frivolity and a greater impending doom?

But adversity and loneliness finally stirred the old spirit in her, and she promised herself she would not leave. She devoted more of her time to her son; she enrolled for night courses in the university; she bought an inexpensive cottage in Virginia; she even began entertaining again with a younger and less established crowd. For such, of course, was the final character of her city that power at its center came and went, as since its first orgiastic beginnings it always had, power that flickered and waned and disappeared, change being its last and rudimentary sustenance, and gradually in time she became once more a little of the radiant girl of her younger days; she baked cakes and took gifts to the maimed soldiers at the military hospitals, and she looked the gossips in the eye and shamed them again with spontaneity. A year went by, and when she turned thirty-three the journalists gave a party on a farm in Virginia, where she was toasted in ribald verse and all the guests ate steak with their fingers.

Yet in her vacillating heart she felt something had been lost to her forever, some prideful trust perhaps in the arrangement of things. She had become precarious. *What did the woman want*, they asked. Life had assumed a new edge. She was feeling her own mortality.

# 5

IT WAS A SUMMER of wilting humidity and languorous winds, oppressive even in the earliest mornings of June. The statues and monuments shimmered in little waves of heat, the pavements were too hot for the bare feet of children, and the streets gave off the sweet smell of tar from the endless repairs and the construction of the new subways. Everywhere there was the whine of drills, and the ripped concrete and demolished sidewalks gave Washington the atmosphere of a bombed city in the wake of a small air raid. At night in the woods and quieter places there were katydids and fireflies, but when the breezes ceased and the broad green trees were still, even the nighttimes were uncomfortably heavy.

She had been to one of the hospitals that afternoon, and now as she drove down Constitution Avenue toward Georgetown, where she was to meet Jennie Grand and Elaine Rossiter for cocktails, she was in a state of despair. Everyone in town was short-tempered. Anger flared even in the calmest of circumstances. It was the war, which seemed to drag on forever, draining the country of its vitality, so that now it seemed impossible to exchange opinions about it without the most impossible bitterness. There was something brutalizing in the spirit of people; fear was everywhere, and even in this city, so cushioned by its professional composures, everything threatened now to collide. *The damned war,* she thought, and then she remembered she and her son would be leaving for her cottage on the shore soon, where she intended to lie on the beach until autumn and tempt the sun to burn away her merciless grievances.

From the car she looked about her at the familiar landmarks of the city. How long it seemed since she had emerged with such bustling confidence from Union Station with her new luggage given her by the Elks Club. She felt so much a part of the struggle for existence; the things she saw now, all around her, only confirmed her distress about life. The angry rush-hour traffic filled her with horror, as did the tawdry cut-rate stores on F Street, the sudden empty places, the vacant shops all boarded down after the desolating exodus to suburbia. At a corner of Constitution a group of Negroes with their new Afros stood talking among themselves, and across the way there was a blind man with a tin cup and a yellow dog, and further on a cluster of boys and girls with shaved heads and togas beating on drums; and then a congregation of tourists gawking at a statue, all of this stirring in her a biting contempt. For the thousandth time she gazed at the huge limestone government buildings with their monotonous tiled roofs in the Triangle east of the Ellipse. When she was a girl they had thrilled her with their buzz of well-conducted activity, but now they seemed spurious, their exteriors not unlike warehouses, rife with their bureaucratic malfeasances, and the humanity pouring out from them, all the coatless GS9's who worked fifty weeks a year for two-week vacations which they spent around development swimming pools, black lunchpails now in every hand, was a specter to her.

That afternoon at the military hospital where she went once a week she had stood by the bed of a boy whose features had melted away, whose skin from the waist up was the texture of the scorched surface of an apple, with mounds of pink, seared wrinkles and scars. She had talked with him for five minutes before she knew he was blind; he was nineteen and from Topeka, Kansas. She had seen boys paralyzed in wheelchairs who smiled at her, and ravaged torsos who asked her to come back as soon as she could, and to bring some books next time. Now, on the drive through the city, she wondered why she had gone there these past months. The nurses said the soldiers adored her, and talked about her in her absence, and the nurses themselves said they admired her good cheer, but was it charity alone that had prompted her visits? Perhaps it was something much deeper, some purging inside herself, some harsh assuaging of her own wants and fears, of her own feelings of shortcoming—a quest for her better nature. "I think you're doing them more harm than good," Jennie Grand had told her a few days before, "because you remind them they can never again have a woman like you." Jennie was probably right. Her cheerful benevolence was nothing more than a mask for pride. She had even spent some time for a while with several of the wounded veterans' wives who lived in Suitland far out on Pennsylvania Avenue, once a genuine old town with the dim remains of a general store but now a ruined, haphazard maze of garden apartments like chicken houses. Finally the wives, whom she had come briefly to comfort out of all the impulses of her own discontent, began to horrify her with their constant talk of menstrual pains and the bargains to be

had in the military PX's, and she had fled from them as
surely as she might flee some premonition of destruction.

   She turned now on Pennsylvania Avenue and moved in
the direction of the White House, remembering all she had
read or been told about the pomp this stretch of pavement
had known, the march of grand armies, the pageants of the
inaugurals, but what returned to haunt her now were the
muffled echoes of drums, the caisson and the riderless horse
on that November day of 1963. She had lost her husband in
the crowds along the avenue, she remembered, and finally
she had found him standing very quiet and alone.

   "Let's go live somewhere else," she had said.

   "Where?"

   "I don't care. Chicago. San Francisco. New York. It won't
matter."

   "I thought this was your town. If it is, you've got to take
the good with the bad."

   She had started to cry then, and when he reached out for
her she had instinctively withdrawn. A more perceptive man
would have understood, that there was no affection in her
for him, that even in grief she could not respond to his
gentleness. And yet it was he who had said to her: "Sometimes I feel I married you and became your mistress."

   And now, in the past months, she had turned to her son,
and found in her boy Templeton something she had forgotten of herself. He evoked her own childhood. He reaffirmed
the contours of her own existence.

   She had always loved children. Even when she was the
high school favorite in her town in Arkansas the little children followed her about. She had treated them as rambunctious equals. When she grew older, whenever she was in
their company she envied them their innocence before life,
their brief invulnerability. No one could tell them, she

thought now; they would discover soon enough for themselves the miseries of living. Yet she had also learned that they are bewildered by death, that they cared deeply about the things that really matter: the heart in conflict with itself, the suffering of people and animals, justice, the purpose of life. Much of this her son had taught her.

Not too long before, shortly after he had turned seven, he had come home from the private school he attended and reported that one-third of his class was celebrating Yom Kippur.

"What are we?" he had asked.

"What do you mean, what are we?" she replied.

"I mean, *what are we?* We're not Negroes, we're not Jews, so what are we?"

She had come close to laughing, but then it struck her as a question of some importance. She did not quite know how to reply, but she tried, and the more she tried the more dramatic the answer became, the more she remembered of herself. She began with all the innumerable forebears who had settled Carolina and Virginia, and the later migration southwestward, and the guilt of the land, touching on the whole chronicle of patriotism and rebellion and family decay as she herself had been taught it a quarter of a century before: their volatile, close-to-the-skin people. She reminded him of the day the two of them had gone all over the city together—the Smithsonian and the Capitol and the wax museum and Ford's Theater and Old Treasury and the top of the Monument. And that they had gone to the Episcopal cemetery in Alexandria to look for the grave of his great-great-great-grandmother. And how they had separated to look for her and after ten minutes or so he had shouted across all the old weathered gravestones: "Mama, I found her!" And sure enough he had: *Sarah Gibbs Templeton.*

*Born 1775. Died 1800.* He had picked some wildflowers that day for the grave and then stood next to it and after a moment said: "Boy. Eighteen hundred!"

Still, he had remained unsatisfied. "But what *are* we?" he persisted.

"Well, if you want a word," Carol had said, "I guess you'll have to say we're Wasps. You spell it w-a-s-p-s."

"*Wasps!*" He laughed very hard. He went, "zzzzzzzz." Then he said: "There sure are a lot more Jews than Wasps."

He had sharp blond features and pale blue eyes and straw-colored hair worn long. He walked like his mother, on the tips of his toes, and he even moved his arms and shoulders the way she did, and sometimes he mimicked her accent. One day that winter, she had watched as he skated on the reflecting pond by the Lincoln Memorial, flicking effortlessly over the ice, greeting everyone within the distance of his shouts. She was feeling lonely, and had been thinking again of her comrade Buddy Carr, remembering him as he was when they were her son's age. She knew in that moment, having never acknowledged it before, that her son was the most treasured of her fellow beings. He was the only one she would willingly die for.

On their trips around the city, she had taken him one afternoon to the Woodrow Wilson house on S Street. Here Wilson had spent his last years, and even with its happy Victorian blunders the old house set in a glade of thick green trees cast a shroud of unhappiness about itself. It was Memorial Day, a crystal blue afternoon filled with the fragrance of flowering shrubs and bushes, and when Carol had signed their names into the guest book she noticed they were the only visitors who had come there all day. The thought saddened her a little, and as she made the rounds of the rooms and the glassed display cases crammed with artifacts, she felt sorry for the three cheerful old ladies who were so eager to interest her in Mr. Wilson's days of decline, who hovered about her, drawing her attention to this or that, as if they had been waiting for hours to share all this with someone. Later, on the terrace, she sat in a lawn chair and drank thick sweet tea with them, and the ladies chattered on endlessly, vying with one another in their desire to entertain her.

"I adored Mr. Wilson," one of them said. "Sometimes on fine afternoons like this the neighbors could catch a glimpse of him sitting out here in the sunshine. See that balcony? He fed his birds there."

"We come here every day," another added. "Bring your friends some afternoon. Do you like the house?"

"I like it very much," Carol said. "I never expected such hospitality."

"And do *you* like Mr. Wilson, young man?" one of the ladies said to her son.

"I'd like to have some of his medals."

The most frail and retiring of the three said: "Well, perhaps *you'll* be President some day."

"I can't do it," he said, after earnestly pondering the possibility. "I'm a Wasp."

More titters and laughter. "So was Mr. Wilson!"

Carol had watched as her son strolled into the sunny back lawn and began playing with a large white dog who had come out unexpectedly from a row of hedges. The bright sun streamed down on the boy and animal tussling in the grass, and the ladies also observed this scene wordlessly, caught perhaps as Carol was by the same simple emotion.

"Can't you stay a little longer?" one of them asked as Carol stood to leave.

"I wish I could, but I have to go now."

"Who were they?" Templeton asked as they walked toward the car.

"Three lonely and nice ladies," she answered. "I may be doing that someday," she added.

"*You!*"

She had seen that afternoon how certain shreds of the Washington past linger on and on, and a thrill of desolation had swept her. "We'll bring some people out here next week," she said. And she had, returning the following Tuesday with a party of ten.

Now, released from these reveries, she was aware that the rush-hour traffic had broken, and she drove across the bridge into Georgetown and found a space to park on Wisconsin Avenue. She walked into the Georgetown Inn and found Jennie Grand and Elaine Rossiter at a table in the bar.

She had only lately become on friendly terms again with her old friend Elaine, whom in a fit of anger she had called a "clerk of the obvious." Elaine, in turn, had told her that she was like someone going through a lighting plant turning off all the switches. Now Elaine, with Jennie's skeptical encouragement, was trying to persuade Carol, for she had become as proprietary as before about her well-being, to return to what she called the "red-hot center."

Carol slipped into a chair beside them and sighed. "That's the last trip I'm making to the hospital," she said.

"Don't take too seriously what I said," Jennie replied.

Elaine rustled in her chair. In the flickering candlelight her dark features gave her the visage of a seer.

"You're impossibly out of touch. It doesn't become you. I've been spending more time than usual on the Hill and I know some good responsible people who'd go on their knees to get you back."

"A dentist on Massachusetts Avenue has asked me to be his receptionist. That's all they want, isn't it?"

"She's half right," Jennie said, laughing in the lilting way she always did when she was the recipient of truths.

"No, I'm serious, damn you, Jennie," Elaine said. She entered into a lengthy analysis of the partisan politics of that particular moment, building detail upon detail as a bricklayer applies his bricks to mortar. She discussed various political contenders. "I'm sure one of them, maybe two, would offer you a job tomorrow."

"They've forgotten all the foibles of the past?" Carol answered.

"I've told you before," Elaine said, with unusual vehemence. "I'm an authority on the subject. In another six months you'll be able to turn all that to your advantage."

Carol gazed into her glass. In a discreet corner of the bar a pianist began playing some of the tunes from her adolescence, and her remembrance of the events from her years in this city seemed merely like the old vanished hurts of childhood. She might feel different tomorrow, but her intuitions had told her to live day by day, in the moment. Now toward her allies at the table, each so different from the other, she felt a gentle wave of trust and affection.

"I have a suggestion," Elaine continued. "There's a very promising new Congressman. Jennie and I know him. He's trying to fill a job on his staff." He was from a large city of the newer South then bursting forth with change, she continued, an uncharted place, which the newsweeklies forever were praising with the adjective *progressive*. "All I ask . . ."

"Now really. A first-term Congressman?"

Elaine Rossiter was poised to reply, but as she did so a balding figure appeared at their table.

"Are you Mrs. Hollywell?" he asked.

"Yes, I am. Do I know you?"

"I recognized you from pictures."

"Yes?"

"I thought they booted you out of town."

Instantly Elaine and Jennie exchanged knowing glances and, in subtle concert, leaned across to restrain their companion. They were too late.

"Why, you bald-eagled son-of-a-bitch!" Carol said. She stood up and kicked the man, not once but twice, in the shins, then picked up a straw bowl of pretzels, which she proceeded to rain upon his head. The cocktail hour patrons at adjoining tables turned to stare, and as they did so the man, dazed by the audacity of the counterattack, retreated out the door and into the lobby. The piano player, who had not missed this Washington display, brief though it was, bowed his head in her direction and began playing "Ain't She Sweet?"

"I should have gone for the balls," Carol said.

"Couldn't you have smiled and told him you were someone else?" Jennie asked.

"No."

"I'll order you another drink," Elaine said.

She settled into her chair, as suddenly placid now as a landscape after the passing of a storm.

"Only if you promise not to talk any more about the red-hot center. Fill me in on the news, Jennie."

"Where shall I start?" Jennie said.

Jennie began speaking, passing along her information in the noble tradition of the Pony Express and the Committees of Correspondence, but Carol did not listen closely. Her thoughts took her far away, and soon she went home. Deep inside her, she was waiting for something to happen.

# 6

ON A PROSPEROUS SWEEP of the Eastern Shore, not far from the tip of that tapering peninsula which separates the Atlantic Ocean from the Chesapeake Bay, Carol and Jennie lay motionless in an early summer noon. The sky and the bay were hazy blue, there were the distant silhouettes of fishing boats along tiny islands in the darker waters, and from the houses beyond the dunes the strains of faintly wistful music and the voices of families sitting down to lunch. Fifteen years or so before on such a day in July this stretch of shore would have been empty, but now there were dozens of people in varying groupings, under broad striped umbrellas or scorching their bodies without caution or mercy. The houses on the curving promontory below loomed ghostlike, far above them an oceanic jetliner left a thin swath, and her son carried a rubber football and danced in the water of the bay.

It was a place of marshy flatlands, narrow inlets and bays, of neat white cottages dominated by blue-green piney woods. Sweeping inland from the dunes was the flat farmland, where the descendants of the early settlers still worked

the ancestral ground. "The country itself," said its first dia-
rist, "sends forth such a fragrant smell that it may be per-
ceived at sea before they make the Land." Farmers working
these fields near isolated villages saw white-sailed sloops and
schooners passing always before them on the far horizon,
cargoed with slaves from Africa, wines from the Mediterranean, and spices from the South Seas. On this terrain, only
miles from where the founders of Virginia first arrived on
American soil, they had built houses with brick and with
cedar shingles and tiny apertures of imported glass. They
were not given to the severities of their Puritan countrymen
to the north, and they fought hard during the wars of the
revolution, for they were bold in spirit, having sacrificed
everything for what they believed. The land they had forged
and fought for may now have been approaching its final
doom, the doom of the spade and the bulldozer and the
developer, but in its tentative reprieve it was still a land of
lingering orange twilights, of moisture-heavy air and swirl-
ing seafogs, of the deep howling of the night wind.

Carol stretched her arms and sat up, leaning slightly
toward the sun. She was as brown as she dared be and moved
into the shade of the umbrella. She wore a red bikini and
purple sunglasses, grotesque after the fashion of the day.
She watched her son somersault in the water, disappear and
emerge again a few yards down the shore.

"He pretends he's playing football and the water is the
Arkansas Razorbacks," she said.

Jennie Grand stirred uneasily for a moment and said
nothing.

Carol gazed for a long time at a group of shore birds
standing lazily with their heads in their back feathers, or
preening and dozing in the sun. She had been there a week
now and felt drowsy the whole time. It was the air, they told
her. She fell asleep.

"*Carol.*"

Jennie tugged gently on her arm. She raised herself from under the umbrella and saw her friend peering down, her blistered face shaded by an immense straw hat. The sun was still high, and more people had arrived now and settled on the beach. She looked up and again saw the slender figure of Templeton, brown as a berry already, curly blond hair and large blue eyes and slouching frame, seven and going on eight. He was walking now in the water in their direction, slouched over the way he walked when he was showing off. Directly behind him, also in the water, was a large black dog. The boy threw a stick far into the water and the dog went after it.

"Where did he get that?"

"That's Andy Jackson," Jennie said. "He belongs to these people I know down the beach. I'm going for a swim."

The boy and the dog galloped across the sand. He came to a sliding halt in front of her. The dog licked his ears.

"Don't let him do that," Carol said. She leaned back, her eyes barely closed, letting the sun bake into her face. Suddenly she sensed that someone was quite close to her, and when she looked up there was a man.

"Are you Carol?"

"Yes I am."

"I thought so. I'm looking for a black dog."

"Oh."

She looked up at him. He stood in front of her, bending slightly. An expression in his eyes caused her to stare.

"*Jack Winter!*" The boy jumped at him from nowhere with a flying tackle and came close to knocking him off his feet.

"I won't tangle with you," he said.

He was of medium height, with blond hair streaked light from the sun. His face was wrinkleless except for the faint suggestion of a furrow across the brow. What kept him from being straightforwardly handsome in the simple American grain was a distinct crack in the noseline, that and his curiously assessing eyes. He had the body of an athlete.

"I want you and Jennie to come to my house if you can. It's right in a swamp. A friend's letting me use it. I'll only be here three days."

Carol was about to speak, but he laughed and shrugged. "I've got to go." Jennie returned from the water and he kissed her on the cheek and said goodbye. "Come on, dog!" He and the dog walked away down the beach. The boy reappeared then and raced in their direction, and for one explosive moment the boy, the dog, and the man wrestled in a heap on the sand. Then the man and the dog were gone.

She and Jennie lay back on the sand. For a time Carol read in her book. She sat up and counted six fishing boats in the distance.

"Who is he?"

"He's that new Congressman Elaine dug out of the grime," Jennie said.

"Another of your intellectuals?"

"From *that* place?"

"Don't be harsh. It's made remarkable strides since Sherman."

"Well, he's not what Elaine Rossiter takes him to be. Who am I to judge a Congressman?"

"Is he married?"

"I believe divorced like everyone else. Down there these days it's become a political advantage."

Carol made a gesture of annoyance. "The more they change the more they're the same," she said, repeating Jennie's favorite phrase.

"I believe you're finally growing up," Jennie said.

"Still, you know what they say about the incumbents from

down there—the only way to beat one is to catch him in bed with a live man or a dead woman."

"There's no danger of that in this case. I wish he showed more taste in his preferences. I believe there's something a little cheap about him. I suspect Elaine told him you were coming and he followed."

That night Carol gave a dinner in her cottage. She rustled up a couple of journalists, and a professor from Georgetown and his wife. She gave the sociology professor a difficult time. Whenever he made a point about the Negroes being matriarchal she looked at the hair in his ears, grimacing each time he used "norm," "patterns," and "charisma," and when he embarked on a solemn discussion of his recent investigations into the ghetto life style she began to ply the journalists with enormous quantities of after-dinner Bourbon.

"The old verities," Carol said to them. "Give me one old verity."

With that, one of the journalists began describing his travels in Alabama.

"Do you remember Kissin' Jim Folsom?" Carol asked.

"Who wouldn't?"

"He was my hero. When I was little my uncle went with a delegation of Governors to an aircraft carrier in Mobile Bay. It was a big official 'air show' to unwrap the new jet airplanes. Those Governors watched twenty planes take off in fine order, and then the last one got about two hundred yards in the air and nose-dived into the water and exploded. Kissin' Jim had been on the Bourbon all day and he turned to my uncle and said, 'Kiss my ass if *that* ain't a show.'"

The professor's wife was shocked. Carol was happy when midnight came and everyone departed, an unpropitious beginning to her summer. She resolved to savor her solitude.

The next morning she was shopping at a grocery in the village. She felt an unexpected touch on her shoulder. She turned and saw the Congressman. "You have a beautiful suntan," he said. He wore a large, dirty straw hat like Jennie's and a blue jersey with VISIT NATURAL BRIDGE written on it.

"A girl has to watch her skin."

"I've got to work today, but can I meet you on the beach tomorrow? I'd love to talk with you."

"I may not go."

"What's the population of De Soto Point, Arkansas, anyway?"

"I don't know. I suppose about 12,000. Why?"

"I was there once. Do you know a place on Main Street called the Dew Drop Inn?"

"I was raised in it. What were you doing there?"

"It was an unusual mission. I went with a football coach to talk to a boy named Freddy Luckett. A tackle, I believe."

"I know Freddy Luckett. I graduated from high school with his brother."

"He couldn't pass the entrance exams, and that's saying something."

"The Lucketts never were very bright. Freddy Luckett once identified Theodore Roosevelt as a colored Senator from Tennessee."

"He picked Baltimore as the capital of the U.S.A. and the coaches wanted to give him a seventy since Baltimore is only thirty miles from Washington."

"His father was a bookkeeper and once added the deficit to the date."

He pointed to the items in her shopping basket. "I can see you're serious about cooking."

"I've been that way a long time. That makes it easy to poison freshmen Congressmen."

"I don't blame you," he said. "We rank between the janitors and the receptionists."

She stopped to get some Coca-Cola. He picked up one of the old-fashioned bottles and looked at the bottom. "*Muncie, Indiana,*" he said.

"Then make a wish."

"I wish you'll be there tomorrow. You're really marvelous to be with." He abruptly walked out the door, and from the window she saw him slide into a car next to his black dog.

She was at her spot on the beach. Her son was playing with the neighbor's children on the dunes, and Jennie had gone into the village to fetch beer. The day was dry and a little cool, with a freshness that made the blood tingle. She watched a fisherman down the way angling in the bay. She returned to her book, feeling quite healthy and content.

"Hello."

He had come up behind her. His salutation was tender, almost sad.

"Hello." She barely hid her disappointment that he had come.

"May I sit down?"

"Yes."

"Where's your son?"

"Right over there."

"That boy and I have a feeling between us. I think I could be his father."

"No you couldn't." The remark did not amuse her. She looked at him leaning slightly back in the sand, arms extended to support his body, and she sensed what Jennie Grand had said of him.

"I brought you something." He reached in his pocket and handed her a plain silver necklace, very old and fine.

"It's beautiful!" she said, taken by surprise. "Why are you giving it to me? I've done nothing to deserve it." She looked at him suspiciously.

"It belonged to a great-aunt of mine who died in the insane asylum on V-E Day. She bought it in New Orleans a long time ago. Ever since I was a boy I've used it as a good luck piece."

"And now you no longer need good luck?"

"It got me elected by 1,222 votes." He shrugged. "I considered that much too close."

"Well, I love things like that."

With a sudden movement he brushed the top of his head with a palm. "God, I hope I'm not losing my hair. My great-aunt was bald."

"You've got more than enough."

"Have you noticed that you and I look alike?" he said.

"Oh, come on." Five minutes before she had been pleasantly settled in the sun, enjoying her loneliness in the cooling breezes, and despite the fact that she was a master of such buffoonery, she was not in a mood to waste such a perfect day with a total stranger, especially a stranger she was unable to assess to her satisfaction.

"Look at the skin. The same texture and everything. Look at the face and the hair and the arms. And the ears and the toes. We're siblings."

"I never wanted a brother," she said.

"I once had a sister, but she married a civil engineer from Dallas and joined the John Birch Society. I think she was the one who spit on Governor Stevenson and jabbed Mrs. Johnson with a hatpin."

There was a silence, as if he expected a reply, but she had

looked away, toward the tiny islands in the distance. She heard him sigh, and then with the same strange tenderness as before he said, "I know a few of those around Washington, but not many. Washington gets them confused because they don't know where to start. I imagine you know that town pretty well."

"Why haven't we bumped into each other?"

"Because I'm back home all the time."

"How long have *you* been there?"

"Only a little more than a year. First a special election, and now for the whole endless two years."

"I know it better than any woman *my* age. I've been on the make and that gives you a lot of insights because most everybody else is too." She had wished to be imperious, but something in his expression made the words a little tentative.

"Maybe you were better," he said finally.

"No. Just more rambunctious."

"I'll bet more *imagination*. Imagination gets you into a lot of trouble, especially when you're around people without it. Sometimes it seems I've been slowly drowning for a whole year just to stay out of trouble. So many people tell you to go along or get along that it's no longer a cliché, to them it's the universal truth. It makes me a little guilty to take three or four days off to lie in the sun. But imagination makes you play around with other people even when you're not especially cruel. It can't be helped. The Lord knows it. He doesn't hold it against you, I don't think."

"Where did you pick all that up?"

"On the river. We should compare rivers."

The laughter of the children drifted down from the dunes. He turned and waved toward her son.

"I have a daughter," he said. "She's the best thing I ever

did. Her name is Annie Winter. She's ten. I've learned a lot from that little girl."

"What have you learned?"

"I don't know you well enough to tell you. But down on the Gulf one summer she'd play on the beach with a very smart little boy from Memphis. We'd been looking all day at outcroppings and talking about sedimentations and such things. A family from Birmingham was watching. The woman turned to the boy and said, 'What do you want to be when you grow up?' and he said, 'I want to be a geologist.' She asked my little girl the same thing, and she said, 'I want to be a rock.' "

He got up and applied some suntan lotion, then settled next to her again on the sand. He brushed the sand off her shoulders. "You're golden. Look at you."

"Is that how you get the female vote?"

"I'm glad to be out here with you. I'm glad not to be in Washington today. I have a friend there who's very small and he went to study karate to protect himself against the Negroes and Puerto Ricans and found there was no one else in his karate class but Negroes and Puerto Ricans."

"I don't have an inkling how bright you are," Carol said, "but you're certainly the strangest Congressman I ever met. We've been sitting out here for half an hour and you haven't talked about politics yet. Don't you believe in it?"

"Of course I do. Of course, when I won it seemed so important, and then when I got up there I saw I'd sort of overestimated myself. I'm on a four-day vacation. It's the first one I've had in two years. Please be patient with me."

"How are you on abortion?"

"I'm getting better all the time."

"How precisely do you earn your $42,500? You haven't even told me your committees."

"Post Office and Merchant Marine and Fisheries."

"My God."

From behind the dunes Jennie Grand arrived with a cooler full of beer. She sprawled in the sand and looked at them.

"Are you enjoying it here, Congressman?"

"Very much. It's where it all started. But have you noticed all the old racists have stickers of the American flag on their car windows? Five years ago it was the Confederate flag. I guess they believe the rest of America's changed its mind."

"When do you go back?"

"Tomorrow. I've been in my district since the Fourth. Do you want a job?"

"No, thank you."

They drank their beer, in a silence that threatened to become embarrassing. Jennie continued to stare at him for long moments. Suddenly the Congressman picked up one of his sneakers. "Let me show you something. I've got it written down somewhere." He shook his shoe and a scrap of paper fell out. "I found some termites in my friend's cottage yesterday and looked in the telephone book for the exterminators. I wrote down the names. Look: there's the Dynamic Exterminating Co. at Chincoteague, the Atomic Exterminating Co. at Eastville, the Exterm-All at Virginia Beach, and the all-embracing Global Exterminating, Inc., at Newport News, to which the more modest Belt A Bug Exterminators of Hampton enter the competition." He put the paper back in his shoe.

"Where'd you get those awful scars on your foot?" Carol asked.

He lifted his leg and pondered a line of deep, jagged scars on his ankle. "Damned if I ever noticed it before."

"Probably in a coup in the hinterlands," Jennie said.

"It looks more like a deer trap," Carol added.

"Better than that," he said.

"A race riot?"

"No. On Halloween of 1954. *Ole Miss!* In Oxford, Mississippi. It still hurts when it rains."

"1954 . . ." Carol said. "Do you know something funny?"

"What?"

She shook her head in such merriment that her hair tumbled into her eyes. "I was there."

"Where?"

"*There.* At that ball game."

"Jesus!" Jennie said. "I'm not believing this conversation."

For the first time Carol noticed a look of annoyance on the Congressman's face, a hard, calculating gaze in Jennie's direction, a gesture of distrust that passed as quickly as it had come, followed by a glance toward Carol.

But then he picked up her book and looked at it. "*Absalom, Absalom,*" he said.

"Have you read it?" Jennie asked.

"This is no place to be reading this book," he said. "Listen!" He thumbed to a page. "*It was a summer of wisteria. The twilight was full of it and of the smell of father's cigar as they sat on the gallery after supper . . . while in the deep shaggy lawn below the veranda the fireflies blew and shifted and drifted in soft random.*" He stopped, then turned to Carol. "You know, there was a time I could not only read and pretend that but also smell and touch it."

"I guess me too," Carol said.

Her son raced down the dunes and landed at their feet. "*Jack Winter!*" he shouted.

"Templeton Hollywell, my good sir. I know you'd probably want to play with Andy Jackson today, but I took him to the vet for his bad breath."

"Come on, you Jack! We're building a tunnel," and dashed away again.

The sun was settling slowly now to the west. Already the water was a darker shade of blue. A flock of gulls flew downward at the reaches of the horizon, and a man with a prominent stomach succeeded, after a lengthy hesitation, in walking into a wave.

"I've really got to get my dog," he said.

"Look," Carol said on an impulse, "why don't you come to my place for dinner?"

"I'd like to."

They walked toward the road. She gave him the directions. "Can I give you my compliment for the day?" he asked.

"Yes."

"I believe you're the most beautiful woman I ever saw in my life. But everybody's told you."

"No. Not quite."

"Wear your green dress with the silver buckle your mother bought you in Memphis."

"How did you know I had one?"

"Because I've known you all my life, and you don't even have the sense to realize it." With a wave he walked away, running toward her son and whirling him twice in the air, then disappearing beyond the dunes. Carol returned to Jennie.

"Why on earth did you do that?" Jennie asked.

"I don't know. I think I feel a little sorry for him."

"*Sorry?*" Jennie sharply exhaled. "He's glib."

"He was trying hard to impress me."

"I believe he's weak."

"No. Selfish, maybe, but not weak."

"Well, in Washington they're a dime a dozen. I'm glad I'm dining out."


FROM THE MARSHES and the pines behind the cottage came the sound of katydids. They sat at a large round table in the kitchen and drank a martini. The Congressman was more guarded than before, even a little moody; she had the most curious sensation that they were each, with considerable wariness, looking one another over. She was glad when the food was ready and she could call in her son.

"*Templeton Hollyw-e-e-e-l!*"

And from the wall of pines, far in the darkness: "*Wh-a-a-t?*"

"*Come to the t-a-a-ble. Mama wants to spank you.*"

"The cooking is wonderful," he said, and indeed it was: pork chops and salad and corn bread and squash done in the Arkansas way, and much cold white wine.

"I have a daughter named Annie who's a little older than you," he said to the boy.

"My mother was an Annie," Carol said. "Annie Templeton."

"Where's she now?" the boy asked.

"Honey, she's dead in her grave."

"What's she doing?"

"I suppose she's doing very little," Carol said. "She never did too much when she was living, bless her soul. In summer she drank a case of Nehi Strawberry a day. They delivered it by the case like milk."

"Where do you work, anyway?" the boy asked the Congressman.

"In that big white building in Washington with the round top."

"You play for the Redskins?"

"I'm talking about the Capitol, not the stadium."

"Do you make a lot of money?"

"I'm so much in debt I have to go home all the time to make speeches."

"You mean people pay to come hear you?" the boy said.

"Reluctantly."

"Have you met the President, Jack?" the boy said.

"I can't remember."

"Come on."

"Not this one."

"Where's that dog now?"

"He's home watching television."

"Is that dog any kin to you and Annie?"

"*Kin?* He's my brother. He's my daughter's uncle. We're not so far removed from good old Andy Jackson in evolution. He thinks he's ahead of us. It gives him a sense of power. I even let him run wild in Washington. He goes to the bathroom every morning under the statue of Mr. Taft. I once saved him from drowning last Christmas."

"How?"

"When we go back home he likes to walk on the pond behind my house way up in the pine country when it's frozen. He likes to skid around on the ice. I believe it makes him feel he's walking on water like Jesus' dog. I was walking along the pond and he was on the ice and it cracked, and poor Andy Jackson disappeared into the water and he tried to climb back on the ice but he couldn't make it. I threw off my coat and shoes and tried to pull him up, but he kept biting me. I jumped into the water and tried to push him onto the ice from his rear end, but that didn't work either. By this time I was getting a little worried. Then we both started sinking. I prayed but the Lord didn't get the message. Finally I bit him as hard as I could on his neck to distract him and then barely shoved him back on the ice. After a while I got out too. Was I glad! You've probably heard about dogs saving men and dogs biting men, but this was the first time a man saved a dog and had to bite him to do it."

"I don't believe a word of it," Carol said.

"I believe it," Templeton said, having followed the Congressman's narrative with much concern.

"This boy's great-uncle, Tolbert Templeton," she said, "used to save people from drowning all the time during floods. He'd go out in a skiff with the firemen, and sometimes they'd be waiting for him on the top of their houses with snakes all around the top too. During floods was the only time snakes and people got along."

"I don't believe a word of it," the Congressman said.

"Why do I have a name like Templeton, anyway? It sounds like a cat's name."

"It's a noble name and a noble family," the Congressman replied. "Making fun of your name is like making fun of your nose."

Carol took off her apron and sank into a chair at the table.

"Your mother's very pretty."

"She was once named one of the ten best legs in Washington," the boy said.

"You've got it wrong," Carol said. "It was one of the ten women with the best legs. I beat out Margaret Chase Smith."

"Well, the boy's right. Her left leg's a lot better than her right one."

"Let me see!" Templeton said, reaching under the table.

"Leave me alone," Carol shouted. "That's no decent way to treat a lady."

"Yes it is," the Congressman said.

"It sure is," the boy added.

"Would you mind if I took her to that fancy roadhouse down the way for a little while?" he asked the boy. "I'm leaving in the morning."

"No," she said. "I can't leave him here anyway."

"Yes you can," the boy said. "I'll watch the TV. Jack Winter likes you."

"What if I don't like him?"

"Then why did you make him come see us?"

"Come on. I don't bite."

"You bit the dog," she replied.

"The dog was *scratching*," the boy said. "You don't scratch."

"Yes I do."


THEY SAT AT A TABLE outside, on a gallery lit with candles and Japanese lanterns. She smelled the leaves of the red maples all around them, sensing the soft warmth on her body from the day's sun; she felt very healthy, but she intended to do nothing whatever to reassure the handsome young Congressman who was sitting next to her in the Virginia summer night.

"This is the first time in a long while I've been with a woman and everybody stares," he said, gesturing to the vacationing couples all around them, the skin textures ranging from bright tangerine to deep brown.

"Don't let it go to your head."

"You can be rude."

"You wear a disguise. You're much more intelligent than you want people to believe, and I don't like that at all."

"Intelligence isn't enough. Some of the meanest people I know are very intelligent. Also some of the narrowest."

"I believe you're quite proud of yourself," she said, assuming for the moment an air of boredom, as if to show him she was there because there was nothing better to do.

"You're one to talk!" he said. His aggressiveness surprised her. "I have reason to be. Do you know I hold the record in my State Senate for a filibuster?"

"Where's your string tie?"

"Twenty-eight hours and eleven minutes. It got a great deal of attention because it was so unusual."

"What was so unusual about a filibuster?"

"I filibustered against some bills aimed to hurt our colored brethren. And believe me, Mrs. Hollywell, I have sense enough to know I'm in Washington City because of that." He added: "That and football."

"My heart's always yearned for reformers."

"I'm no reformer. I'm a politician. I became a politician at the university and I'll undoubtedly be one all my life."

"I could teach you some things about politics."

"I'm aware of that."

"I also suspect you've been pursuing me the last two days because of your career. I know I'm glamorous."

"And where did it all get you?"

"That's something you have no right to say."

"I'm sorry."

"Men like you on the Hill remind me of the old town character in Arkansas who'd corner my uncle on Main Street and say, 'Tolbert, can I have a dime for a cup of coffee?' and my uncle would say, 'Sure, but coffee's only a nickel in the Dew Drop Inn,' and the man would say, 'I know, but won't you join me?'"

"Maybe you're right. Who knows?"

"We don't have a very high regard for Congressmen in Washington, except the very rich ones. Senators, yes. But *Congressmen!*"

"Well, hell. That's where Kennedy started out. So did Mr. Johnson. And Lincoln. John Quincy Adams even went back there after he was President."

"He craved obscurity. He deserved a rest."

"I forget what rest is."

"How did you get elected, anyway?"

"Maybe you've been at the top too long. I could tell *you* some things. I was practicing law, you see, and teaching a history course a couple of nights a week out at the university, and then in the State Senate long enough for people to remember who I was. I also got involved in a couple of strange law cases that made the papers. I defended a bookseller in a little town forty or fifty miles south of the city. The fellow was an eccentric, I guess. He was about sixty-five and chewed tobacco and had a Ph.D. from Chapel Hill in Greek, and he'd decided to open his bookstore right across from the courthouse. Word got around that he might be a Communist. The police seized his books, including Thoreau, Ralph McGill, Lincoln Steffens, Pope John's encyclical, and a copy of a dissenting opinion of Hugo Black. I took that case all the way to the U.S. Supreme Court. Justice Stewart asked me, 'Did they return the dissenting opinion of Mr. Justice Black?' and I said, 'No sir, I have high hopes they'll read that opinion and grow in stature.' The same old man was tried in district court on some other unusual charge. I remember it was right after the assassination and feelings were tense. They had plainclothesmen and detectives planted all over the courtroom to keep me and my client from being hurt. In the middle of the trial a very sinister man walked in wearing big black eyeglasses. At that very moment I was at the bench, right in front of the judge, whose name was F. Barbour Mendenhall. The judge whispered to me, 'Mr. Winter, please move to the left or right a few feet. If you get shot now I will get it right between the

eyes.' This so unnerved me I had a paralysis of my vocal
cords and had to go in a conference room and lie down to
recover my voice. Not long after this, the incumbent in Congress died of a heart attack on the golf course. An hour
before the filing deadline for the special election I went
home and shaved and changed suits and trimmed back the
hair a little from around my ears and listened to Mahalia
Jackson on the record player singing 'Abide With Me.' I got
very mystical. I showed up at the Capitol three minutes
before midnight and filed my name. A week before the election it came to light that my toughest opponent hadn't filed
an income tax in eight years. He went into hiding with his
lawyer and then they had a drunken press conference, and
he said damned right he hadn't paid taxes in eight years,
that with him it was a matter of principle, and in fact the
first thing he intended to do after his election was to go to
the well of the House and introduce a Constitutional amendment to abolish the federal income tax. This didn't sit too
well. There were twenty-three of us and no provision for a
runoff, and I finished first. A politician's got to sell out to
somebody unless he's rich, but the problem is selling out to
the right people. A few years back I picked the teachers and
the liquor boys. The advantage there is that if you vote
against your conscience for the teachers, you can go out and
get drunk on it free of charge. But you don't know what it's
like to turn up in Washington after a special election in an
off-year and be four hundred and thirty-fifth in seniority.
Four hundred and thirty-fifth! My reserved parking place
was so far from my office building I couldn't see the Capitol
dome on a clear day. For an office they almost put me in a
kind of broom closet. For a couple of weeks the janitor was
using my sofa at night to accommodate him and his woman.
I was so powerless that when I found out about it I had to

make a deal with him to use the sofa only at certain pre-
arranged hours. I believe the elevator operators laughed
behind my back. One of them started calling me "Mr. President.' I was a celebrity. People all over the Hill pointed me
out as the one who was last in line. One day I took a walk all
alone out around Arlington. I turned to the skies and said,
'Lord, Lord, what have I done? My colleagues don't speak
to me. I'm the most powerless man in Washington. My dog
has a hernia and I'm getting pimples on my shoulders. Lord,
why have you done this to me?' And from high in the skies
came this rumbling bass voice: 'Because there's just something about you that pisses me off.'"

"I can tell it bothered you."

"Not at all! I took advantage of it. I learned things fast.
And then, guess what? After a while there were the usual
deaths, and I moved up to four hundred and twenty-ninth. I
felt the Lord was gradually taking care of me. I was going
up one step at a time. And then several of the old ones
decided to retire. They turned their backs on all that golden
*seniority* and decided they'd rather walk out than be carried
out. You don't realize what an old institution it really is.
Why, it's like a geriatric ward! They've got stretchers and
oxygen tanks and God knows what else in a special room
down there, and then the pressures have grown so much
lately that the old boys simply aren't venerated the way they
used to be. Two or three months ago one of them had a
seizure right on the floor of the House. It was like the dance
of death. That spectacle alone caused a couple of retire-
ments by the end of the month. So that almost before I knew
it I was four hundred and twenty-one. And when the time
came to run for a full term it was all different. *I* was different. I'd been to the Jefferson Memorial in the moonlight. I
knew the reprobates from the heroes. Sometimes I liked the

reprobates more than I did the heroes. This time I was more grandiose about myself. And a lot of people liked me back home. Some of the banks said they liked me because I made a good image for the city—very progressive and contemporary without wanting to throw things. A lot of young people liked me. Our black brethren liked me because of the way I voted and the things I said and because they knew I liked *them.* Nothing patronizing at all. The hardest part was persuading them not to put a candidate in the race. When the bankers talked about Henry Grady, I quoted Blanche Bruce. I got to know more about Crispus Attucks than anyone in town. Of course I drew the line at Nat Turner."

"Opportunist."

"Never that. You misunderstand."

"And then?"

"I mastered TV and I never lost my temper. And I worked hard! Harder than I'd ever worked in my life. Up at dawn and never asleep before two a.m. Willing and anxious to talk with *anybody.* My opponent in the runoff was a distant cousin of the U.S. Senator. He said I was the agent of outside interests. For some reason I never understood, he placed these outside interests in Indiana. It was an uninspired notion. Couldn't he have picked New York? I said on television that if I was the agent of these interests, how would he explain the two touchdowns I made in 1954 against Notre Dame? I finally won by my 1,222 votes. I sweated my heart out for every last one of them. I'll never run that close again. And God how I learned!"

"What did you learn?"

"The secret is pure diligence. That and not to let the diligence get the best of you. Now I've gone and made myself thirsty."

They looked into their brandy in silence. Then curiously,

without expecting it, Carol felt a warm surge of serenity. She recognized the feeling. She was enjoying his presence.

"It's just that I don't like your nose," she said.

"I haven't looked in a mirror since I was sixteen. I bend over to comb my hair and I shave in the bathtub. I'm half Jewish. I used to get into all the bar mitzvahs back home at half price."

"You're not half Jewish."

"There were times I wished it. By my calculations, and I mean all things considered, our Southern colored brethren are the best people in America. The Jews are second, and the white Southrons are third. We're catching up on the Jews but it's going to take a lot longer. I never liked those rich Eastern Wasps. They're always overrating themselves. It didn't take me long to figure out that the Civil War was a war between the Southern whites and the rich Eastern Wasps, except they paid off poor little Irish boys with crooked teeth and bad skin to do their dying for them. They owned the factories where they worked little girls fourteen hours a day. And now they have field houses named for them at Yale, or maybe it's dormitories, and their grandsons inherited all they've got. Have you ever known a rich Eastern Wasp our age who inherited all his money?"

"I married one."

"I've known a few. They stick together. I'll take the coloreds and the Jews."

"Don't provoke me with generalizations," she said. Then she looked across at him and whispered, "Damned if you don't remind me of a little boy I once knew back home. I trusted him so much."

"That means you don't trust me."

"Don't take it personally."

"I'll make you trust me. *Listen.*" He leaned over conspiratorially. "My great-grandfather was wounded at Kennesaw Mountain. Captain Winter! My great-uncle died at Champion's Hill. I've got all that in my blood. Of course I seldom mention this at civil rights rallies."

"My great-grandfather was wounded at Petersburg and went back to Arkansas and became very rich."

"A toast to our great-grandfathers. I'll bet anything they knew each other."

"To our great-grandfathers," she said.

He stood slightly and waved his glass, and as the waiter came by he said to him: "Lest we forget."

"Forget what?" the waiter demanded.

"Forget it." He laughed. "He doesn't like me. The other night I said, 'Waiter, what time is it?' and he said, 'I'm not your waiter.' "

From inside she heard the pianist playing one of her De Soto Point River Cat country club songs.

"Would you like to dance?" he asked.

"I suppose so."

They embraced on the crowded dance floor.

"I'm thinking about not doing anything constructive this summer," she said. "I intend to be a recluse. I won't be mean to anyone because I plan not to have anyone around."

"I wish I could say that. Most of the time you don't even have the chance to think."

"I thought you said you were a politician. You already sound like a has-been."

"How old are you anyway?" he said.

"I'll be thirty-four on October 28. What I lack in maturity I make up in one important quality."

"Which one?"

"I have the rare ability not to give a damn."

"I have one year on you."

"I like them older, but only in nonelective positions."

"I know."

On the way home, having skirted the potato fields and vegetable patches, he stopped at the beach near her cottage. "You can't refuse a walk," he said. "I may disappear in the bureaucracies tomorrow afternoon and never be seen again."

The night was resplendent with stars. The Big Dipper could have been right above the point, and the half moon broke through a tuft of clouds and touched the water. It was such a lovely Virginia night that it seemed to her to promise a procession of them forever.

They sat on the sand near the dunes. "I know a lot about you, you know," he said.

"I don't consider it your business."

"I've made a lot of friends in Washington, and then Elaine Rossiter's told me the rest. If I were you I'd trust Elaine Rossiter."

"That's the thing about Washington friends. They feel it's their duty to spread the faults right along with the virtues."

"Being with someone like me after all you've gone through must be like getting sent back to the minor leagues."

"I suppose I *have* lost my touch. Don't be so obsequious."

"I've never been obsequious. It's just that I'm putting so much of my soul into that town up there I'm finding it difficult to see where vanity ends and business begins."

"Well, Congressman, you have many precursors. Only they seldom get around to asking the question."

He kissed her gently on the lips. She pushed him away.

"No," she said.

"Why?"

"I'm still old-fashioned."

"I hope not too old-fashioned."

"I have to go home."

He walked her to the door. "Maybe I'll see you in Washington when the summer's over."

"I'll come to your next filibuster."

"I'm afraid you've got the wrong chamber."

"Do I?" She took his hand and gave him a brisk squeeze. And from the porch, for little reason at all: "Take care of yourself."

"I intend to."

"You didn't have to tell me." And with a grandly executed wave and a slight bow she let herself into the house.

For a time she lay awake. The moonlight drifted through her window onto the bed, and the branches of the big pines rustled in the wind. She remembered one night a long time ago when her husband had tried to make love to her and she had slapped him across the face. The dance in Georgetown when she was twenty-two. All the parties on Embassy Row. All the people who had wandered through her life and disappeared forever. Well, there may be something about this one, a resilience, a tautness, an absurdity that was refreshing after the owlish solemnity of so many of his fellows. Still she could not help feel that something, deep and complex, was askew in the man.

She drifted into a light sleep. Then there was a stirring at the door.

"Did you have a good time?" her son asked sleepily.

"So-so."

"I love Jack Winter."

"Oh for God sakes, such nonsense! It's midnight. Go back to bed."

She stretched her limbs and watched the play of the moonlight on the green needles of the pines. With the frivolous spirit which had been her bulwark against many things, she dismissed from her drowsy consciousness the past three days, and felt only the promise of bright summer beaches.

THE WEEKS WENT BY, and in her rare solitude she enjoyed the small pleasures. In this isolation she believed the treacheries of display were now behind her forever. She had brought a suitcase full of paperback books, and she languished in the literature of excessive women, punishing herself all the while with fifty sit-ups daily and rounds of volleyball with muscular beachboys or sad-eyed hippies white as the bugs that scurry from overturned stones, all of them relishing her presence with undisguised expressions of lust. As the days waned, sometimes she would lie quietly in her bed and hear the midnight flight of birds passing through the darkness overhead, the rush of vast companies of wings in the forlorn season. At the end of the summer she took her son for a brief visit to her hometown in Arkansas, and she told her uncle in the presence of her child, "I could just stay here and grow up all over again." But finally it was to Washington, as always since the liberations of her girlhood, that she returned.

There is a bustle to Washington at the approach of autumn, the Indian summer briskness that slowly sheds the torpid layers of August and deepens somehow the hopes and renewals of the official city, as if the health of the Republic itself depends on such simple cycles. Washington at the first touch of fall was like the new school years of one's childhood, when even the most perfunctory rituals are for a time fraught with possibility. Perhaps it was this air of exhilaration that prompted her to accept a luncheon date at La Niçoise with one of the most ponderous First Secretaries in town, a plump intellectual from the Middle East, or that induced her to give an elegant buffet for several young wives from the Hill, or that caused her to display such unexpected good will in the telephone call that came to her the second week after her return.

"Carol. This is Jack Winter."

"My favorite Congressman! The wives over there believe you're another Senator Lamar."

"Lucius Quintius Cassius Lamar?"

"Yes. And that you're bringing all sections together in harmony."

"Have you been drinking?"

"Not at all. I've merely been convinced that someday you will also appear in marble."

"If that's the case you'll go to dinner with me tomorrow night."

"Of course I will."

"You *have* been drinking."

"No I haven't."

"I'm giving a reception here for some women constituents at 6:30. Can you meet me here? It won't last more than an hour."

"I'll come for the end of it. They might draft me."

In the same gay mood the next afternoon she put on a tight red dress and a bronze belt and a white shawl, and left for the Hill. She found his office tucked away inauspiciously at the end of the long corridor on the fourth floor wing of the Longworth Building, and a secretary directed her to the reception room. "It's for the leaders of the state PTA," she whispered. "They're here for a convention."

As Carol slipped into the back of the room she saw the Congressman surrounded by three or four dozen ladies, some of them with drinks in hand, seated in a circle about the host. They all seemed to be talking at once; like so many conclaves of middle-aged women she had seen from those environs, she knew that the ladies had arrived en masse with cerebral intentions, but that at some point in the proceedings their conduct had resorted at last to the girlish. As she took a drink from the bartender and sat down unobtrusively in the back, she noticed that many of the women had turned in her direction and were appraising her openly, some with apparent admiration but the majority with a certain hostility, as if she were an intruder now on a delicious tête-à-tête. The Congressman had been bantering with them, and there was an atmosphere of fun in the room; he was holding them in his sway, however, and as she looked at him she knew why. He had lost some weight since they had met on the shore, he had allowed his blond hair to grow longer, and in his blue blazer and striped tie he was a study in assurance. On the shore she had thought him dapper, but here on his home ground she was forced to concede him his looks.

"Let me ask another question, Congressman," one of the ladies was saying. "Do you think politics is really the art of the possible, as most people say? I voted for you, you know," she added, "which may be something many of my colleagues here can't say."

"Mrs. Ledbetter, I *know* you voted for me, and I also suspect many of your friends here voted for me too, but have kept this a secret in their inmost hearts." More titters. "I believe the key to politics is understanding, not moralizing. I feel I owe it to you to be seriously concerned about the deep questions of politics: what moves men? what advancements do they covet? when are they fearful? when bold? what inspires them to love? to hostility? I try to translate these things to our own district. I'm only one Congressman in four hundred and thirty-five, but I also feel a responsibility to the whole nation. Of course, too often in Congress we don't so much act as we're acted upon. Everything was precisely this way before we came, and sojourners aren't expected to defy the old ways."

He took a sip of his drink. "Of course I believe in compromise, because that's the basis of our system, but I also believe with Mr. Jefferson that often we have to discard the dead weight of the past to keep the system vital. I think you have to remember that Washington is usually about half a generation behind the rest of America. There's a strange kind of *amnesia* to this city. I haven't quite figured it out yet, but people forget important things. We're too clogged with everything immediate. We can't *concentrate*. Everything moves too fast. I suppose it's a reflection of the country. And also I guess we're hampered from time to time by the suspicious way Americans look at politics. Americans still like to think of themselves as simple and innocent, and somehow they believe politics is very secret and Byzantine. I believe in politics. I like its responsibility and thrall."

The ladies dutifully applauded.

"I think you deserve both effectiveness and courage in the Representatives you send here. I admire the passion of men who see the absurdities of politics and who still feel the nation can be governed to good ends. I also can't help but feel that our office here on the Hill is somehow involved, no matter how modestly, in the great flow of history on this continent."

Carol stretched her legs in the hard-backed chair and caught his eye, giving him a gesture of her hand with her thumb pointed down, to let him know she had heard all this before, and in more lordly surroundings. As she did so, another of the ladies posed a question of some moment.

The Congressman crossed his legs and brushed back his hair. "Well, as you all know," he said, "we come from a place that derives considerable riches from military bases and spending. For more than a generation we've been spending our money for battleships and bombers and air bases and tanks and bombs, while the civilian aspects of our society have gone into decline. That's the truth we have to face sooner or later."

One of the ladies began to speak, but he interrupted her with a small movement of his hand. "Read your Bible. The human race has known fire and scourge and pestilence and famine before. Just because we feel ourselves so secure in our own intelligence is no reason we should be exempt from history. Sometimes I think the sheer intelligence of the human race will lead to its destruction. Our brains have gotten too big for our hearts. And then there's that other terrible consideration, something D. H. Lawrence once said, that the majority of our fellow beings pull life down and destroy it like vermin."

There was an uncomfortable silence now. Carol moved embarrassedly in her chair, thinking him foolish. He must have sensed the mood. "Anyway," he said, "I'm on the House Committee which decides who will survive, and you ladies of the PTA are at the top of my list, God bless you."

"Congressman," the leader of the group asked, "do you think the South will rise again?"

"I most certainly do, but I'd rather direct that question to my adviser Mrs. Hollywell, who's sitting in the back and is an authority on the subject."

"We started rising with the first inoculation against hookworm," Carol said, "that, and when Dr. Carver found more in the peanut than was in the peanut before he started."

The response from the ladies was friendly, suggesting to her that she may have saved the occasion. He signaled for her to join him; she wanted to shake her head, but it was too late. They stood close together and shook hands with the ladies, who surrounded them now, pressing closer, openly admiring the handsome young couple who dominated the whole room with some subtle electricity. But the excitement she felt surprised and frightened her a little, causing her to evoke wordlessly to herself, as she first had as a girl: *I have this power over people.*

Later, as the two of them were leaving together, he turned to her. "I guess I shouldn't have said some of those things. Hell, it was a long day. We had eight roll calls. Some of the old bastards who were absent one day last week kept demanding the damned things to build up their *percentages.*"

"Three or four times I thought you were the assistant Baptist preacher."

"It was thirty percent bullshit and seventy percent gold."

"Fifty-fifty," she said.

They drove to a restaurant on the waterfront, walking along the whitewashed wharf, stopping once or twice to look at the fish markets which were just beginning to close for the day. They took a table by a window. In the fading light, filled with the fresh promise of autumn, they saw a dozen sailboats and three or four barges churning away in the distance.

"I missed you very much," he said. "I even started to write you once or twice."

"It's just as well. It was the best summer of my life. It would've threatened the mood."

"How is your son?"

"He wanted to come tonight."

"And Jennie?"

"She's always the same. She doesn't like the fact that people here like you."

"I don't like her, for that matter."

"Don't criticize my friends."

"I've been home about eight times since I saw you. I spend half my time on the way to airports. God I'm tired."

"Do you have a speech writer?"

"I can take a hint."

"It would be amusing to see you out campaigning."

"Maybe you'll get the chance."

As they were finishing their dinner, he waved at someone across the terrace.

"Who is it?" she asked.

"Ruth Ann Pennebaker. Here she comes."

"Oh no. I haven't seen her in a long time."

The effervescent friend of her girlhood, looking matronly now in a dark gray suit, swept over to embrace her, then shook hands with Congressman Winter and without an invitation took a chair.

"Carol! Let's see more of each other. This is such nonsense. Guess what?" she whispered to them: *"We're running for the Senate!"*

"That's wonderful. Where's your husband?"

"Picking up votes in the bar. There he is!"

The two Congressmen sat at the table talking to each other, while Ruth Ann Pennebaker prattled on good-naturedly. "Oh, Carol," she said, "we had such good times, didn't we? I was fresh off the farm. I thought you were the most sophisticated girl I'd ever seen. I learned a lot from you."

"You haven't changed."

"And you? Have you changed?"

"I believe I have."

Ruth Ann Pennebaker leaned over, once again whispering lustily. "Carol, we've got such a good chance! Just think of it. I'd give anything if you'd come home when the time comes and help us. How we could use you!"

"Who knows? Maybe I will."

"And *The New York Times* had a little editorial on him today. Did you see it?"

"No, but that's marvelous."

"And, Carol, I had no idea you knew Jack Winter. He's going places, you wait and see. I can just *feel* it." Ruth Ann looked over at him, then turned to Carol and, licking her lips, muttered: "*Ummm, Hmmm!*"

"Well, I don't know," Carol replied.

"Will you and Jack come to a dinner party at our place sometime?"

"Give me a little while to get settled."

"Do you remember that funny time we went to Mount Vernon together?"

Carol thought back to the untroubled moments of those days. "I'd almost forgotten," she said. "Of course I remember."

"Do you know that was eleven years ago?" Ruth Ann tried to look sad, tried again and failed.

"*Eleven years,*" Carol repeated.

Then, with a swirl, she and her husband were gone, leaving the two of them alone.

From somewhere in the darkness there was the mournful signal of a boat's horn. Far out in the water a green buoy tossed and bobbed. She watched it come and go, feeling again how much she loved and needed being close to water. The ripplets lapped gently on the wharf, and the sweep of lights far away lulled her.

"You talk and talk and then you have these strange silences," she said.

"Sometimes I'm all talked out."

"The fifty-fifty ratio's responsible."

He took her hand. "Carol?"

"Yes."

"Let's go to my house."

She did not answer. She looked away. She was suffused again with the past, with anonymous automobiles at public corners, with affection betrayed and emotion denied, with her own small triumphs and unfulfillments.

"If something's bothering you, let me help. I love you very much."

"That might make the damned dog jealous," she laughed.

Later, in his apartment, he brought her very close to him and kissed her, and then again with deep warm movements. "*Jack. Please be careful with me.*" It was the first time she had called him by his name.

# 7

In her first days with Jack Winter she was irritable and afraid. She goaded him and occasionally made jest of him, just as she had done before with others, but all the while she was anxious for herself, not even certain that she liked him, only that she was drawn to him by something deeper than her impulsiveness or her curiosity. Then, quite suddenly one day when she was alone in her own house, passionately considering her own nature, and his, she decided that she had never known another being who was so much like herself.

At first she was unfulfilled. She tried magnificently to bestow and receive the full ardor of love. Then, imperceptibly, with the most delicate subtlety, something began to turn within her. Sometimes it would be slow and tender, drawing everything she was out of her, and then an unimaginable wildness, on an edge of madness. She gradually grew to know how nearly perfect their bodies were together. Outside was the rush of traffic and the sound of birds in the red and golden trees, and the fading sun streamed through the leaves and made dancing movements on the walls. She loved to touch him everywhere for long moments, to be next to him and to look at him while she lightly felt him, and sometimes the things she did and said made her blush with surprise. He controlled her, measuring her with himself and taking care of her, until she shuddered deeply in her body, feeling the soft agonizing pleasure for the first time in her life. Then, in his own passion she looked into his eyes and held his back in her arms. Once she kneeled over him, her hands lightly touching his shoulders. They were distended in a rigidity and softness of extraordinary possession. She looked down at him, moving gently in his embrace, her hair fell over her eyes: as if from far away she heard herself whispering his name. And later she pulled him fiercely toward her, touching his lips until she turned her head and cried softly, and cried again.

It was this for her. Was it he? Or was it, she asked herself as their days together unfolded, that she at last was ready? She only knew she was feeling things she never believed existed, some deep new web of experience. Out of all her strident gratifications, she believed she had come to the most elemental thing of all, the thing she had least known.

She whispered to herself: *I didn't know.* In her past she thought it was sometimes good. She would have small pleasant feelings. But sometimes she had thought it might be a fraud against women. Or she would read things and feel something was against her. Now (as she later told an uncharacteristically subdued Jennie Grand) it was like something she had discovered, something that had always been buried there in her, but that she had abandoned any hope of realizing, as one might search for a ring or a pin lost many years ago, but with no expectation of finding it, until suddenly one day there it was. She could do anything with him she wanted. She demanded, lechered, whored, fantasized. She believed she trusted him.

At his apartment one afternoon she looked at her face and

her body for a long time in the mirror, and then she turned to him and laughed. "My God," she said, "I look loved."

And then near sunset on those days he could leave his work early they would build a fire in the fireplace and drink white wine, and prop up their feet and listen to Mahalia Jackson, watching the autumn lights on the trees. On these first days of love they might sit and say nothing, sipping the cold wine in a twilight breeze, or she would remember things she had long forgotten, about Ole Miss or De Soto Point or some exceptional event from Washington, and she would tell him all about them in vivid detail. She told him how her great-grandfather had climbed to the top of St. Paul's and carved his initials in 1868. She told him about the dead child in her uncle's arms, and about Buddy Carr and the giant Indians. One night that autumn she told him about all the men she had known, and what her life had been to her.

"Tell me some more about Washington." The days had grown cool, and in the fire there was always the smell of old wood. "I want to learn as much as I can from you." He stoked the fire and came back and stood over her.

She looked up at him, tieless in his shirt sleeves, his hair disarranged and his eyes a little red from a long day's work, and she was overcome by contentment, welling inside her like waves, washing out the frivolity of her years. She began to cry.

"Don't."

"I can't help it."

"I'll make a face, the way I do in my office. I've been looking for you all my old life."

"Have you?"

"I didn't count on this at all."

"I didn't either."

From the tiny garden patio in the back there was a clamorous scratching and pounding on the kitchen door. He got up and opened it. "Well, my good Andy Jackson! Please come in." The immense black dog entered in a rush. He sat down there before them: brown liquid eyes and shiny black mane and a long moving tail knocking a stack of documents off the coffee table. He bent down and grabbed the dog's muzzle. "You've been gone all day with your girl, I can tell. Running amuck in the parking lots. My girl's better than yours. She smells better. Look at her lovely legs. Look at her ears and teeth. Keep your lecherous paws off my girl. This one's *my* girl . . ."

His comfortable rooms seemed perfect for their passion. For long days she neglected her son. She reflected on the extraordinary nature of the emotion of love. She relished it, examined it from afar, pondered the strange new layers of sensation, felt the wonder in her. She believed few women had known this before. Only the great ones! And it had come upon her without warning, with one she least expected.

"I don't care to see anybody," she said.

"I know. All this makes a person very private. I suspect most public people don't have it."

"Well, *you're* public."

"I'll fight for enough privacy to be with you."

"I haven't been very virtuous, you know. I've been rowdy and mean."

"I never liked people who had nothing to regret."

"But where does one go for redemption?"

"I believe in the redemption of love."

She laughed.

"No. I'm serious."

"I'm beginning to believe you are."

Only now could she begin to understand how the South of her day had damaged the sexuality of its girls, how uncomprehending fathers, and the strictures of the church, and male supremacy had left so many of them baffled before their trepidations. Little around her had changed, yet she seemed to have undergone some chemistry, and as always when the arrangements of life went well for her, she was glad when others noticed it. They talked lightheartedly about physical encounters from the past, and this to her was like the sealing of a pact, a wanton communion that made them comrades in the sensual.

She admired the edges of his assertion, and there was a private side to him which appealed to her, so totally lacking in most politicians with their emotional austerities. His mind was speculative and objective, with a good feeling for history. And like her he was haunted by the Brady photographs, the landscapes of sorrowful American places, the famous men rooted in the American earth. He took Jefferson's alternatives very seriously, and his idol was Lincoln. He had visited Gettysburg five times, once on the centennial re-enactment of that confrontation, worrying all the while that the innocent charade might undergo some transfiguration and start the whole business all over again, and on the latest pilgrimage there wandering the contoured valleys and ridges of the battlefield alone at midnight, only to be arrested and interrogated by the enterprising federal constabulary. From the lexicon of the Mavericks he called the more exotic manifestations of the Eastern mind "gobbledygook," and his best friend back home, he told her, was a Negro poet out of Mobile and Tuskegee who warned him soon after his election never to turn his back on seed stores, feed stores, and courthouse squares, and to always be one, boy, on whom nothing is lost.

WHY, THEN, even in the first days of her new happiness, did she wish so to ferret out his faults and uncertainties? She would continue to have suspicions, as she had voiced them so mindlessly that night in the roadhouse on the shore, that he wanted her for what her worldliness might profit him. "I'm very proud of you," he said to her one day during a reception for his state delegation, where crusty politicians and their wives and helpers had watched her by his side, and flashbulbs burst in front of them for newspaper consumption in the home district. He had said it with affection, but also, she believed, with a keen self-satisfaction. Everywhere they went together in those days, she felt, people were bestowing more and more attention on him; surely she was the reason. Elaine Rossiter devoted a column to him in her prestigious New York journal as "one of the best of the new breed," making uncharacteristic note of his "friendship with the remarkable Mrs. Hollywell," and whenever she took him to the important dinners to which once again her company was solicited, she watched him captivating important people as she herself had done in her girlhood. They embraced and kissed in secret alcoves of the Georgetown houses between dessert and brandy, later walking hand-in-hand down balustraded staircases under the gaze of their hosts and hostesses, stopping alone for nightcaps at the bars on Wisconsin or M—Clyde's, perhaps, or Mr. Smith's—to appraise irreverently the personae of the evening, and then on to renew the deep pleasures of their unforeseen love. Surely her questionings were unfounded. Was it that she had never before been so at the mercy of a man?

She loved to watch him on such evenings alone in discourse with some garrulous Washington stereotype, conversing assuredly with him on the politics of the instant while smoking a thin brown cigar, standing next to his elderly companion, patting him gingerly on the collarbone to make a point while his friend draped an arm about his shoulder, then breaking into laughter over some incidental indulgence. How true this must be to this city, she thought, this small casual drama, acted and re-enacted since Washington began. In such moments, hearing out the observations of his companion, he might look in her direction, as if he wished to wink, causing her to smile whimsically. "What did you say to the Senator?" she would whisper to him later, more from the momentary affection than from curiosity. "I told him I admired the fact that he understood all the congestions of cruelty and ignorance, and that knowing them so well he could hate them so much, and that I was learning from his example." "And the Senator? What did he say?" "He was saying that the trouble with all the liberals in his state wasn't the notions they had but the liquor they drank. And he said the wave of the future in politics was women, Negroes, and youth between ten and twenty-two, but he wouldn't be a party to it. And then I asked him for his advice on what to do when the things I believed come in conflict with the political realities back home."

"And how did he advise you on that?"

"He looked at me as if I were God's greatest fool and whispered, '*Lie, Congressman, lie!*' "

Or she might see him with a writer for one of the slick new journals of the day, a redoubtable figure with that pointed cruelty of certain intelligent drunks who after considerable experience have developed the expertise of knowing precisely where the knife hurts the most.

"What was the conversation?" she would ask.

"He said he knew people liked me here but that I'm going to suffer the sophomore jinx. He said he'd kept an eye on me and I was fragile where it mattered. He also said the word was out that I'd won by 1,222 votes."

"What did you say?"

"I told him he was a failed poet."

"How did you know?"

"I told him not to disappoint his following and to go ahead and get whatever emotion he was feeling at the moment into print before it got cold. I told him he was teaching me the one lesson we all have to learn by ourselves, about the morality of the professionally moral."

"And then he wanted to fight."

"How did you know?"

"This is my town, remember?"

On other occasions she might see him in conclave with one of the truly distinguished figures, but then he would be entirely absorbed, with no glances toward her nor the faintest suggestion of a wink, until suddenly they too would break into laughter, the Washington laughter that always shaped the exposed surfaces of its icebergs, and she knew then that they had been in riposte about some person or public consideration or remnant of history, for such was the talent with which he endeared himself, as she once had, to the notable veterans. "Tell me about the conversation," she would again demand. "We were talking about Congressman ———, who happens to be the Senator's enemy. I told him Churchill said of Lord Ponsonby, 'He's neither here nor there.' Then the Senator said, 'Congressman, do you know just what it was John Randolph remarked about Henry Clay?' I said I didn't. 'Well, sir, he said he shines and stinks like rotten mackerel by moonlight.' "

"So you think this is quite a town," Carol said. "You're beginning to think it belongs to you."

"I want to stay here all my life."

"Then you've been claimed by the virus."

"I'm afraid so."

"Whatever it is, it's a good old town to love in."

Later that night at the dinner table a visiting intellectual from London said: "I believe your two most overrated Presidents are Truman and Lincoln. Truman bores me, but Lincoln fascinates me, and in many ways he was an exceedingly calculating and even evil man."

"That amounts to a heresy," a Harvard historian laughed.

"Calculating, certainly," Congressman Winter said, "but not evil."

"The only thing I admired about him," the Englishman continued, "was the way he used those apocalyptical animals. He didn't say after Gettysburg, for instance, 'General, you let the enemy escape across the Potomac.' He said, 'Meade, you shooed the geese across the river.'"

"Yes—and more to the point, slavery was a whale. 'With one flop of the tail it will send us all into eternity.'"

"But look at the things he did to preserve your Union," the Englishman argued.

"He was consumed with suffering for having to do them."

"Yes, and he revoked *habeas corpus,* surrounded the statehouse in Maryland, and didn't issue an emancipation until the third year of that war."

"And I would have done precisely the same things."

"You're a most curious Rebel," the Englishman said.

"Most curious," Carol added. "Shall I prepare a letter to your constituents on that?"

THEY SPENT A WEEKEND in the cottage on the Eastern Shore. He had just been slapped down badly in a committee hearing, by a consummate pragmatist whom he described as a "Cagliostro and a Rasputin, mixed in with a little Billy Graham," and he felt the need to lick his wounds. By the time they arrived, late on a Friday afternoon, the last big storm of the autumn was raging northward from the Caribbean and then Cape Hatteras toward the east. In late morning the skies had grown murky and black, covered with a thin veil of fog, and twisting winds from the south stripped whole trees bare, bending them into the most painful shapes until they groaned. The thunderstorms started again at dawn, and the flat fields all around them were wet with ponds in the low places, and here and there was a lonesome shorebird left behind. They drove into Cape Charles early that day, and in the stores people listened to radios, charting the route of the storm and passing along all the latest warnings. Human beings are paradoxical creatures, for they are closer together and often at their most generous under conditions least propitious to them. The elements were once again beginning to work against them, and there was a poetry in their souls.

Carol was overjoyed by the setting: the hyperbolic power of it and the loneliness of the land without its summer people. She felt the need to be very near the man who was with her there. They bought groceries and candles and firewood and returned to the cottage. They sat in front of the fireplace and heard in the distance the cascading waters of the bay. Claps of thunder roared down from the clouds. Everywhere around them was noise and motion—a vibrating hum. The pine trees surrounding the porch rustled before them, the shutters of the cottage suddenly butted against the clapboards, and gusts of rain swept across the lawn and down the wooded lanes.

They sat by the fire.

He laughed. "Look at Andy Jackson," he said. The dog had crawled under a sofa, and only his nose was showing.

"Put on some music," she said. "Something out of the 'fifties."

"All right."

"This is silly to tell, but a day like this makes me feel all the songs and everything I grew up on are right after all."

"That's a funny thing to say."

"If you open that briefcase you brought I'll murder you."

"Then be damned if I'll risk it."

He put on a heavy raincoat and went outside to latch the shutters.

He shouted to her: "Put on your coat and come outside. It's something to see."

She winced against the driving rain. "It's so frightening it's lovely," she said.

In front of the fire again she shivered and leaned against an easy chair. "I'm cold."

He got up and went to his suitcase, returning with a heavy red and black jersey with the number "44." He put it on her, drawing it down over her face very gently until the bottom of it stretched to her thighs.

"They let me keep it. It makes me feel like a boy."

"What is this?" she said, pointing to a big stain on the side.

"It's old blood."

"Well, wash it off. It's filthy."

"Hell no. I want to remember who I am. Sometimes I'm not sure."

"As of yesterday you're three hundred and twentieth."

At the height of the storm, in late afternoon, the lights went out, and now they were sitting by candlelight in the darkened room.

"Do you know what my mother did two weeks before she died?" she said. "She gave a big party and invited all her friends. I came down from Washington to help her. She talked to all of them one by one. The next day she locked herself in the house and never saw anyone again. I'd come in and give her news of the people who'd been at the party, and she'd say 'Oh?' She no longer cared."

"Here. Number 44's all disarranged." He pulled the sweater more closely around her. "Why do you come from such an outrageous place as Arkansas?"

"Well, don't be too righteous. I've seen the Acropolis at sunset."

Now the wind was at its peak, and the dog began to howl along with it. They listened as the storm battered in its fullness, then gradually diminished, as if victimized finally by its own strength, leaving the earth hushed again in the dark October night.

SHE LUNCHED THAT AUTUMN with Elaine Rossiter, whom Jennie Grand had begun now to call the Iron Virgin and who unmistakably, from the ruddy flush on her dark features and the curious giggle and the things she chose to discuss, was involved in her first real infatuation. She had more or less adopted the Congressman, much as a high-minded household in Westchester might take on a child from the Harlem backways from June 15 to Labor Day.

"He's just so damned *busy*," she said to Carol, over a leg of lamb in the Sans Souci. "He gobbles down lunch in the cloakroom, and all the trips home, and office hours for constituents. It's bone-wearying work, you know."

"He gets out enough."

"His office is a horrible mess. Do you know he spends nearly an hour every afternoon with one Southern leader or another? They drink neat Bourbon. He's even started calling it 'striking a blow for freedom.' He's out for the next spot on Ways and Means."

"I'd imagine they drink from jelly glasses. Next thing you know he may be voted most likely to secede."

"It's no laughing matter."

"There's only a certain amount he'll give in to. Then his instincts take over."

"I think you should go down there and try to smooth things out. Last week he had some love child answering the telephone. I realize she's the daughter of a big banker down there, but the girl actually got into a long argument on the telephone with a constituent about whether we should have dropped the bomb on Hiroshima, and the Bay of Tonkin, and the laws on marijuana, and God knows what else. The poor man was a peanut farmer."

"I wouldn't feed his monumental arrogance by telling him, but he's learned more about this town in two years than I did in eight."

"But if he's fool enough to try for that Senate seat next year . . ."

"He won't."

"Well, he's seriously thinking about it, and if he does he's got to get his office organized. Of course, quite a number of the good ones were that way at first. When Lincoln was in Congress he used bread crusts for book marks."

That was how Carol started coming to Jack Winter's quarters on the Hill. She arrived unannounced one Monday morning at nine, and by the end of the week, since she knew better than most that even on this level power is as power does, residing as it must in whosoever occupies the avenues of access to the leader, she had made friends with his administrative assistant and displaced, in authority if not in name, the elderly Southern widow who managed his office. After a few days she had straightened out the correspondence and the flow of telephone calls, advised him to replace three or four inefficient souls on his small staff, and interviewed applicants for the vacated jobs. All of this harkened back to her youthful days with the senior Senator from Kentucky, the years dissolving for her as a stream slips again into older contours, and from time to time she experienced the sharpest *déjà vu's.* She remembered long-ago conversations with constituents from Paducah or Louisville, the way her Senator sallied forth into the outer office on the merest excuse the way Jack Winter did, all the aspirations of that unanxious time when they shone through the many drudgeries.

Sometimes at lunch they would bring in beer and sandwiches. A few of the younger Congressmen started dropping by, and after a time the casual lunches in Congressman Winter's office, presided over by the Congressman and his lovely companion, became something of a ritual, relaxed occasions to discuss bills and committees, all the complex minutiae of daily life in that gregarious community which was the Hill. Sometimes the quorum bells would ring in the middle of one of these sessions, and he and his fellows would tarry as long as they dared, then dash down to the subway to the Capitol, up the escalator and into the elevator, to the second floor and on to the House, returning a little later slightly windblown to resume their conversations. And sometimes, when they were uninterrupted, the talk would move beyond the workaday considerations which are the preoccupation of all Congressmen no matter how weak or strong, to the sweeping questions which embraced the future of the nation, the quality of the society, the thin skeins which held America together, the tensions and bitterness just beneath the surface, and it was after a number of these meetings that Carol gradually began to perceive the brilliance and distinction in the complex creature she had so unexpectedly grown to love. The thought of it both disturbed and exhilarated her; she began to brood upon where it might lead.

One afternoon, after a lengthy meeting in his office had dispersed, he called her in to see him, closing the door as she came in.

"Will you draft me a reply to this?" he said, handing her a letter. "Put it in free verse."

He placed a quick telephone call while she read the message.

*Dear Congressman:*

*The South is changing, according to the* Commercial Appeal's *report of your speech at the college auditorium in Memphis last week. Frankly, I don't think it is.*

*Lonely little towns still support oligarchies. Preachers commit suicide. Female teachers run away to New Orleans with high school principals. Rich children fail to return library books. Society matrons are often drunkards. And the common people work on.*

> (*Mrs.*) *Phoebe Cartwright*
> *Midnight, Mississippi*

"You're wrong and the lady's right," Carol said.

"Little lady, I have to give a speech to the Rotarians in Lynn County next week, and I want it to be a memorable one."

"That's not even in your district."

"I'm expanding my hegemony."

"So? Aren't you big enough for the occasion?"

"I have a job for you."

"What is it? I'm about ready to retire from this whole operation. It reminds me of an Arkansas revival tent."

"I want you to go out and do me a memorandum on all of Churchill's speeches."

"Go to hell."

"Then I want you to sample my colleagues about putting the flags of all the states around the Monument."

"It won't go over."

He reached for her and pulled her toward his chair.

"For God sakes not here, you fool."

"Why not? Politicians and their wives have got to learn to live in the goldfish bowl. Love in it too, sooner or later."

"You've gotten way ahead of me."

The next day she lost her temper at one of the secretaries, insulting her in a voice that echoed down the corridor outside and almost throwing a bottle of blue ink at her massive breastworks.

"You can't do that sort of thing," he said to her.

"Why not? She lost five letters I spent a whole afternoon on. Besides, I don't like the way she paints her fingernails and the way she flutters those insipid eyes when she drawls out her inanities."

"You can't insult someone before a whole office. She's probably gone to the bathroom to cry."

"I'll do what I damned well please."

He looked at her harshly. "Her grandfather is my largest contributor."

"You're a sellout like all the rest." When she was angry there was a sharp nasal whine to her voice, and just now she realized he had wounded her.

"I'll sell out any time for five letters, even if you did write them yourself."

Yet these were happy days for her, filled with a warmth she had seldom known, and she wished deeply to take them for granted. Once or twice a week they worked together late at night, and on these nights sometimes she brought her son to be with them, when he would dawdle in the office or try out the typewriters.

"Why do you get so many letters, Jack?"

"They're not for me," he said from behind his desk. "They're all for your mother."

"Seriously?"

"We all expect her to do things for us. The nation slows to a halt every time she leaves to powder her nose."

"Then it sure does slow down a lot."

Later that night, under an enormous harvest moon, they walked to the Capitol. The moonlight through the oaks and elms cast the dome and the wings below in deep shadows. He had her son by the hand, and he said, "On nights like this it makes me mystical." He took them inside, and up an elevator to the chamber of the House of Representatives, empty now, tempting the three of them to whisper among themselves before its grand sweep, before the starkness that touches great places in such desolate moments with a trace of awe and sadness. He led them down the central aisle and placed the boy in the middle chair at the top of the big walnut rostrum.

"This is where the Speaker of the House sits," he told him.

Then he led Carol to a place to the side and persuaded her to settle into it.

"This belongs to the parliamentarian."

He stood to full height behind the rostrum.

"And this is where the President of the United States addresses the joint sessions of Congress."

Carol, from her perch below, looked up at Jack Winter, and a tiny shudder coursed through her body before she managed a loud laugh.

"Mr. Speaker, Madame Parliamentarian. Damned we'd make a great team!"

"Give us a speech, President!" the boy shouted.

Jack Winter paused dramatically, then spoke in a voice that echoed through the hall. "I believe I interpret the will of the Congress and of the people when I assert that we will not only defend ourselves to the uttermost but will make very certain that this form of treachery shall never endanger us again."

Far back in the chamber, where three or four of the guards had gathered for this curious spectacle, there was enthusiastic applause. The Congressman bowed low once or twice before requesting, in that day of infamy, a full declaration of war.


ONE SATURDAY late in that autumn, starting early on a crisp Washington day, they drove into northern Virginia, planning to tarry along the way before reaching Harper's Ferry for the night.

They let down the top and took back ways. The land was moist and clean, and the breezes whipped her hair so that she tied a green bandanna around her head. In the prime and beauty of her womanhood, she absorbed this bountiful day, the sunswept fields with shocked corn and pumpkins, the flaming Virginia creepers, the horses in neatly circumscribed meadows with whitewashed fences, and it left her a little breathless, for she tingled so with the majesty of living. She had never looked so lovely, an aura of beauty that comes from pleasure and joy and the repose of a lavish temperament. She looked at him, his blond hair streaked with the sun blowing into his eyes and over his ears, and she poked him affectionately in the ribs.

"What's wrong with you?"

"You're so damned pretty when you're messed up."

For a while they were in the neighborhood of Dulles Airport. Big jets swept over sleepy hamlets lying between low ridges and the rolling country of Second Bull Run, rising slowly through a terrain of small farms toward the Blue Ridge and the Shenandoah Valley. That morning many years ago when she had come to Washington, she had awakened at dawn in her Pullman on the train, slowly drawing back the curtains as one might open a present from a person one loved, to see what might greet her eyes, and she remembered the echo of the whistle and her own quick surge of happiness in this country which was so new to her, a country so deeply, poignantly American.

They drove past Civil War cemeteries, through little towns with general stores from a past generation and trees arched over narrow mainways, the dead leaves whirling on streets and sidewalks, and everywhere the sight of little boys in bright sweaters throwing footballs.

"God, how I love the integrity of these places," he said. "Let's go on down to Lexington and see V.M.I. play The Citadel. And the bones of Traveler at W. and L."

"No. I want to stand in the moonlight where John Brown did. I want to soak in the decay."

"This state is one great big cemetery."

"Well, don't let the ruined gray ghosts of our people carry you away."

As they drove westward the outlines of the Blue Ridge foothills loomed before them. On one of the back roads they suddenly came across a small pond shaped in a slight crescent, set under several towering oaks, with ducks among lilypads and a little boy at the edge sailing a toy sailboat. Six or eight large dogs were sunning themselves and swimming, churning the water and keeping the ducks at a respectable distance. He stopped the car for a moment.

"The little boy's lost his boat," she said. "He's crying."

"I'll go get it."

He walked out to the pond, rolled up his trousers and waded in, and handed the boat to the little boy. Something there that moment touched her deepest heart. The whole tableau, the crying child and the man wading in the water and the dogs and ducks against the blue horizons of the Old Dominion autumn, made her feel vulnerable, as if she were at the mercy of things beyond her and far away.

He got back in the car. "Those old country dogs have the best life there is. Rolling around in the sun scratching their backs. I imagine they just wander around for days in packs getting handouts at all the country houses."

"They remind me of politicians I know," she said.

"I've even spotted the leader. The big brown one with the floppy ears under the tree."

"How do you know?"

"By his air of studied nonchalance. If he got up to go somewhere else they'd all come after him. But he wouldn't get too far ahead, and he'd make damned sure they were following."

"Please leave the political parables alone. It's a holiday."

Now they were on the main road again, cruising among dairy farms and stone-walled orchards, the apple trees crimson and gold in the morning light, spreading away as far as the eye could see.

"Oh hell!" he said. "Spare me another one of those today."

He pointed to a large roadsign done in garish colors, slowing the car to read it:

Coming Soon!

BOUTIQUE PLAZA!

Created by G. H. Stogbach

Loudoun and Culpeper Counties' Most Complete
Shopping Center

Thirty Acres, Twenty-five Stores

Largest W. T. Grant's in the South

KING KULLEN IS COMING!

650 Cars

Complete Living

Ecology Development Corp.

New York City

Beyond the sign was a gaping hole in the earth, acre upon
acre of it, and yellow bulldozers like dinosaurs.

"G. H. Stogbach!" he repeated. "Indeed."

"Do you know him?"

"Dozens. Maybe after the next fire and ice they'll start
from scratch and do better, even if they do have fins."

"Well, do something about it. Don't just bitch. Aren't you
a public servant?"

"Well, damn it, I *will*."

Now they were in Leesburg, driving past old houses set
far back from the road with their air of permanence and
vanished luxury. It was a Southern country town to its core,
bustling now with all the urgency of a Southern Saturday
noon—the wonderful Saturday noons of one's childhood,
filled with the fresh odors of percolating coffee and freshly
laundered country clothes and the throaty shouts of the
Negroes milling on street corners.

Closer to the center was a large crossroads grocery, with a

dozen or so men in khaki clothes in front, whiling away the time.

"Look at those damned old hardnoses," Carol said. "They'd just as soon rape you as look you in the eye."

"No, no!" he said. "You've forgotten. They're Tom Jefferson's yeoman farmers."

"Yeah."

Now the streets were shaded by oaks and elms, and there were older houses of stone and brick with ivy on their walls, and people walking toward town.

Suddenly Carol said, "It reminds me of home!"

The streets and the sidewalks, the houses set out in a line, the sharp feel of isolation recalled the villages of her youth. "I can't believe it. This street is like mine. It's Boulevard. It's the same old feeling of it. See that little girl? That's *me*. I wonder where she's going. Maybe to catfish."

"We'll ask her." He slowed the car. "Little girl, are you going to catch some catfish?"

The skinny little girl looked at them. "Catfish?" she exclaimed. "What's that?"

"So much for your *déjà vu*," he said.

Chimes began to peal from somewhere in the distance, and Carol touched her face with both hands, whispering:

> *"Lord through this hour*
> *Be thou our Guide*
> *So by Thy power*
> *No foot shall slide."*

"Have you been saved?" he asked.

"I remembered it from home. Leesburg makes me remember."

Soon they were curving the edge of the cemetery, rimmed by turn-of-the-century houses. "Look at that one!" She pointed to a weathered gray colonial with a sweeping front gallery and a large weathervane on top. "Let's buy it. We'll completely renovate it inside. I'm good at that." Then, in feigned disappointment: "No. It won't do. It's right across the street from the new part of the cemetery. I prefer the old."

"We'll renovate the cemetery."

"Let's get out and take a walk."

Carol took off her shoes and felt the cool grass between her toes. They walked among the old gray stones. *John Edwards, 1719–1760. Phebe daughter of Josiah and Annabelle Rogers died Oct. 20, 1801. We loved her. In memory of Mrs. Samuel Pelham, Relict of Mr. Elijah Pelham, who Died of the Smallpox in the 60th year of her age: 1820. In loving memory Capt. William Davis died April 29, 1863. Age 20 years. Killed at Battle of Vicksburg. Rebeccah Russell wife of John Russell who Departed this Life Sep. 19th A.D. 1741. The righteous shall be in everlasting remembrance. James Ludlow, died June 20th, 1815. Soldier of the Revolution. Caroline Mercer, 1835. Aged 30 Years wanting 15 days:*

> *Peace and Kindness her mind inspired*
> *Which made her Life by all Desired*
> *But Death our Pleasing Hopes did Cross*
> *And we with Grief Lament our Loss.*

"I wonder why I'm so comforted by the dead," she said. "We put such burdens on them."

"Hell," he said.

"What's wrong now?"

"After all we've been through we've got to be stretched out by the undertakers and pumped and excavated. I can't do anything about *that*. It'd never even get out of committee. It's a pain in the ass."

"Well, let's forget about that today."

"I feel like a beer."

"I feel like buying antiques. Death makes me want material things."

They drove around the courthouse square with its white-pillared buildings, its closely set elms, and its Confederate soldier. Across from the green, in the center of a row of businesses, Congressman Winter saw the Jeb Stuart Bar and Grill.

"I really do want to mingle with the local constituency," he said. "I need to keep in practice."

They arranged to meet after she made the rounds of the antique stores. An hour or so later, in a mood of acquisition, she returned to the car with a box full of bric-a-brac, an early American footstool, a Revolutionary War letter opener, and six Yankee Minié balls. Then, with her light swift step she walked into the Jeb Stuart Bar and Grill, where she immediately beheld an unusual scene.

There, sitting at a large square table laden with empty beer bottles was Congressman Winter, surrounded by eight or nine men in khakis and blue jeans. The men were listening closely to something he was telling them, and they suddenly broke into laughter.

She walked to the table, through a crowded assemblage standing at the bar, and tugged at his shoulder.

"Who is *this?*" one of his companions asked. They all looked at her now. She heard a kind of community sigh. "Hot dog!" one of them said. "Is this the one?"

He stood up. "This is Mrs. Hollywell, of Washington, D.C. Mrs. Hollywell, I've made some new friends, and I want you to meet them. This is Tommy, who went into exile from Norfolk to run this bar. This is Cotten, who's a farmer. John, who raises horses and paints pictures on the side. Ribeye and Clarence, who also farm. Leo, who drives a truck to Front Royal and is on parole for hijacking. Al, who is a policeman.

Dave, who claims he's a descendant of the Chickahominy Indians. Look at his mustache. He's a hippie Chickahominy."

"Hello," she said. "I think I'll join this good-looking group."

"Which do you think is the most distinguished?" he asked.

"Well, every last one of them. I couldn't begin to decide."

"John once did a painting of Clarence here standing across the street from the courthouse. John says it actually hung in a gallery in Richmond for two weeks but Clarence was so ugly they took it down by popular demand."

"It was a lousy painting," Clarence said. "Not a good likeness at all. It was fuzzy. My face looked orange."

"I had to get the sunset in," John said.

"You could've put it someplace else."

"I hear you got a lot of niggers in Washington," the man named Al said to her.

"Well . . ."

"Listen," the Congressman said, "if there's anything I can't stand it's an amateur bigot."

"So?"

"They tell me Al's so conservative they won't let him use the Key Bridge. He's to the right of Mussolini, except he doesn't believe in public highways."

"Don't tell her that," Al said.

The farmer Cotten was asking him about crop supports, and as he was replying she looked about her, at the sawdust on the floor and the dark bar extending the length of the room and the farmers and workingmen in various stages of celebration all around them. From the jukebox Johnny Cash mourned the sadness of early Sundays and the vicissitudes of vanquished love. Every so often one of the men would steal a glance at her. She wore a white cotton dress cut low and when she caught her image in a mirror she was tempted to linger on it for a while.

"Leo, stop it!" Jack was saying.

"Stop what, Jack?"

"Stop looking that way at my girl. I'm going to report you to the parole board."

"I don't mind it, Leo," Carol said.

"See?" Leo said.

Tommy walked to the bar and returned with a new tray of beer.

"Leo, damn you!" Jack said.

"I can't help it."

"Is he really a Congressman?" one of them said to her.

"Yes, but he thinks he's much more important than that. I wouldn't begin to tell you what his dreams are. There are only six members behind him in seniority, and they're all diseased or mental invalids."

"Yeah?"

"What about the state of the Union, Ribeye?" the Congressman asked.

"I'll tell you what it is. Nobody remembers the Depression. These little hippies are all rich. Their daddies send them an *allowance*. I like the nigger hippies better than the white hippies."

"Between the hippies and the Russkies," Clarence said, "I don't know which I'd take. Neither one's got no respect."

"Everybody wants a handout," Al said.

"Well, what are poor people to do when they can't work?" Leo said. "I seen niggers and whites over in West Virginia who don't get enough to eat."

"The richest country in the world and some of our own people are starving," Jack said. "Tell me what we should do about that."

The talk settled into flurries of argument and retort, encouraged by Jack Winter. Carol took a long sip from her mug of beer and watched him at work. He was being quite corny. She pondered this for a while, and then began to notice something akin to respect in the men's glances, the tentative expressions about the eyes, as if they awaited his word.

"My girl is from De Soto Point, Arkansas," he said finally. "Could you tell them about it, Carol?"

They pulled their chairs more closely about her.

"Well," she said, pausing briefly to consider. "I grew up on the Mississippi River. My father was the pilot of a steamboat."

"Seriously?" Leo asked.

"When I was eight years old I found Hernando De Soto's bones. I learned that something silver under the pillow prevents nightmares. Smoke and buttermilk fight delta chills. The powdered lining of a chicken gizzard will cure hives. Red flannel in a hollowed pecan hull dries out boils. Rotted apple skins drive away female ticks. Bark from a sting-tongue tree cures toothache. I had a grandfather who used to say he was raised in the wilds of Arkansas, uncultivated as a poke stalk, unlettered as a savage, birthplace caved in when he was young, father shot from ambush while asleep at home. If the sun sets behind a bank of clouds on Sunday, it will rain before Wednesday. A red sunset brings wind. When smoke hangs flat and geese fly low, it's about to cloud up. A morning shower never lasts long. If the river's up, spirits are down. Three months after you hear the first katydid, frost will fall."

"My God!" Jack Winter said. "I can't tell you how that impresses me."

"I'm a farmer," Ribeye said, "and I never heard that kind of talk. Give us a little more."

"Moonlight during Christmas means light crops. If the

wind is from the south on the twenty-second of March, the whole year will be dry. A halo around the sun brings a quick change of weather. If smoke and birds fly high, watch out for sleet. If the fifth of January is rainy, expect a rainy May. Plant cotton when the cottonwood blooms. If lightning shifts to the south, it means good planting." She paused to catch her breath. "And please don't be the last one to leave a funeral."

"Why?"

"*You'll be next!*"

"I'm going to write all this down," one of the farmers said.

"I think it only applies to Arkansas," the Congressman said.

"It's universal," Carol replied.

By this time a number of the men at the bar, attracted to the soliloquy, were milling about the table in rapt attention.

"Tell us more!" Leo said. He had the look of a man who five minutes before had been smitten inescapably by love.

"Oh Leo," she said, smiling at him and at the newcomers. "One of the worst days in the history of De Soto Point, Arkansas, was the morning the firehouse burned down."

"I never heard such a thing," Leo said.

"I'm a volunteer fireman!" one of the men at the edge of the crowd exclaimed.

"It burned right to the ground. I was ten years old and went with my Uncle Tolbert Templeton to look at it. I felt sorry for the poor fire chief. He looked so sad. We asked him how it happened. He said, 'Well, we were all asleep and then we smelled somethin' burning. The whole place was on fire. We tried to get the firetruck out, but it was too late. That's all we had to fight the fire with. We were lucky to get out ourselves. We lost all our clothes.' "

"Who is she?" the volunteer fireman shouted again. "Who's that guy with her?"

"He's a United States Congressman!" Leo shouted back. Now there were whispers and gestures across the bar, a subtle agitation that vibrated across the big room and out into the street. From everywhere heads craned to get a better look.

"Where'd you meet her, Jack?" Tommy asked.

"I found her on the beach while looking for my dog."

"Is she always this pretty?"

"You bet."

From the back of the room one of the farmers suggested boisterously: "You better get a haircut, Congressman!" There were whoops of irreverent laughter.

"Never!" he said. "When I go home I wear a cowboy hat. My people know that the meanest cowboys in the world are cowboys with long hair."

"You ain't one of them liberals, are you, Congressman?" another demanded.

"*Liberals?* From where I'm from? I'm a states' rights Democrat." This was greeted with vigorous applause.

"Well," Clarence said, "there was a time when the only thing around here protecting Republicans was the game laws. Now I might be one of 'em."

"The niggers are takin' over the Democrats down here," another said.

"Don't jump on the colored," Jack shouted back. "Why, the white Southrons and the coloreds are the oldest minorities in this country. We're here together and we've got to work together. Deep down we love each other. You sure can't say that about the North."

"Somebody once told me in the North they love the coloreds as a race and treat them bad as persons," a man in a broad straw hat at the bar shouted.

"Sir, you're right," Jack Winter replied to this fustian old bromide. "That's a profound observation."

"Well, I like the Republicans," Clarence persisted.

"You mean the party of *Grant* and *Phil Sheridan?*" the Congressman said, in a voice heard far into the street.

"Well . . ."

"Remember what they did down here? Pillage. Fire. Raped our great-aunts. That's why there're so many red-headed people in this country."

"In Arkansas," Carol said, "they kidnapped babies. They tried to change the course of the Mississippi River. They twisted railroad tracks around trees and stole all the chickens and ate them raw."

"What would Jeb Stuart say to this?" Jack said. "We had the greatest fighting men in the field in the history of warfare. Only our machines failed us. What would Tom Jefferson say, Clarence? This wonderful Old Dominion, his native ground. Are you asking us to choose between you and Tom Jefferson?"

"I guess so," Clarence said sheepishly.

"Well, you're making it awfully tough on us."

Now there were more shouts and clapping, and catcalls in the direction of the hapless Clarence.

At this juncture Carol stood up, and the melodrama of this sudden gesture quieted the crowd, so that each man in it looked solemnly at her to hear what she might offer them. With much deliberation she recited Lee's farewell address to the Army of Northern Virginia. *"You will take with you the satisfaction that proceeds from the consciousness of duty faithfully performed; and I earnestly pray that a Merciful God will extend to you His Blessing and protection."* A wave of emotion swept the place. Two or three grown men, who undoubtedly had settled in at the bar in the earliest hours, began to cry. From the kitchen, mysteriously, came a blood-chilling Rebel yell.

The owner Tommy broke this improbable spell, perhaps

deliberately, for purposes of avoiding mayhem. "Congress-man, tell everybody that story you were telling us a little while ago, about the time you were playing football in Alabama and that halfback lost his pants."

"I can't today," he replied. "I'm afraid Mrs. Hollywell and I have a schedule to meet. I promise you we'll be back." He stood up and took her by the arm. They shook hands with their companions at the table, mingling briefly with the others standing around them, and the throng parted deferen-tially as they walked together into the sunlight of the street. From behind them a man yelled: "I'm for you, Congressman. You're a good ol' boy!"

"You better be good to that girl!" Leo shouted.

On the way to the car Congressman Winter sighted a large group of Negroes standing on the corner. He dipped into their midst, introducing himself and shaking each hand in turn, until suddenly a plump young man in a green shirt caught up with him. He was carrying a camera.

"I'm with the paper, Congressman. I heard you were here. I wonder if I could take you and your wife's picture."

"Of course. She's not my wife, she's my assistant."

"Let's walk across the street and take it in front of the Confederate monument."

Congressman Winter looked at him, and after a heavy silence replied: "No, not in front of the Confederate monu-ment. Why not in front of our car?"

Carol laughed and clapped her hands together, causing her hair to tumble over her nose. "He doesn't have the courage of his own rhetoric!" she said. "He's a modern demagogue."

"Beg pardon?" the man asked.

"I have an undisciplined assistant," he said.

With the popping of several flashbulbs another crowd, by

now biracial in composition and in a festive Saturday temper, a mixture of curiosity and mischief, gathered around them.

"They're TV stars!" a Negro woman shouted.

"Can you tell us why you're in our town, Congressman?" the man with the camera inquired, withdrawing pencil and paper from his trousers pocket.

"We're on an informal tour of the area," he said, "sampling the feelings of the people at the grassroots. Sometimes I feel we're a little removed from things in Washington, and I want to know what the citizens are thinking. The Congressman from your district is a friend of mine, and I intend to tell him what a wonderful city I've found this to be."

"Where are you going next?"

"We're on our way to Harper's Ferry. Our feeling is that a town like Harper's Ferry is an ideal place to visit. It's rooted in our history. Famous men like Lee and Jefferson and Brown and Stuart and Stonewall Jackson figured prominently in its past. I think it can teach us politicians a great deal about America in these perilous 1960's."

Carol, who by now had opened the door of the car, said to the crowd, just as reverentially as she had spoken in the Jeb Stuart Bar and Grill: "Let the word go forth from Leesburg, to friend and foe alike, that the torch has passed to a new generation of Americans."

"Get in, Carol," he said.

"Thank you, Congressman. Come back and see us."

"I'm sure he will," she said.


Now THE COUNTRY began to rise and fall, with pleasant orchards and farmlands, patches of rocky land here and there, and trim villages like studies in miniature at the foot of the mountains, the road winding and dipping as it rose gradually toward the hazes of the Blue Ridge.

"*Jesus!*" Carol said.

"What?"

"Back there. You impress me sometimes despite myself."

"You should hear me be bipartisan. I guess we riled them too much."

"You, not me."

"You're deluding yourself. You liked it more than I did."

"And did *you* enjoy it?"

"I was trained for it. That's the sort of thing that keeps the country going, but your intellectual friends don't know it. I've always liked the image of de Gaulle getting the votes of the Frenchmen in Algeria when he was planning all the time to give them the axe, listening all intently to their demands and lifting his big arms wide and high and saying, 'I understand you! I understand you!' It ain't an exact science."

"Come now. Aren't you an intellectual?"

"I believe in the whole process."

"I can't decide whether you're the most calculating bastard I know or the kindest."

"Well, hurry and make up your mind."

Beyond Winchester they stopped at a roadside store for a glass of cold apple cider, and as the shadows lengthened across the mountains onto the stone fences they were welcomed by a large sign to the State of West Virginia. The happy mood of the morning was upon her again, and she moved across the seat and sat close to him, the way they used to do it in high school.

"So you suddenly get very quiet again," she said after a time.

"Well, I liked those people. And I entertain myself thinking. I just put my head on something and I think it right through. I'm better at it than anybody."

"That makes good sense, I guess."

"Take you. I can sit and think about something you've told me, one of those things out of Washington, your husband at a dinner party, that assistant and the place in the mountains, or the night you threw the frying pan at your daddy. I elaborate as I go."

"Did you like the way I did Lee's farewell?"

"It would've warmed the heart of an abolitionist. Marcus Garvey would've cried."

"I memorized it for my junior high graduation."

"I thought so."

It was twilight when they reached Harper's Ferry. They checked into a rambling inn with a gallery all around it, on a high bluff overlooking that dramatic terrain where the Shenandoah meets the Potomac. Then they emerged to take a walk.

It was cold now, and they huddled closely together as they strolled down an abrupt way leading to the town. No one was in sight. Out beyond the rivers toward Maryland there was the beginning of a quarter moon, hovering amidst pillowy clouds, and from all around them there was the sharp rush, like an exhaling sigh, of water tumbling across desolate shoals. From a cluster of houses on the ridge came the smell of leaves burning, and out in the distance the barking of dogs, and the clanging of an anonymous bell echoed off the very walls of the earth down through the empty streets. They walked past the stolid buildings of the old village, that juncture which had led the settlers through rocky passes toward the valleys and plains beyond, that ghostly concourse across which our deepest history had converged: revolution and conspiracy and rebellion, and the drama of bloodshed through which this deceptive little point between its rivers and mountains had barely endured. The moonlit night seemed dark in faraway events, and when they reached the brick structure where John Brown and his conspirators had finally surrendered to Colonel Lee and Lieutenant Stuart, Carol took him by the hand.

"None of this is lost on you, is it?" he said.

"I hear things out in the gloom."

Later they climbed the steps carved from the outcroppings of gray mountain rock past the Harper house restored now to its former distinction, above the brick church on the bluff to a commanding eminence with a view of the two rivers. She was silent before all of it: the walls of rock angling earthward toward the lofty trees, the tiny village set fortuitously in the valley, the moonlight on the surfaces of the Potomac coursing eastward toward northern Virginia and Washington. As Carol looked down from the rock on which they stood into the mists gathering among the trees along the banks, she felt this was the finest day of her life, a day of mirth and silences and dalliance to come.


THE WEEKS PASSED, and now they were in the slushy, unpleasant days of December. They practically lived together. Often he stayed overnight at her house, and when he went home on his frequent flying visits to consolidate and mollify, he would telephone her twice a day, telling her he knew he must mend his fences on all fronts. Her heart was strangely assuaged, and although she could still be as brusque with him as she had been with others, these others now seemed transformed into a superior mold. They were a well-regarded pair in the city; his calling, as usual, meant much hard work and commitment and a procession of minor crises in that day familiar to dozens of other young men in similar circumstances. The two of them had frequent dinners with their companion Elaine Rossiter. He assiduously picked Elaine's brain, exploiting it as one would seek out the mineral rights lurking within some well-regarded promontory, tapping her dossier of knowledge on the practical workings of power and influence and the less functional details of ambition and compromise. The Pentagon, the Treasury, the Asian desks of State, the Bureau of the Budget, Agriculture, the circumlocutions of the latest Governors' Conference, the most recent cloakroom maneuverings in the U.S. Senate—all these were easily within her purview, and she mapped them out for him as diligently as a geologist might deal in delicate contours.

"Who do you contact in the White House on aid to education?" he would ask Elaine.

"Ferguson."

"Who on mental health?"

"Kyle."

"How's the best way to see the Secretary of Defense?"

"Call Schmidt."

"Who in the press corps knows the most about the bombings?"

"Golden."

"What's the best cure for hemorrhoids?" Carol would interrupt.

"Come off it, Carol."

"Who procures for the Congressman from Denver? Who promoted Peress?"

"Have another drink, Carol."

"Does Elaine know that Washington and Lafayette were lovers? Remember their wigs?"

"Damn you, Carol."

Occasionally he angered her, by thoughtless acts or his schoolboy's zeal for facts or even by political gestures she deemed amateurish, but she tried hard to curb those scornful impulses which had so long been the best weapons in her arsenal. Even if at times she secretly felt superior to him, how in a matter of months could she have transformed her very nature? It was impossible. It would simply have to be handled with discipline. In a word, a détente with herself. She must never allow herself to forget that she was linked with him, a curious partnership, but no less genuine for that. She was living from a new catechism, which embraced affection and friendship and sex; she must never ignore their love.

"I'm partaking for the first time of pure feminine elegance," he said to her one day after the champagne at a hotel ball. "I've never had this with such a beautiful woman. I've never known a woman who dressed so well. Or who could talk better, or was smarter."

"Please go on."

"But mainly it's the elegance."

One day on a visit to Jennie Grand's he embarrassed her by reaching into his coat pocket and presenting Jennie with an emerald brooch. "I thought you'd like it, Jennie. It belonged to my great-aunt."

"How many great-aunts did you have?" Carol asked.

"This one tried to teach her birddog how to drive a pickup truck. Anyway, it'll go well with Jennie's black dress."

Later, on the way home, he told Carol: "She's the first woman who's made me feel like Chinese Gordon at Khartoum."

"That's because she's jealous for my happiness."

"Do you think she's relenting?"

A week or so before Christmas they went to a holiday party at the British Embassy. In the dark of the early afternoon, beyond the statue of Mr. Churchill, a large Christmas tree shone in the courtyard. Inside, amidst all the baroque appointments, she greeted their host.

"Mr. Ambassador, I haven't seen you in months."

"Carol. I miss those gay dinners. We've thought of you. We couldn't do without you this year."

"I'd like you to meet Congressman Winter."

"Congressman, it's a pleasure."

"Sir, I'm honored to be invited. Especially since I'm nothing but a country boy."

"Only when it's convenient," Carol said, smiling coyly to the Ambassador and leading him away.

"Why in God's name did you say that?" she asked.

"You told me they dropped you like all the rest."

"That's no cause to be such a bumpkin."

"I've met him before. I asked him what his politics were and he said, 'I'm a true-blue Tory, which I understand is considerably to the left of anything you have in America.' I didn't like the way he said it. Besides, they never did a damned thing about the Yankee blockade."

Despite herself she laughed and squeezed his hand. "You're simply childlike," adding, "so it wasn't loyalty to me?"

"As if I haven't proved my loyalty to you by now."


IT WAS LOYALTY that was keeping them together: the loyalty of their circumstances, the security of their passion. They talked and loved, loved and talked, as always lovers have, and in the memory of recent ardor, they lay together and confided:

"Jack?"

"What?"

"Can I ask you something private?"

"Please do."

"Did you ever . . ."

"What?"

"You know . . ."

"No I don't."

"*Masturbate.*"

"In high school I'd do it after every football game."

"No kidding?"

"I had to wind down I guess."

"Did it make the sports section?"

"Basketball was worse. I'd get aroused just a few seconds before the tipoff."

"Would it get in the way?"

"I had bad first quarters."

"I have a big confession."

"Tell me."

"I'd get naked and look at myself in a long mirror."

"What's wrong with that?"

"I'd kiss my own image."

"Lucky image."

"Do you think that's sick?"

"I think it's the best thing I've heard today."

The night of their unsuccessful party at the Embassy they went to a bedraggled restaurant far out on Connecticut Avenue. A bill he had sponsored, having to do with allotments for peanuts, had just passed both houses of Congress, and he was in a mood to celebrate. They had enchiladas and tacos and margaritas and sangría, and when they had finished they were in excellent spirits.

"What now?" she said.

"I'm going to take you to a dirty movie."

"You are?"

"Please don't tell any of my Baptists."

He chose one on Fifteenth Street near the old Willard, rated high, as a Republican Congressman from Michigan had told him, by *Screw* Magazine's Peter-Meter, paying five dollars apiece for the privilege of enjoying the fruits of our latter-day revolution. When they were inside the darkened cinema they chose a sparsely populated back row.

"I was embarrassed walking in," she whispered. "Did you see that man taking tickets looking at me?"

"He's used to it."

"I'm scared, too. I'm the only woman in the place. You're corrupting me, you know."

All around them were middle-aged men, sitting alone with newspapers in their laps, gazing at the screen. Occasionally someone coughed or lit a cigarette, or the men glanced furtively at one another, but otherwise nothing broke the silence except for a small group of Orientals who sat together and giggled from time to time.

"It's safe. I'll take care of you."

"It's a long way from the Pic Theater in De Soto Point."

Lights flashed from the screen and she turned to it now as if magnetized. Her eyes grew wide at the scene before her. An exceedingly large man was in bed with two shapely women, the women taking turns with him and gratifying his numerous whims.

"My God!" she whispered.

The scene shifted. Now the three of them were in the woods. One of the women was tied to a dangling trapeze-like mechanism from a tree, and the man and the woman titillated her with unusual stratagems until she requested the more straightforward gratification.

She leaned over. "I never saw anything so big."

"Be quiet!"

Now a handsome young couple not more than twenty performed in Eastman color on a divan in Haight-Ashbury of San Francisco. Their bodies were very beautiful, and they made love with an innocence and spirit which reached high crests. Next a couple copulated on a vinyl table in a kitchen in Los Angeles, the camera taking unerring aim at the heart of the action. Then Candy Barr in a Texas motel with Mr. America, summoning company later from a blonde lady of the night, and three randy soldiers satisfying the wants of a lovely mulatto in South Side Chicago, and a multilingual poetess in the East Village using, for want of proper company, a battery-operated vibrator, which she had bought in the drugstore of the St. Regis, and two rhythmic Negro males, footloose on Manhattan Island, exhibiting the efficacies of black power to a Southern society lady from Charleston, South Carolina, and an unfortunate professor of philosophy from the University of California at Riverside tormented by eight Amazons who had not seen a male since the golden age of Juan Perón, and three happy couples from Berkeley, California, smoking bushels of marijuana and applying organizational principles on a thick carpet on the fringes of Oakland, and an unfulfilled housewife in the suburbs of Evanston, Illinois, who had been Homecoming Queen at Northwestern circa late 1950's, posturing on the television set for the television repairman. And finally the handsome young couple again, reaching the supreme moment from the Old Testament's holiest stance.

"How far is the nearest motel?" she whispered. "You've ruined me forever."

That night she discovered there were no limits to herself. The pleasures of her being were limitless, fibers of pain and ecstasy never known to her.

Later she said, "What will the people in the next room think?"

"You're an exhibitionist. I knew it all along."

She opened her eyes wide and said, "Can we go to another one tomorrow?"

"We'll go to the matinee."

·  ·  ·

"ANNIE WINTER'S coming today!" he shouted at the boy. They were shooting baskets in Rock Creek Park in the sunshine of a cloudless Saturday. It was four days before Christmas. From far down the hill on Wisconsin Avenue came the good sounds of Christmas songs. The big dog sniffed squirrel trails in the woods beyond; everywhere about them were the rustlings of wintertime creatures. Carol, in faded blue jeans and a heavy pullover, reclined against an oak tree and read her mail. There was a letter from her former husband, some unexpected communication; as any member of that vast constituency, the great American community of the legally divorced, might perceive, she did not want to open it. She laid it aside for later. There was a Christmas card from the wife of her Kentucky Senator, home for a long holiday vacation:

*Everyone here remembers your visits such a long time ago and asks of you. Did I tell you before I left that two of the NBC boys are in love with you? Bring your Congressman down here next spring for the Derby. It does me good to get away from there. You really must do it more often for your own sake. One more Georgetown dinner party and I'll . . .*

She browsed through others: a newsweekly editor asking her to visit him in Virginia over New Year's, a rich hostess giving her advice on fashions, a bachelor in the State Department wanting her to plan a large dinner for him in January, Christmas cards from specters far in her past, including her college roommate and the Johnnie Reb linebacker now making his third million in Memphis, poor defeated Sidney Ricks from Pennsylvania and Ruth Ann Pennebaker mending fences in Oregon. And then, unex-

pectedly, a message from her old lover, the young Senator
from the Midwest:

*I haven't seen you in a year, since the dance at Jennie's. I
suddenly have this urge to see you. Can you be persuaded to
meet me in New York early next week . . .*

She arched her back against the tree. Washington, its
small pleasures and grand designs, flashed through her memory, all the happy days of her youth, the despairing days
of her maturity. A year before she undoubtedly would have
caught the plane and met her young Senator at the small
hotel in the Village.

A letter from her Uncle Tolbert:

*Dear Carol. I read your last letter aloud to everyone in the
Dew Drop. We all miss you and enjoyed your visit. You stay
away too long at a time. Here's a funny story. The new
owners of the old house dug up that boy in the side yard!
There was a story about it in the Memphis paper which I
enclose. . . .*

### BONES OF SOLDIER
### DISINTERRED IN
### DE SOTO POINT

The remains of a Confederate lieutenant from
Humboldt were disinterred today near the house
in De Soto Point, Arkansas, formerly belonging to
Colonel D. R. Templeton, cavalryman in the Civil
War and brother of Shays Templeton, U.S. Senator from Arkansas 1878–1892. The new owners,
Mr. and Mrs. L. O. Castle formerly of Memphis
wished the remains of Lt. Robert Marmaduke,
who died according to town records at 20 of saber
wounds incurred in the Battle of Helena . . .

*P.S. They found an earring in his hand that must have been your great-grandmother's. What in hell should I do with it?*

She laughed out loud and thought: he'll have to see *this*, remembering the summer days she and Buddy Carr put flowers by the round stone and read from the Anglican Book of Prayer and ate crackerjacks and moonpies on top of the lieutenant. She reached in her bag for a notepad and scribbled:

*Dear Tolbert. I promise I'll come down in the spring with Templeton. I miss your stories. I want him to hear them all over again because he's old enough to remember. There's also an exasperating Southern boy I think I want you to meet. . . .*

The object of this latter declaration was standing at some imagined line teaching her son how to shoot a basketball. They moved about each other in circles with the ball and talked relentlessly:

"I can't."

"You can."

"It's too tall."

"Are you afraid to fail?"

"I'm not big enough."

"Midgets play it."

"Midgets don't."

"They use ladders."

"They're too tiny."

"Then try this."

"The ball's too big."

Suddenly there was a movement from the woods, and the dog came out proudly carrying a turtle in his mouth.

"Look at Andy Jackson!" the boy shouted. The dog carefully put the turtle at his feet. "Where did that come from?"

"He smelled him out in the leaves. Last year one of those turtles bit him on the nose."

"Can I have him?"

"He's got a wife back there."

"What does he eat?"

"Hamburgers."

"He does not."

"Play with him."

He came under the tree and sat down. They sat there watching the boy and the dog with the new acquisition.

"I never can tell which one of you is the seven-year-old," she said.

"I hope you'll will your tongue to the Smithsonian. People should come from miles around to watch it move."

"I never gave a filibuster."

"Only informally. You're too lewd for formal locution."

"And still you'll trust me with your daughter at Christmas."

Union Station was busy at that hour. They were early and they stopped for coffee. All around them was the rush and flow of the great terminus, the staccato announcements of arrivals and departures, all the urgency of dislocation. Carol watched Congressman Winter surveying the scene, like a hunter squinting out from a cover of brush.

"This is where it all started for me," she said.

"I should have been here to meet you."

"Jack Winter," the boy said, "I don't think you made those ten shots in a row."

"You saw it with your own eyes."

"But I still didn't believe it."

"You'll have to, that's all."

"Is your daughter pretty?"

"Wait and see."

They went to the platform, and soon the train appeared, rumbling to a halt. In the midst of the throng, a slight figure with a straw suitcase and a red hat emerged and looked around. He and the little girl walked toward each other, and when they met he leaned down and held her in his arms for a long time. Over the noise of the crowd she heard them laughing. With his arm on her shoulder they came her way. The boy saluted and snapped his heels.

"This is Annie Winter, of the sovereign state of . . ." he said.

"Annie," Carol said, and then, without planning to, kissed the girl lightly on the cheek.

"What's he doing?" she said, laughing extravagantly at the little boy the way her father laughed. Her flaxen hair flowed in a ponytail from under the red hat, and her slender limbs in a white dress were brown as if she had been much in the sun.

"I like trains," she said.

"Your second trip to Washington," Jack said.

"Daddy. I've missed you and dreamed about you."

Night came early and they drove around the city, absorbing all the fine sights of Washington at Christmastime, the White House tree and the trees in the Ellipse, the smartly decorated shops near Dupont Circle, the lights on Embassy Row, the hippies with twigs of mistletoe in their hair and beards on the dense thoroughfares of Georgetown.

"Have you been in there, Daddy?" Annie asked when they drove by the White House.

"Only as a tourist." And pointing to Carol: "Now *she's* been in there on official errands."

"Really?"

"I got kicked out the kitchen door," Carol said.

"Seriously?"

"I almost landed on my arse."

"She always lands on her feet," he said.

They went to her house for dinner, and afterward, in front of the fire, she served Russian tea the way they used to in Arkansas at Christmas, and he gave the boy a gift: a tiny short-wave radio that received all the police messages. He bent low with the earphones on.

"That man says there's been a stabbing out in Zululand," he said.

"I'll hold you responsible for any new terminology," Carol said, sitting on a sofa by the fire wrapping presents.

Then he brought out one of his daughter's presents, a radio with a long antenna. They listened to all the different languages and the brisk codes and then the rhetorical music of love.

"This old radio will pick up anything," he said. "Yesterday it got Mogadiscio, Somaliland. Now I think this one is New Orleans, and I'll bet Carol Hollywell grew up on it just like I did." The dance music wafted through the room, and then the voice: *WWL, Loyola University of the South, with studios in the Roosevelt Hotel.*

"That brings back things," she said. "Don't make me suffer the past."

"Is that it?" the boy asked. He had ignored the police reports and was picking a flea from the hide of the exhausted black dog.

"That's the one."

"Here's Andy's flea."

"Quick. We'll roast it for dessert."

"Oh no!" The girl turned to Carol. "He always says he

makes tick stew, and redbug gravy, and flea soup. I don't believe half of him."

"I'd forgotten all about redbugs. *Good night, sleep tight, don't let the redbugs bite.*"

"But redbug gravy?"

"I don't take your father seriously. Neither do his constituents."

"I take him seriously," she said, "but sometimes I have to get away from him."

He caught her by the ponytail and tugged. "You're going to have a marvelous Christmas in Washington. You're nothing but a little old girl."

"Little old girl," the boy said. "I don't want to be some little old girl."

"I never thought it possible your father could have such a lovely daughter," Carol said. "Did he really watch you being born?"

"It sounds disgusting," the boy said.

"Well, it's true. He not only watched me being born, he weighed me on the scales and washed me off when I was one minute old."

"What did she look like?" Carol asked.

"She looked surprised," he said.

"I remember what *he* looked like," the girl said. "He had a mask on and his hair fell in his face. Then he smiled."

"He looks for votes early," Carol said.

"You can't *remember*," the boy said. "I just started remembering last summer."

"I remember from before I was born," Carol said.

"No you don't!"

"I was a tiny speck in the sky, out among the planets at Christmastime, just waiting for my summons."

"It don't work that way," the boy said.

"How do you know?" Annie asked.

"Does it work that way, Jack?"

"I know how it works but I'm not giving details right now. Ask me later. I'll take you to a movie."

"No you won't," Carol said. "I'll plot your defeat on that issue."

His daughter turned to him. "People sure are talking a lot about you back home," she said. "You should read some of the bad letters in the paper."

"Just so they spell the name right," he said.

"He believes it adds to his legend," Carol said. "I think he wishes he were a Congressman under King Arthur."

"The Governor's been saying some awful things about you," Annie said, making a face.

"We'll get him back. We're going to surprise the son of a . . ."

"Don't lose your composure at Christmas," Carol interrupted.

"Just awful things," the girl repeated, shaking her head from side to side.

Carol looked at him, then shrugged, and to change the subject: "Annie Winter, I like your drawl."

"I like yours. I like *you*. You're a little devilish, aren't you?"

Later they went into the back garden. In the darkness they heard children caroling down the way. Just beyond the trees they saw the evening star.

"There's Venus, Carol," the girl said.

"It certainly is. The Star of Bethlehem, right over the Chevy Chase Club."

"The first star of my Christmas."

Suddenly she saw a beautiful magnolia tree, its leaves still full and green, towering over the edge of the lawn. "Oh, look at it. It's a wonderful tree. Does it stay green all year?"

"I believe it must have character. Do you like it?"

"Can I decorate it with Christmas lights sometime?"

"Of course you can."

"I'd like to give a party for it, and invite some children."

"Why didn't I think of that? We'll do it on Christmas Eve."

In Washington at Christmastime a vague moratorium comes to our politics, all the better for its being undeclared, a splendid contrast which invests the place and the season with an almost tangible mellowness. It is that one time in the year during congressional recess when its practitioners do not rush home to wave the colors or toil for promotion, and for that reason if no other it has in those brief days a true spirit of community, so absent in its usual harassments. It was in just such a mood that she sat next to him on a bench beside the reflecting pool of the Lincoln Memorial on Christmas Eve morning and watched the two children skating on the ice. A number of politicians and their wives with children similarly occupied had strolled by to pass the time, and now as Carol gazed across at the procession of bright colors whirling across the surface of the pond in a chaotic dance, she devoured the invigorating chill of the day and felt the pleasure of her senses.

"I hate to confess it, but this is the most domestic I've ever been in my life."

"Are you enjoying it?"

"I believe I am."

From far in the distance, against the backdrop of the Memorial, she watched as her son executed some intricate maneuver and landed in a tumble on his rear.

"Carol, I want to have a serious talk with you. I'm afraid I've been postponing it."

"Well, go ahead."

"I'm thinking very much about trying for the Senate seat."

As he spoke to her of it, an eavesdropper on this morning in the final days of that decade might have sensed how often such conversations had unfolded in that most American of cities, the practical confidences exchanged then as now between husbands and wives or lovers about risks and advancements, about moving toward loftier goals, the decision he must arrive at being neither more nor less indigenous to our politics, but basic to the species: the old urge to authority and power. His words were rooted in the moment, in the sensitive politician's deepest reflexes toward a divided land, but for all that the year could have been 1856, or 1892, or 1934.

She listened for a long time. Finally she said: "Well, you'd better be sure."

"You can't ever be sure. You know that. You have to gamble sometimes."

"Then reasonably sure. You've only been here two years. What about your 1,222 votes? Do they really know who you are?"

"They're beginning to. This situation is developing in my favor. It's all changing. It's easier now for an unknown to take on an entrenched old soldier. If I don't now it may take another twelve years. Maybe never. I may *have* to do it now."

"Then let me be frank. Have you grown the big head?"

"I don't think so."

"I wouldn't want you to do anything hasty. Sometimes you're too impetuous."

He laughed. "I'm getting a haircut and I'm going home with Annie after Christmas for a few days. I'm giving myself two months or so to decide."

"Very well."

"Will you stick with me?"

She looked at him. Her whispered words were strangely fragile. "I can't make that promise now."

"For a while then?"

Again she was briefly silent, looking out beyond the Memorial to the hills of Arlington.

"Yes."

Suddenly the children skated to them, breaking the mood. She was glad for the interruption, because the conversation had disturbed her a little, all the more because she had been expecting it for a long time.

"Why do you always sit together and never pay attention to anything?" her son asked.

"We're telling secrets," Carol said.

"Well, stop it," the girl said. "Tonight's my party for a tree!"

THE NIGHT WAS EXCELLENT for it, with a hearty Christmas Eve cheer, and for two hours before the children of the neighborhood arrived Annie and her father and Templeton decorated the magnolia with Christmas lights and strands of crepe and tinsel, and all the ornaments from the Christmas trees of Carol's childhood: a velvet angel and a team of white reindeer acquired in Little Rock, a dancing figure on a sleigh and a golden star from Memphis, three silver Wise Men from Helena, and an array of tiny adornments from McClellan's in her own town, all a little frayed now with wear. A dozen or so children walked from their houses to be there, each costumed as a certain kind of tree. Cool breezes drifted into the garden, and the smell of hamburgers from the open grill brought a group of dogs from down the way, competing momentarily with Congressman Winter's dog for the territorial sway. The lawn sloping away to the ivy-covered walls was alive with the motions of young beings and beasts.

"This place has never seen such activity," Carol said. "Whoever heard of a party for a tree?"

"I never heard of such a thing," the boy said. "That little girl has crazy ideas."

"A crazy little Southern girl."

"I wouldn't want to be her."

"I once gave a party for some dogs and it was written up in *Open Road for Boys*," she said. "But I guess it wasn't this unusual."

"What time is Santa Claus due here?" the boy asked.

"He's leaving your ashes and switches at the Pentagon."

The magnolia, festooned in all its splendor, stood magnificently before them. How many children long since gone had climbed its branches, she wondered. As she looked she saw more than a few living ones poised in its leaves, and near the top, gazing out toward the adjoining townhouses with a telescope, was Annie Winter.

"Jack. Please get her down. She'll kill herself."

Suddenly, from out of the kitchen door, appeared one of Carol's least favorite neighbors, a drunk oil-and-gas lobbyist in a tweed suit. Once, some time before, when this neighbor boasted to all of the fine mileage his new sportscar was getting, Carol and her son had sneaked into his garage every night for a week, surreptitiously pouring gasoline into the tank, so that he actually began bragging that he was getting 135 miles to the gallon on the brand name he represented.

"Oh God," she whispered. "Try to get rid of him."

"What the hell's going on here?" the lobbyist shouted, stumbling slightly as he spoke, drinking from a china Santa mug. "What's going on in that tree?"

"Hello, friend," Jack said. "I believe I've met you on the Hill."

"I never saw anything like this. I can't stand the noise."

"Don't be Scrooge on Christmas Eve."

"Let's go chop down the tree while we've got 'em all in it."

"I'm thinking about introducing some measures on the depletion allowance," Jack said, embracing the neighbor in a strong bear hug.

"Can I borrow an axe?"

"He's a Congressman and wants to increase the depletion allowance," Carol said.

"Seriously?" the neighbor said. "Are you from Texas? Why don't I know you? Are you from Tulsa?"

"Can we discuss it if I walk you back to your house?" Jack said. "I'd go as high as fifty percent if the argument's reasonable."

"Damned reasonable!" he said, and left the garden arm-in-arm with the Congressman.

"That was masterful," Carol said to him when he returned. "Maybe you were right this morning."

"I have experience in suffering fools."

The evening settled now into a languor of quiet, tired children and dogs satiated on scraps of supper and the fresh breezes of December. Finally it was time for Annie Winter's ceremony.

With magnolia twigs tied to her head and mistletoe to her limbs, she gathered the children around the tree and they circled about it in a ceremonial dance.

"Something enigmatic runs in your family blood," Carol said.

Then the little girl led the others in strange incantations. They bowed before the magnolia in obeisance.

"Now," she shouted for all to hear, "my father said I should read from this book of his about trees. Everybody listen."

Slowly, stumbling over and mispronouncing words, she said:

It appears from a tiny capsule more or less the size of a drop of water. It grows with mathematical rhythm, putting out myriads of contact points with the gases of the atmosphere and minerals of the earth. It erects antennae to catch the power of the sunshine. It makes its own food from the elements and reproduces itself with a shower of seeds. This is an expression of the elemental quality of life that gives wings to the thoughts far beyond the commonplace. The spirit of a tree is our spirit. Its art is our art. Its color, designs, and the values of its wood and fruit are ours. If you would discover what kind of life is hidden in the shadows of leaves, and behind tough, silent bark, you must find it within yourself.

"I didn't know you were a conservationist too," Carol said.

"What does that mean anyway, Jack?" the boy shouted from across the lawn.

"It means that old tree is your cousin!" Carol shouted back.


WITH THE CHRISTMAS DAWN came a change in weather, a golden warmth that promised for the day the laziness of Indian summer. Carol yawned and stretched. She looked at the early sunlight streaming through the curtains, remembering the awakenings on such mornings of her childhood, when the world and all its possessions seemed to lie in wait only for her, and the very atmosphere itself was rich with the kitchen smells of Christmastime in Arkansas. Turning, she saw him next to her, and she gently rubbed his back until he too stirred with the day and drowsily turned to her.

"So very good."

"The best," he whispered.

"I'm so sorry. I was selfish. Next time will all be for you."

"No. I love you that way."

"Then go wake up the orphans."

After breakfast they opened the presents. Then Carol said, "We won't have the turkey until tonight. I really want to show all of you my city. I'll probably be here long after Jack Winter's gone."

"It's a strange notion to see Washington on Christmas Day," he said.

"Why not? We'll have it all to ourselves."

"We'll take a picnic," Annie Winter said.

"A picnic on Christmas?" the boy said. "I'd rather stay home and listen to the police."

"Just a second!" he said. "I've got to make about five telephone calls. I have to wish five key people back home a Merry Christmas."

"Well, if you want privacy you'll find a telephone in the manger," Carol said.

With the trees leafless, the sharp glare of the day was reflected on the surfaces of limestone and marble, on all the domes and columns. They did indeed have the city to themselves, almost as private to them as Harper's Ferry on the night in October. They drove past the embassies all closed down and silent, and the empty plazas, and the generals on horseback.

"I sure do feel sorry for that horse," the boy said, pointing to the equine figure supporting the gargantuan General Winfield Scott.

"Why can't every President have a memorial?" Annie said.

"I agree," Carol said. "I've always felt sorry for poor John Tyler."

"Why does the Washington Monument look like different colors?" Templeton asked. He pointed to the obelisk and shrugged his shoulders.

"You're absolutely right," Carol said. "It's made of different kinds of marble. You see? That's why there's a ring around the shaft."

"Don't be too graphic," Jack said to her.

She felt as frolicsome as the children in the back seat. "One more remark like that and you're out," she whispered.

They took a circuitous route around the city, stopping first at the Lincoln Memorial, where the children stood a little in awe and examined the brooding figure.

"Was he really that big?" the boy asked. "Look at his feet."

"Why is he so sad?" Annie asked.

"He has every reason to be," Carol said, standing to the side of the rotunda looking at the Second Inaugural.

"My teacher says he wrote the Gettysburg Address on the back of an envelope," the girl said. "He thought it up in ten minutes."

"Tell your teacher I said he thought about it longer than that," Jack said.

"Well, you see, it sure is a short speech," she said, pointing to the grand words carved in the stone. "I guess he just ran out of words."

"He looks like a big penny," Templeton added.

They walked through the garden of the Jefferson Memorial, a comfortable place at noon, the bare cherry trees all about them and the Potomac in the distance. Inside, Congressman Winter read from the inscription, and his words echoed hollowly through the interior, causing the two children to come suddenly to attention. *"I have sworn upon the altar of God eternal hostility against every form of tyranny over the mind of man."*

"How did I ever get involved with an ideologue?" Carol said.

"What does it mean?" the boy asked.

"Tom Jefferson hated bullies," Carol replied.

"Didn't he find electricity?"

"Sort of," Jack said. "But I believe he wants you to think for yourself."

"So now we've seen a Greek Lincoln, an Egyptian Washington, and a Roman Jefferson," Carol said in the car. "Look at this." She pointed to that monument to the 1960's called the Watergate, a massive apartment complex that loomed now before them. "This is the most American monument of all. A liberal went in there six months ago and hasn't been seen since."

"It looks like a box of Kleenex," the girl said.

"Which President is it for?"

"Garfield."

"I don't believe it."

Now they were in a sprawling black section of the district, row after row of attached brick houses as far as the eye could see, and Negro children of all sizes trying out their new Christmas toys in the streets and on the sidewalks.

"It reminds me of home," Annie said.

"Honey, it is home, whether you know it or not," Carol said.

"Look at all the old beat-up trucks," the boy said.

"They save things to use later," Annie replied.

Soon they had crossed the river and were speeding down
the deserted expressway into Virginia, and after a time they
were in Alexandria.

"My great-great-great-grandmother is buried in that
cemetery," Templeton said.

"Then let's go look at her," Annie said.

In the cemetery the boy found the grave, just as he had
two years before—*Sarah Gibbs Templeton. Born 1775. Died
1800*—under a bare oak tree near the church which Lee had
attended, and Washington before him. Carol looked at the
tombstone, gray now in the warm sunshine, and sighed.

"Merry Christmas, grandmother," she said.

"Where's her husband?" Jack asked.

"He left her here and went to Arkansas. Isn't that just like
a man? My uncle said he was a fugitive from misunder-
standing."

"That probably means he was broke."

"She looks lonesome," Annie said.

"What's she doing down there?" Templeton asked.

"You must have a fetish about that," Carol said. "Maybe
she's wondering who we are."

"We're her kinfolks."

"Yes," Carol said, and gave another small sigh, in Yuletide
recognition of the passing of her generations from the earth.

They strolled through the streets of Alexandria, past the
brick and clapboard houses set flush with the sidewalks, and
the arched gates leading into gardens; they looked through
the open windows and saw families sitting down to midday
dinners. From a transomed doorway down a lane a child
stood watching them, cracking a cap pistol in their direction.

"What did you get for Christmas, little boy?" Carol asked,
interrupting for a moment her light stride.

"Nothing I wanted," the little boy replied.

"Why aren't you eating dinner?" Annie asked.

"I don't like turkey."

"Your modern American child," Carol said.

They wandered through the countryside, and in the middle of the afternoon, on the way home, they reached the heights of Arlington. From the Lee mansion, on the rise above the endless rows of military tombstones, lay the Lincoln Memorial, the Potomac, and the city, sweeping before them now in an unseasonal haze.

Such remote views of great cities tell much about their character. The city that stretched before them now could not be assimilated in the instant; in its gleaming whiteness and its deferential splendor lay the substance of dreams. It appeared before them a little jerry-built and disordered, government and ghetto in fitful juxtaposition, as if its consummations of stone had been contrived to reach away toward a final measure of immortality—a congeries of hopes carved out to last forever, a monument made up of smaller monuments.

"It was built for giants and inhabited by pygmies," Carol said.

"I believe it's the prettiest place I ever saw," Annie said.

"Well, eat your picnic and save room for dinner."

They reclined in a sunny spot on the terrace, looking out from time to time at the view.

"Doesn't everybody love Washington?" the little girl asked.

"Lord, no," Carol replied. "I once visited a town in Oklahoma where people were picketing federal mailboxes."

"Well, it's a nice way to spend Christmas. Thank you, Carol."

"You're welcome."

"What does your daddy do for a living?" the girl asked Templeton.

"He makes money. What does yours do?"

"He makes laws."

"I remember. He showed me."

"He talks a lot. It's part of his job."

"I know."

"Your mother talks a lot too."

"She doesn't get paid for it."

"I'm proud of my father."

"Me too."

"Sometimes he says he has to lose his temper on purpose."

"No kidding?"

"I wish people back home would stop saying bad things about him. They say he doesn't deserve to be in Washington."

"Well, he's sitting right here, and there's Washington."

"Of course he has plenty of friends."

"I bet."

The two adults had been listening to this exchange with a feigned interest, when Jack Winter said: "At least I'm glad you kids aren't adolescents. Thank God you aren't going through puberty today."

"What's puberty?" Templeton asked.

"You'll find out soon enough," Carol said.

"It's when you sprout hair, under your arms and everywhere else," Annie replied.

"Is that right, Jack?" the boy said.

"It's the best definition I've heard."

"I'm never going to bed with a boy unless I love him," Annie said.

"What about Andy Jackson? I've seen him in your daddy's bed," Templeton replied.

"A *dog?* Besides, he's so much older. He's seven years old and that makes him seven times seven. He's forty-nine."

"He's almost dead."

"Is love good?" Annie asked.

"I think love's good for everybody," Carol said.

"No, I mean loving a boy."

"I hope so, but I'm not sure."

"What's the difference between being in love and *making* love?"

"I'll tell you tonight."

"Is there a difference?"

"Well," she said, looking at Jack Winter, "sometimes yes and sometimes not."

"When yes and when not?"

"I can't answer that."

Finally, as the late afternoon settled on the river and the city beyond, they got up to leave, making their way home in a comforting darkness.

# 8

IT WAS EARLY in the new session. Carol and Elaine Rossiter were sitting in the House gallery. They saw Congressman Winter near the brass railing behind the Democratic side of the floor, waiting for his name in a quorum call.

"This is the most physical place I ever saw," Carol said to her companion.

She was right. In the scene before them, the Congressmen were greeting each other with jabs at shoulders, whacks upon backs, masculine pats, and half embraces. Jack Winter had his arm casually draped about the elbow of a slight gargoyle from New York. Soon he was being courtly with a female representative from Massachusetts wearing a dress that extended considerably below her knees.

"I'd be jealous," Elaine said.

"Don't make me laugh."

They had come that morning because he had gotten permission from the Speaker to speak for a "long minute" on an issue before the House. The question itself was not momentous, but when he was recognized shortly before the noon break, Carol and Elaine listened very closely.

Halfway through his remarks Carol whispered, "It's not very good."

"No, it's not."

"It's shrill."

The fact that no one in particular was listening, neither on the floor nor in the galleries, was slightly humiliating to her. She looked at Elaine and grimaced. Something between her and the Congressman was imperceptibly beginning to change. Certain things about him, real or fancied, were beginning to irritate her. She thought of all the happy days, the days of confidence and freedom.

"He's disappointing. He should've told me what he was going to say."

"Forget it," Elaine said. "It's not important."

Now she blurted to Elaine: "He's so damnably self-assured."

"You've always felt you were slumming with him a little, haven't you?"

Elaine's words jolted her. "That's not true."

Her companion's remark, however, made her thoughtful. With her strong powers of visualization she knew she was gradually leading herself to an inexplicable fear of her love. None of this was happening all of a piece, for she knew she cared deeply for him, certainly more deeply than she ever thought she could care for a man. The strength of their physical love was not to be denied. Perhaps her subtle disaffection lay in her acknowledgment that she had found a lover who was an equal, in the slow discovery within her of the deep complexities of sexual love. But when he had returned to the city after his long visit home, the uncertainty of his plans, the magnitude of the decision he was postponing, made her feel he was suddenly equivocal toward her, as if he were beginning to take her for granted. Or was all this the work of her imagination?

"It's none of my business, Carol, but you've changed so much for the better. You're still changing. For your own sake see it through."

"You're changing too."

"We're getting older."

"I love him."

"I know."

On the floor five or six of Jack Winter's colleagues, properly attired except for the tennis shoes they wore in their rush from the gymnasium for the quorum call, were strolling with him toward the Speaker's lobby. He paused briefly to seek out the two of them in the gallery, and when he found them he held up the fingers of both hands and said, silently, for them to read his lips: "Ten minutes."

They met in the members' dining room.

"Guess what I just saw on the wire service ticker?" he said as he took a chair.

"What?"

"The Governor says I'm the man to beat for the Senate, and I haven't even announced."

"Congratulations," Carol said. "You won't even have to go through the motions."

"He says if I get in the race they'll tear me apart on my own weaknesses."

"After that speech," Carol said, "I'd practice up for the Governor."

"It wasn't that bad. I had my reasons for it."

"What reasons?"

"Political reasons."

"You made a few enemies and you didn't have to," Carol said.

"That's the most uncharacteristic thing I ever heard you say," Elaine said.

"Well, Carol may be right," he said. "But what the hell? This place baffles me. It can take all the life from a man. Until not too long ago I've thought you could do it from the inside. See that fellow over there?" He pointed to one of his colleagues at a nearby table. "He's only three years older than I am and he's been here five terms. He's working constantly on the little routine, the amendments, the floor statements on bills. He's courteous almost to a fault to the older members. I like him. I *admire* him. He's absolutely trustworthy. But even in the time I've known him something's gone out of him. Do you know what it is? He's beginning to forget the *country*. He never makes enemies. But, you see, he's consciously isolating himself from the things that really matter. The other day we were having a sandwich and he turned to me and said, 'Damn it, Winter, I could stay here another twenty-five years if I'm not whipped back home, and do you know the best I can hope for when I'm sixty-five? Chairman of the Post Office Committee!' Most of them aren't that honest. He put the fear of God in me."

"It's the story of life," Carol said.

"Not *my* life. And not yours either, be damned. You're like me."

"Two outsiders," Elaine said.

"How I'd love to make it to the Other Side!" Jack Winter whispered, raising his elbows in supplication.

"Elaine, we've created a monster."

"I know!"

"Well, we're all in it together," Carol said, "and we're all in for a tough time."

But before her words were out, Congressman Winter had risen from his chair and walked across to two old leaders who were sitting down at a table. Carol watched his deference to the pair, then looked again at Elaine.

"Be cheerful," Elaine laughed.

"I will."

"And if the time comes you can't, then be impatient with your impatience."

"That's something I've never been able to do."


HER SELF-JUDGMENT was apt. Ever so slowly, one layer at a time, her strange aggravation built upon itself like the depositing of fine sediments. She seemed unable to check these anonymous grievances; by turns she thrived on them and suffered a gloomy contrition.

There had been a night, two or three weeks after their lunch in the members' dining room, when she took sides against him before a group of friends and strangers. It was after a dinner in Cleveland Park; one of the guests, in town for a few days, was an important supporter of Congressman Winter's from his home district, a patrician gentleman of the old school who only quite recently had begun devoting something of his wealth to the commerce of his home state's politics.

The evening had started questionably when Carol asked him how he had made his fortune.

The visitor was silent for a moment, then replied peevishly: "Cotton and timber."

"That's blood and guilt money, isn't it?" The guest did not answer her.

Later they were discussing a topic of apparently little consequence—it concerned a set of minor bills then before

the Congress in which the visitor had expressed an interest—and she was suddenly argumentative about an observation of Congressman Winter's, intimating that he was not
well informed on the subject.

There was an embarrassed silence until he replied, "It just
so happened I spent two hours on the telephone today about
those bills."

He looked at her bitterly. The hostess changed the subject. But later, the first moment they were alone, he cornered
her in a fierce rage.

"Why did you do that?"

"I felt the desire to test you, I suppose. I can't explain
these things."

"I suggest you try."

"I'll search myself."

"You can't be without attention. You're a performer."

"And you? You have your profession and I have mine."

"Do you realize there's something in you that's very destructive? There's something dark in you that I can't deal
with."

"You once called it *imagination*."

"Imagination has its underside."

"So does ambition."

A few days later there was another episode, thoroughly
ludicrous, a burlesque of all the acrimonious junctures of her
life. She was angry with him that day because he had just
told a group of reporters from his home state, when they
pressed him good-naturedly on the point, that he and Mrs.
Hollywell were considering marriage.

"It was inexcusable," she had snapped. "You're getting
mileage out of me."

"I know it. I shouldn't have. I was thinking of the good it
would do."

"It only means you're trying to use me. I won't allow it."

At a cocktail party on the Hill she found herself in conversation with his most attractive political rival from home. Jack Winter had discussed him often with her, finding him shrewd but wanting in substance, tough but ever amiable, sharp-eyed in exploiting the blunders of others. "The only time he ever tells the truth is when he contradicts himself," he had told her. Some fugitive emotion passed through her now, something quite amusing to her even though beyond her own immediate comprehension; she felt the strongest compulsion to belittle her lover in his rival's eyes.

Almost instinctually she began to woo the man who stood next to her. She talked to him flirtatiously. She straightened his tie. She reached in his coat pocket for a cigarette lighter he had just deposited there. With all the empiricisms she had acquired from the debutante balls and country club dances of her past, she took the man by the arm and led him to the bar. A dozen heads turned to observe this spectacle, so fraught with hidden meanings now for those practitioners of provincial statecraft in the crowded room. A moment later, only a few feet from Jack Winter, she kissed his rival on the cheek for a society photographer. Then, as she had anticipated, Congressman Winter deserted the group standing near him, and as he approached she briefed her new conspirator on precisely what he should say.

"Hello, Fred."

"Hello, Jack."

"I see you've finally met."

"Yes. And I read you're considering marriage."

"Oh really?" Carol said. "Who's the girl?"

He had the appearance to her of a man invoking all his professional resources to hide an awesome chagrin. "Right now you lead the list," he said.

"And what do you have to offer me? Wealth? Fame? Contentment in the red clay hills?"

He flushed. "All that and the rewards of public service. Right, Fred?"

"But Fred here—he and I were just considering matrimony."

"It would be interesting if the Congressman and I had the same wife in the same campaign," the man said.

"Oh, I don't know," he replied. "You can have her in the hills and me in the suburbs."

"It's a shame. You'd get the female vote in Utah," she laughed.


IN MUCH THE SAME SPIRIT, one night when he had flown home on a speaking trip, she ran into the famous novelist from New York who had, seven years before, been her dinner partner in the White House. It was an evening in one of the smaller embassies and at first she failed to remember him, but he confounded her with an exuberant embrace and reminded her who he was.

"Mrs. Hollywell, I've thought of you and asked about you. You made the deepest impression on me."

"Of course I remember. It was the night my husband's Packard broke down. But I can't recall whether you were charming or rather trying."

"I was trying for *you*," he replied, and led her by the arm to a quiet corner. "But you had a husband who was a *consigliere* for the Cosa Nostra."

"They finally got him at a toll booth on the Jersey Turnpike."

"And just now someone told me you're coddling the U.S. Congress."

"Yes."

"Why would you want to do that?"

"In the interests of the democratic experiment."

"Well, I salute you. It needs encouragement."

At that moment Elaine Rossiter hovered before them in a garish purple dress with immense embroidered pockets. They embraced, and after Elaine greeted the novelist Carol turned to her and said: "I wish you wouldn't wear pencils with clips on your party dresses." From one of the pockets Carol plucked a pencil and put it behind her ear.

"Where's Jack?" Elaine asked.

"You're my *bête noire*. He had to fly home."

"You should've gone with him."

"He didn't ask me."

"That doesn't mean a thing. Now he really needs you."

The novelist returned with two glasses of champagne, and once again they were alone.

"I wanted to be a Congressman or a Senator when I was a boy," he said.

"And why didn't you?"

"I put away childish things. And I thought I was ugly."

"Listen," she said, opening her bright-green eyes as wide as she could and whispering dramatically. "You're the most distinguished man in this room."

"Then you *are* worthy of me," he said.

She proceeded, quite self-consciously, as if from some newly remembered obligation, to get rather drunk. On the merest caprice she soon decided that she would return to her companion's hotel if he expressed the interest, which she assumed he would, and as inevitably he did. When the two of them left together, balancing themselves with gingerly caution as they weaved through the crowd, she saw Elaine again on the fringes of the party staring haughtily in her direction; Carol bowed toward her friend and gave a lofty wave. She believed she found the evening very interesting. But the next morning, a little to her surprise and even disappointment, she felt the slightest twinge of remorse, and when she opened the morning's mail there was a note from Jack Winter, written at the airport in a hasty scrawl:

*This is written in pain and affection. I love you, and I've assumed what had happened with us might last, for the good of us both. I'm mystified. I have to tell you that some of those things which drew me to you now frighten me a little. I want very much to include you in all of it, in what I am and what I might become.*

Her extraordinary self-regard, so long unchallenged, had been in abeyance since she greeted the first novelties of love. Now this conceit, the giddy conceit of her girlhood and her marriage, returned to bedevil her. Sometimes in these days she scanned the horizons of herself and recognized her more callow impulses; perhaps her very loveliness and invention now, as so often in the past, exacted their cost in mean little moods of ambiguity toward a man who understood her more intimately than any other being she had known. Yet these moods, the urge to be honored and transfigured, seemed dictated to her by some remote presence far outside herself. What was she to do? The more her lover tried in these days to mollify the same hasty compulsions, the more demanding to her he became. How little had changed! Much like the girl in the river town in Arkansas who could not understand how thoroughly she was an expression of her time and place, so the mature woman failed to recognize that her life now was molded by the new day. If in her heart lurked the South, its shadows and remembrances, her fulfillment dwelled in the American age. Release and freedom would fetch their price. She might have been more old-fashioned. She would suffer again.

                              .     .     .

NOT AT ALL by coincidence, she had a long discussion with
Jennie Grand about associating with politicians. They had
had similar conversations before, but this time Carol
searched it out, and in the ebb of a cold February afternoon
at Carol's house, her old friend was more emphatic than
ever, so that when she spilled some tea on her skirt she went
right on talking.

"Look," Jennie had begun, flushing slightly with the passion that was to come, "sometimes you run across the wife of
a politician who's more interesting than her husband, but
how many can *you* count?"

"I don't know. Three perhaps."

"Think what these younger wives will be like when they
pass fifty. Think what it must do to them to see their husbands at parties and everywhere else lying, smiling falsely,
telling the same stories, kissing derrières. Especially *elec-
tioneering* husbands. Do you want a life by rote?"

"You're being very lordly."

"No I'm not. Practicing politics every day has got to close
off some part of the brain. Or maybe it's the heart. It would
ruin everything that's distinctive about you. There's something of the locker room about it. I'll imagine even the best
ones were impossible to live with—Washington, Jefferson,
Lincoln, Roosevelt, you name them."

"And what would the place be like if there hadn't been
those men who were so impossible to live with?"

"Well, I say let someone else do the cohabiting. Elaine
Rossiter. Ruth Ann Pennebaker. Politicians in Europe are
accepted for what they are—cool professionals in the business of compromise. But just look what America does to its
politicians—all the rituals and the glamour, the whole un-

godly process. People in this country don't treat politicians like human beings. They vent all their frustrations on them. They expect them to be the sorriest villains one minute and the most glamorous movie stars the next. No wonder so many of their children end up such a mess. How many of them have friends—I mean *real* friendships? It's not just what the politicians do to themselves. The *country* does it to them. They're what the country has become. It's no surprise so many of them get shot. Or that the most ambitious usually have the worst personal problems. There's practically not a single one of them I can talk to as a human being, and I've been in this town a long time."

Jennie caught her breath. Carol held her hands tightly together. She looked distressed.

"Your friend Jack Winter may be an exception to you, but give him five or six years."

Later that afternoon Carol took a long walk through Georgetown, up the hill past Dumbarton Oaks toward Rock Creek Park. She gazed at the same houses which had enthralled her as a girl. She pondered Jennie's advice—Jennie who had never failed her. She winced against the cold, and in the shadows she returned home with harsh thoughts.

That night at dinner she confronted Jack Winter with Jennie's malediction.

"Now I really do feel beleaguered," he said. "If I agreed with it I'd have to close off part of my brain. Or is it my heart?"

"That's not fair."

"Isn't it? Well, you and Jennie are wrong as usual."

"Maybe."

"Don't worry. Even a broken clock is right twice a day."

"I bring it up seriously."

"Then I'll treat it seriously. You're fighting goblins. The

fact that I happen to be in this line of work has nothing to do with it. You're too damned lofty. I suspect you'd drive yourself to find faults in me if I were a businessman, or a veterinarian, or a music critic."

"That's not true."

"I've taught a little history and I've practiced a lot of law. Shall I tell you what I've seen of the sham in a lot of academics? They're usually the first ones to stalk the politicians for not satisfying their high standards. Or would you care for a lecture on what a lot of lawyers are like?"

"Calm down. I don't like you this way."

"Calm down! Your friend Jennie's a dilettante, especially when it comes to other people's deepest commitments. She's a dilettante about human things. She's been groomed for it. If you're not careful, you'll be a dilettante just like her one of these days. You'll go through life on her same splendid podium. Now, just for instance, my daughter adores you. So do I, and besides that I need you. That's more important than the stories you have to hear all the time."

"I felt I deserved your reaction."

"I wish you didn't feel you deserved so much. Now drink some more wine. I've had a hard day. We'll go see a belly dancer. Or a movie. Or find one of those bars where we won't see a single poor laboring politician. But let's hurry. I've only got five or six years."

SHE DECIDED not to see him for three or four days. At first she thought she might take her son for a while to the cottage on the shore. But she missed him.

On the late afternoon of an uncertain March day, an alternation of sunshine and thundershowers, she went to his office. He was not there.

"He's hiding by himself," his secretary told her.

"Well, I'll just sneak up on him for a few minutes."

"Do you know he's making up his mind today?"

"Oh." She had completely forgotten.

"I think he likes that kind of drama, but don't tell him I said so."

"Where is he?"

"At the Library of Congress. At one of those desks in the big reading room."

The wind blew in sharp gusts as she walked across to the library. She climbed the stairs to the gallery of the reading hall in the rotunda. She looked down at the hundreds of mahogany desks arranged concentrically in the silent room, the same room where she had come so many years before to research the speeches of Sir Winston, and later to gather material for her Senator from Kentucky. She gazed about her now, at the red columns and the vast dome and the old ivory on the ceiling, a composite of dark and bright colors, and as she looked the sun of the dreary day again broke through, making a coral glow on the marble. She paused to remember her early time there, remembering also that far-away day in Chartres Cathedral, a setting curiously not unlike this, when something very subtle had touched her— what was it? She could not recall.

At last she saw him. He was sitting at a desk by himself, reading from a book. His blond hair had fallen slightly over his face, and his brow was furrowed in concentration. The sight of him, so alone there and so small against the monumental backdrop of the hall, filled her with melancholy. She felt the candid laughter of their first days of love, the complexity and the charity of him, Christmas with their children, and, with pain, her own strange hesitations.

She would have made a fine painting just now, with her

slender hands on the railing looking downward, her wind-swept hair in disarray over her shoulders. The rosy sunlight streaming through the dome in this dying hour reflected upon her, and the magnificent chamber mesmerized her.

She became aware in that moment of her own body. She knew then she was at the height of her beauty and power. She remembered how almost every man she had ever met, however casually, had wanted to make love to her, and how almost every woman of every man had suspected and envied her. She remembered the attentions of the so many men, the sexuality of them feeding on her body, the affection of their courtship, their lavish promises, and all this had been mysterious to her, until the man before her, the man on whom her gaze reposed, had led her in pleasure and affection to comprehend it all. And her mind drifted back to the casual inanities of Ole Miss when she was the reigning belle among all the double-named belles, and on to her own town and the bluffs by the river, when her spirit had never failed her in her timeless quest of . . . *what?*

A cloud must have swept the sun, for the chamber darkened, casting her briefly in shadows, and she thought now of the years ahead, the time of growing old, the narrowing peripheries of age, the death of friends, her own mortality, and her son's. Everything she had touched, it seemed to her, had turned sour, spectacular beginnings and sorry deteriorations: were there seeds of destruction in her that she could not acknowledge to herself? Out of all her years on this earth, from the tow-headed girl walking down the street called Boulevard to the beautiful figure now standing in this vast monument, from all her ambitions and imaginings, through all the successive phases of her girlhood and marriage and love, she had grown into a mature woman of distinction and complexity. Yet she only knew her silent plea against the echoes in the rotunda that day: *God, who am I? God, what do I want?*

And in this mood of self-contemplation, soft as the rushing of wings, fragments from the past returned to her: the stricken look on her Congressman's face when she warned about the flags at the Monument; the evening with the old Senator from the deepest South whispering to her, "Sometimes I think I failed, that what with all the little things the big things passed me by"; her excitement in the taxicab on the way to her first Georgetown party, her companion telling her he wanted to be President of the United States; her husband speaking to her in her days of prominence: "You're spending a lot of time with them. Won't you wear out your welcome?"; the assistant standing closely at her side, above the darkened valley in Maryland: "I'm the happiest I've ever been in my life, and I say to myself, who would've thought?"; she and her son and the lonely old ladies at the Woodrow Wilson house on Memorial Day; the mutilated soldiers in the military hospitals and Jennie Grand's fearful admonition; Harper's Ferry ghostlike under the autumn moon; Jack Winter's belabored speech in the well of the House; Elaine Rossiter saying so unexpectedly to her: "You've always felt you were slumming with him a little, haven't you?" . . .

The grand edifices of the city might someday fall into ruin, the very nation it epitomized might descend at last into oblivion. She felt the penetrating damp and cold, and she shuddered now in her deepest being. Only later would she come to know, long after Jack Winter, long after her memory of this day, that all of it, all of what it was—the monuments and inscriptions in stone, the marble and bronze, the parks and boulevards, the toils and maneuverings, and deceits and nobilities—all of it, in that time granted her to see it and live it, was not what it seemed but dwelled in fleeting mists: affirmation against the darkness.

But now she must do what she had to do, whatever it was she had to do.

She walked down the stairs into the reading room. She circled the long rows of desks and stopped behind Jack Winter. She touched him on the shoulder. He looked up in surprise.

After a pause he said: "Do you want a false smile?"

"Come on outside."

He followed her into the hallway.

"Well?"

"I'm sorry for all those things."

"Then you're forgiven. But don't talk that way again."

"What were you reading?"

"You wouldn't believe it."

"Tell me."

"Walt Whitman and the Book of Psalms."

"Lord God! And so you've made up your mind."

"Yes."

"And you and I both knew all along."

"Probably so."

"And now you want me to help you."

"Only if you really want to."

"Then I will."

"You're the most changeable creature I've ever known."

"I know."

"Are you really sure you want to stick with me on this, Carol?"

She embraced him, holding him close to her for the briefest moment, then answering, almost as a sigh: "I think so."

He laughed and shook his head. "I don't really believe

you, you know. I won't ask for anything in writing. Just come back with me now to my place."

"Yes. I was hoping for that," she said, in a whisper that lilted down the breezy hall, then faded away.

# 9

IN THE GEOMETRY of American politics, as we all know, the task of gaining recognition falls heaviest on the newcomer, no matter how able or well regarded in the best quarters. But the tactical advantages which offset this—fewer enemies, for instance, and less identification with bedeviling issues and predispositions—can sometimes make a significant difference. In the two months until the party primary in which he was one of several contestants, Congressman Winter, with a substantial if inexperienced personal organization behind him, would be faced with the enormous need of making himself known in environs far removed from his own constituency.

Carol left her son with his father and went to the state to help in the campaign. The novelty of it at first charmed her, and with her wide knowledge of the calling she became a barometer for the candidate and his advisers, and more than that, not surprisingly, an attraction in herself. Since this was no accident, for indeed she had fully expected it, she chose her wardrobe carefully, one for the larger cities, another for the outlands—the pine thickets and the swamp bottoms and that whole world, bred in her bones in childhood which now seemed so remote to her, of cotton gins and courthouse squares. She went openly with him, and his daughter when she was not in school, and the coteries of preoccupied campaign workers, and practically as a matter of course it was assumed they were engaged to be married.

At his first press conference in the largest hotel in the capital city, she thrilled as always to the crowds and the klieg lights; her abbreviated red dress and her jangle of trinkets, as she knew better than anyone else, were far from common to provincial politics. She stood far off to the side while he read a statement and answered questions, and when he had more or less finished, a group of home state journalists who were based most of the year in Washington, captivated by her history there, turned their attention to her.

"Mrs. Hollywell, can you tell us why you're helping the Congressman in this campaign?"

Flashbulbs popped, blinding her for the moment, and she squinted out grotesquely at them, then said: "Because he's so good-looking, and he's named his dog Andy Jackson and calls me Woodrow. He wants to rename his daughter Eleanor. But more important, he deserves the female vote in your state because he believes, as most Americans now believe, that women deserve a crucial role in running this country."

"Are there any personal reasons?"

"Most certainly there are. He's my fiancé."

"Have you set a date?"

"No. The deal is that I won't marry him unless he wins."

This pronouncement was greeted with appreciative laughter, a good-natured shrug from the candidate, and more flashbulbs.

"Will you predict the outcome of this election, Mrs. Hollywell?"

"The Congressman is the wave of the future. Of course he's going to win! And when he does," she paused and finished with a flourish, "he'll never for a moment allow himself to be locked in his bedroom against his will."

Now there were thunderous laughter and applause, for it was well known in the capital city, as she had been told in much detail since she arrived, that the shrewish wife of the Governor of the state, whose husband was a candidate in that very race, had recently locked him in a bedroom of the Governor's Mansion, from which he had telephoned the state police to retrieve him.

Later that night she and his daughter and he strolled down the main thoroughfares. It was Saturday, and she looked about her at a city bursting forth everywhere with bright skyscrapers and merchandise marts and affluent shops and plazas with fountains and restaurants with European names. All around it were suburbs springing fullborn from weed patches and cotton fields, with no one at all knowing quite where it would all end. He had grown up a city boy, he told her as they walked, or at least by comparison with what lay around him, for the country boys had deemed it a city: once a sleepy Southern capital, then in the full tide of a boom, making it more brisk perhaps than it had bargained for.

Already, looking around her now, she missed the serene countenances of Washington.

"It depresses me a little," she said. "It could just as well be Indianapolis, or Dallas."

"We've paid the price," he said. "But it's the best we have."

She pointed to a restaurant called Scandinavia Limited,

set back from a line of palm trees in garish urns. Inside there was violin music, and a long line of customers waiting to be seated.

"I'll bet if we sent in and asked them to play 'Battle Hymn of the Republic' nobody would notice," she said.

"I'm sure that's true, but don't say it in public."

On the sidewalks all around them was a procession of people with a wide range of skin colors, and every so often he paused among them to introduce himself and shake hands.

"Don't you ever stop working, Daddy?" his daughter Annie asked.

"Honey, you'd better get used to it."

"We'll try," Carol said, "but I wish you'd experiment with different kinds of approaches."

They returned to the lobby of the hotel. The lobby itself was enormous, with more trees in urns and running fountains and restaurant tables arranged to resemble sidewalk cafés, and anomalous chandeliers dangling from long cables, and wild birds in an aviary, and balconies on each floor overlooking the main floor and leading upward in a high well that caused a kind of vertigo in reverse, and hanging gardens, and four exposed glass elevators allowing their passengers an unencumbered view on all sides (making a soft whistle as they moved toward the sky not unlike the sound a balloon makes when being deflated), the whole feel of the place suggesting it was actually the *outdoors*. Long lines of people waited for the elevators, handsome couples in evening dress heading for the top and couples with the look of the country upon them: square haircuts and necks burned red from the sun and Saturday clothes, accompanied here and there by children in khakis or blue jeans.

"What in the world are they doing?" she asked.

"They come in from little towns on Saturday to ride in the glass elevators."

All over the lobby were great masses of Negroes, many with Afros and outlandish clothes, and more white country people, and proper patrons waiting to meet someone, all of them lounging on the Danish sofas and chairs or standing about in conversation. Whites and blacks sought out one another in casual chatter; bellboys darted among them on aimless errands; occasionally someone would withdraw a sandwich from a paper sack, or shout in greeting, and from the edges of the scene came an exclamation which sounded very much like "*Hee-haw! Sani-Flush!*"

"It looks like a picnic," the little girl said.

"Well, I guess this has replaced sitting around the wagons by the courthouse on Saturday night," Carol said.

"That's the real truth of it," he said.

"The New South!" she said. "Welcome to your larger constituency."

"Speaking of that," he said, and peremptorily wandered away from them, saying hello to several friends drinking coffee at a table, then moving down the lines waiting for the elevator, shaking hands and fondling the heads of children.

Carol and his daughter found a sofa and sat down next to a Negro man in a green suit and red shoes.

"Look at my father. He's funny when he does that."

"My God, look at him now!"

An old woman in a tiny black hat set at a jaunty angle was embracing him, and as she did so a small crowd suddenly gathered around them. Two teenage Negro girls shook his hand, and in the midst of this activity a little white boy with a camera began snapping pictures.

"He's enjoying it, isn't he?" Annie said.

"So he is, sweetheart." There was a dim look about her eyes when she said it; she looked closely at him again, oblivious to everything except the flesh milling about him, and watching him so immersed there she felt again the familiar stab of apprehension.

THE DAYS PASSED in a flurry of motion. The terrain of the state flashed before her so swiftly that from one moment to the next she was not quite sure where she was, or where she had been the day before. At first she sensed the tremor of the crowds, that electric flow of anticipation, so unmistakable when everything proceeds by expectation. People she had never met appeared from nowhere and briefly became members of their entourage, and he seemed always to be several movements ahead of them, rushing from one engagement to the next, from public meeting to private conference, from one interminable coffee party to another, so that after a time he became a kind of oblong blur, and although she was with him every day, she was seeing less of him than ever before.

For several days in a remote byway of the state they had the use of a private plane, sitting in the back seat with the campaign manager in front by the pilot, moving about the courthouse towns in a torrent of heavy thunderstorms.

"Well, what do you think?" he asked, taking her fingers in his hand, doing his best to stifle his yawn of fatigue.

She yawned too. "Can't we go to Washington for a couple of days of rest and recreation?"

"No, seriously. What do you think?"

"I like just about everything you've done except that damned jar of strawberry jelly." He had gotten in the habit, in the small towns on their itinerary, of using this unusual stage prop, swooping down and picking it up from the platform and saying he believed in putting the jar of jelly "on the lower shelf for the little man."

"Are you happy doing this?" he asked.

"I'm so tired I can't tell."

"Do you remember that day last fall when we drove through Virginia? That bar in Leesburg?"

"I remember it very well."

"It's not much like that down here now. I feel something strange in things. I hope it's not me."

One afternoon, after an appearance in one of the larger country towns where for the first time he was seriously heckled, they were flying at three thousand feet over a ragged landscape of red hills and deep valleys when suddenly they were caught in particularly vicious winds, and then the worst thunderstorm of all. The tiny plane bobbed and tossed against the elements, coughing like a tubercular, and the rain drove against the windows in an ominous dark. She was seized with the most horrible fear she had ever known, and her head felt strangely light, just as it had that afternoon so many years ago when she saw her friend Buddy Carr stretched under the tree in the swampy woods.

She reached across the seat and held him close to her; yet in the instinctual act of needing him she could not help asking herself what she was doing here. Then, when they came out of the storm a few minutes later, she was ashamed she had shown her fear—angry with herself, and with the two men in front who were laughing now, angry also with him for subjecting her not so much to danger itself but to the discomfort of which this most recent hazard was but a momentary component. Never once, even in her awareness of that danger, could she keep Washington from her mind. The contrast between the familiar contours of her whole life there and this new unsettling experience, their ceaseless travels in darkness toward unknown places, made her sense she had come south again to discover something hidden in herself.

When she had seen he was not afraid, this too maddened her. "Why weren't you scared?" she demanded.

"I *was*. I was scared because you were in here too."

"I'd like to shake you out of that equilibrium," she said.

But at the airport of the next small town, as they slid to a halt on the muddy runway, to be welcomed by a delegation of his organizers and a sparse crowd of two or three dozen supporters, she regained her composure. So that when a drawling reporter in a wet seersucker asked her about the storm they had survived, she replied: "I've just switched from a low Episcopalian to a high Episcopalian."

Much of the time she found herself in shopping centers on the peripheries of the larger cities, one like the other in its barren expanse of concrete and asphalt, and the ubiquitous national chains. The crowds they tried to attract there were the most fickle she had seen, as arbitrary as they seemed to be placeless, victims of that catastrophic wanderlust of this generation of Americans, an unknown breed to be pampered and won, by turns hearty, sullen, and malicious. Dappled heat waves shimmered all about her from the sun on the surfaces. Never once did he lose his balance, telling her later that these denizens of progress at the last edge of the great American schizophrenia were well worth winning over, but she could hardly control herself against provocations. In one such place on a scorching afternoon on the edges of a city whose name she had long since forgotten, a large man standing next to her in the front row shouted a savage racial epithet at the candidate, showering her dress with spittle.

"You throwback!" she snapped. "Gorilla!"

Several in the crowd turned at this sudden commotion, and as they did so the man whispered something inaudible to her.

"What did you say?"

"I said, *screw you, bitch.*"

"No." She felt sick.

"Want me to stick it way in?"

She tarried a few moments before stepping backward into the crowd. Reaching far out, she jabbed him in his buttocks with the pin on a campaign button. With his squeal of pain she vanished into the crowd.

On another afternoon at a shopping center the mood of the gathering was curiously festive, as if they expected less to be edified than to be entertained. A large group of Negroes applauded almost every phrase, and far in the rear several hippies had made peace symbols out of long sticks of licorice. Several dozen farmers, in town that day for a meeting, were caught in this contagion. Carol was standing next to his daughter in the crowd, and in the middle of his speech the two of them slipped to the side of the speakers' platform and took the jar of jelly, which had been sitting unnoticed near the edge of the rostrum. Soon he promised the crowd he would leave the jar on the lower shelf for the little man, and reached down for his prop.

"Where is the damned thing?" he whispered, his words coming out clearly over the loudspeakers. Carol had rehearsed his daughter well, for she shouted now for all to hear: "How about leaving it on the bottom shelf for the little woman, too?" to many roars of laughter.


THEY SAT late one afternoon in a private club high atop the capital city of the state. Below them the lights twinkled in the dusk. She looked down in a reverie, at the phantasmagoric place before them, wondering where its history had gone, only half listening to the conversation between Jack Winter and his most loyal financial supporter.

"I've got to have another twenty-five thousand dollars by the end of next week. Either that or cut back to nothing."

The man sipped on a martini in concentration. "Okay," he said finally, "I think I know where to go."

Jack Winter nudged Carol. "We'll be late." Then he sighed and laughed, turning to his friend. "You know something?" he said. "Most men who can get the money necessary to be elected U.S. Senator don't deserve to be in the U.S. Senate."

They drove late into the nights. Bugs splattered on the windshield. The speedometer stayed at seventy on the flat empty highways, and they wheel-straddled dead dogs, cats, and snakes, switching the radio to Del Rio for the gospel singing and the religious advertisements. One Confederate statue faded into another. Somewhere there would be an enormous road sign saying JESUS SAVES! in large block letters, sponsored by the local Ford dealer, and far out in the distance a solitary brick building, an old courthouse in some forgotten town that had been abandoned years before when the railroad went the wrong way. Everywhere were the ghosts of Sherman's soldiers, and old men in khakis under awning shades, lost in a loneliness too big to understand.

They rode into country where the wind whistles when you drive through it and the old people sit around tables in railroad towns playing dominoes in general stores. They had an appointment with a former Congressman who once represented that district and who was now supporting Jack Winter; for a whole afternoon he was going to ride with them.

From the back seat Carol and two workers drowsily watched the red country roll away before them. In front the candidate and his manager talked on.

"I wish I knew half what this old man knows," Jack said. "They were a breed to themselves. They were born poor, educated in the little colleges or not at all. Full of common sense and the Bible. He had ten terms before some rich bastard got him. At first his platform was the Golden Rule. But he got smarter in Washington."

They drove into a little town, all vacant and dusty, with stores boarded up, giving it a look of despair and age. Jack Winter pointed to the Blue Front Café. "He'll be in there," adding, "maybe Carol will tell Jennie Grand about him."

The man who got into the car with them was skinny and wrinkled, with a devilish grin and a long, beaked nose and skin like old leather. He said hello to everyone all around, then took Carol's hand and bowed deeply.

"Well, Congressman," he said to Jack, "anybody put any dead cats on your front porch lately?"

"Can you get me some votes around here, Congressman?"

"I can rustle up a few. Maybe not an absolute plurality."

"That girl back there's from Washington City."

"Bless her soul. See that courthouse square there, Miss? Back in '42 one night there were eight thousand people there at a rally for me. I was a little late and I walked up to some fellow in back and said what's goin' on, and he said they'd been waitin' three hours to hear their *Congressman*."

"I would've waited too, Congressman," Carol said.

He sat on the edge of the seat. He was excited, and he pointed out old landmarks. "When I first came here from Virginia, this was lush country. It's not much to look at now. There ain't enough money to put up a white frame church, but I still think it's the greatest country in the world. It still reminds me a little of those Blue Ridge mountains. I just can't be away forty-eight hours without missing it."

"The Congressman's a Primitive Baptist," Jack said.

"We believe in the final perseverance of the saints. We

believe that what *is* to be, will be, even if it never happens. Stop! Let's go into this old store."

It was the first of several stops that afternoon in weather-beaten crossroads towns, all of them much the same. Carol followed them at a distance. She smelled the dry pork and bacon and saw the same wrinkled faces. He introduced himself simply and said, "This young boy's runnin' for the United States Senate and I'm with him one hundred and three percent." All the faces in the store would come to life, and the old people would get up slowly and shake his hand, then the candidate's. "And he played football at the *state university.*" Many of them had met the old man and shaken his hand years before. The man who sold groceries in Leon had met him at Winfroe in 1944. The son of the farmer in Lonny once went to one of his rallies in Franklin, six years old and bawling all the way through the speech. Sometimes they would not say a word, but just stand there and stare at him. A group of old people at a café further on gathered around him to remember the campaign of 1940. "No livin' in the past!" he admonished. "Vote for this boy. This boy needs you."

"I'll *swan*, I thought you was dead," a woman behind a meat counter said. "Why'd you quit runnin'?"

"I decided to retire against my will, but this boy, he's on his way to the top. Remember his name? Can you spell it?"

Carol began taking him by the arm before the long afternoon was over. "I could support *you*," she whispered.

"It's a rough business, girl. There's meanness in it. You got to get used to it. You got to love it. It's *violence*—it's rhetorical violence and physical violence."

"Were you ever afraid?"

"Sometimes."

"What would you do?"

"I'd remember the Humble Master. And sometimes St. Paul. They wrapped snakes all over him, and threw him in the Mediterranean Sea, and he kept right on goin'."

She was almost asleep, her head propped on a cushion on the back window of the car, when they finally returned to his town in the darkness; she heard the conversation from the front as from afar.

"Did we get some votes today, Congressman?" Jack asked.

"I believe we did. But it's all changed. I'm not sure."

"How do you think I'm doing?"

"Run scared, boy."

Awake now, she leaned over in the seat and touched him gently on the shoulder. "And remember the Humble Master and St. Paul."

"That's it. Remember!"

SHE FOUND IT more and more difficult. The cities were at least reasonable, but in many of the raw country towns of the interior the undertaking they had embarked upon became progressively more somber. He was working harder than she had ever seen a man work. From dawn until far into the night he toiled among them, so that by noon or earlier each day he was drenched in sweat, with swaths of dust on his face and his shirt, his right hand red and swollen, his voice harsh with strain. In such moments, when he returned to some cheap motel for fatigued lovemaking or four or five hours of fitful sleep she began to wonder why he was doing it, pondered the sources of an ambition that could carry a man to the farthest edges of collapse.

In her own weariness the pursuit became grimmer for her. Before a nasty crowd in a middle-sized city he was struck by several raw eggs. The beseechings of wretched people began to strike despondency in her. An unemployed young veteran with a twitch in his cheek approached him in front of a drugstore one day, spelling out his troubles in angry sobs. People approached him in the streets for handouts, so that he began carrying both pockets full of quarters. An old woman described her difficulties, 120 dollars a month in social security and hospital bills she could not pay, growing so hysterical she almost threw herself at his feet.

With mounting horror she watched an episode unfold before a civic club in a town near the state line. It was a weekly luncheon, and four or five dozen men sat at two long tables and heard him out in hostile silence. At last one of them, a twig of a man with a reedy mouth, stood up and interrupted:

"Who brought this man here?" he demanded. "It's the duty and the honor of every young American to die for their country."

She saw Jack Winter grasp the rim of the podium so hard that his knuckles turned white. Then he said calmly, emphasizing each word:

*"Old men babble while young men die!"*

From all sides there was an angry outcry. Two husky men left their tables and approached the candidate menacingly. The resident preacher managed to mollify them. The meeting was quickly adjourned.

Outside, as they were getting into their car, several of the group stood to the side and gazed at them with open contempt. One of the men brushed past her and said: *"Slut."*

In that instant something snapped in her. In the car she began to cry. She felt like a child, and she wanted to go home.

The contrast between all that Jack Winter was exposing

her to here and the place in which she had grown to maturity—Washington with its settled ways and its civilized façades—was becoming too vast a chasm for any act of hers to bridge. The rawness and desperation had surprised and stunned her. Washington at its pinnacle, even Washington at its most restricting, had isolated her. The ambivalent world of her city's politics, muted as it was by the careful forms to which she had grown inured, had over the years deluded her, for beneath its pleasant Georgetown dinners, the play of its banter and gossip, its careful parliamentary devices, lay all the madness and cruelty of an uncertain society.

Once again she wondered why she had come. She had misgauged herself, and now she was genuinely frightened. The fear that had grown in her since her arrival must have spoken much in that moment about America. She had not expected to see how fragile it all was, its rampant tensions and antagonisms. Had she become too fine to descend into its mire? Had she lost something of her own inheritance?

He leaned across the seat of the car. "I'm sorry, Carol."

"Please take me back to the motel. I'm very tired."


SHE MOVED ABOUT with them as before, but with a new uneasiness. Along the way she examined the faces of people in a different light; they baffled and repelled her. She had forgotten the impoverishment of these small Southern towns; she had forgotten their suspicions. He took her to meetings in Negro churches in the countryside echoing with their *amens*, and on endless walks in early mornings around the courthouse squares, where inevitably he would finish in a private meeting with the town's party leader, in a law office or a barber shop, a pool hall or a JP's court, never once allowing her to accompany him to these sessions, but leaving her instead on a street corner with an ample stack of circulars.

She was distributing circulars in just such a town when she felt an unexpected tug on her elbow and a familiar voice which said to her:

*"I never would've thought it."*

Turning, she saw Elaine Rossiter, notebook in hand, sweating with uncertain dignity in the dusty country noon. The sardonic visage of her friend comforted her. They embraced. "Elaine, I'm so glad you're here. I can't tell you how out of character you look." Indeed, in her Lord & Taylor apparel, and with her expression of Yankee incredulity, Elaine Rossiter had all the appearances of a Georgetown dandy who was roughing it.

She had driven in a rented car from the capital city, and she was briefly there to assess one manifestation among many of "the new breed in an election year." They retired to a café for tumblers of iced tea.

They talked for a time about Washington. "Seeing you makes me homesick," Carol said, and this was true, for the sudden appearance of her girlhood friend whom she had associated for more than a decade with the agencies and the embassies and the townhouses and who had always seemed a monitor to her very existence, sitting now at a table in the Bon-Ton Café with several flies vying for better position at the sugar bowl, caused Carol to feel just how much she might be roughing it too.

"Where is the candidate?" Elaine asked.

"He's making a deal with the ruler in the Duggett and Permenter Feed and Seed Store."

"And where are all the young people?"

"Honey, they left the farm long before you arrived. Look for them in the shopping centers."

"It's going to be very difficult for him, you know," Elaine said.

"How do you know?"

"It's my job to know. It appears they're beginning to gang up on him."

"Oh." She stared vacantly at the courthouse across the street.

"You look tired. It's the first time I saw a Southern belle with big circles under her eyes."

"I guess I am."

"How *are* you?"

All the travail of the last days bore upon her anew, so that in a great rush she described her feelings for Elaine, all the scenes she had witnessed, and her own doubts.

"Do you really want to see him elected?"

"What a terrible thing to say. Of course I do."

There was a long silence now, until finally Elaine said: "I was never jealous of you like the others. I respect you, and I understand."

"Understand what?"

"That there's a trap in being golden."

"I don't . . ."

"You learned so much so fast, and you got what you wanted so quickly. You never for a moment stopped believing in your own wonderment, or that it was enough to carry you wherever you wanted to go."

"No."

"Grime and toil. That's what all greatness takes. My people are sufferers."

"And mine?"

"They have too much pride."

"I don't agree."

"Do you hate me for saying this?"

"No. You make me sound like an aristocrat."

"I may be a bitch, but I believe in you."

"Well, thanks for that."

"Let's go find the statesman."

Later that night the three of them, with two of his assistants, met in one of the rooms of the motel. They indulged themselves in the rare pleasure of cocktails from a flask. He and Elaine drifted away to a corner for a long conversation, and when they returned he was worried.

"What is it?" she whispered to him.

"She confirms my feelings. I've got to get some more television money."

"Shall I telephone my ex-husband?"

"I wouldn't mind if you telephoned Goebbels."

They walked down a farm-to-market road to a restaurant for dinner. From all around them came the sound of katydids, and in the still summer twilight dark thunderclouds gathered at the horizon. Elaine, trying valiantly to lift the spirits of the group, said: "Do you know I've never believed in drinking red wine at room temperature?"

"Is that right?" he said, with abstract courtesy.

"I'm going to order us two of the biggest bottles of Beaujolais in the Scrubbs Restaurant."

"That's wonderful, Elaine," Carol said.

"That's really good of you, Elaine."

The waitress, a buxom country girl with long yellow hair, came to their table. "Do you serve your Beaujolais cold?" Elaine asked.

"What's that you say?"

"Your Beaujolais. Do you have any on ice?"

"Bo-*what?*" By now the girl seemed to fear she was at the mercy of rogues.

"What do you serve to drink?" Elaine persisted.

The girl gazed blankly at her for a second, then said: "*Coke . . . R. C. . . . Nehi Strawberry . . . Orange Crush . . . and Dr. Pepper.*"

Carol and Jack looked at each other knowingly, then doubled up with laughter. It was their first real laugh since she had purloined the jar of jelly, and their last, possibly, for a long time.

TWO WEEKS OR so before the election she flew back to Washington for a few days to visit with her son. She telephoned Jennie Grand; they chatted for a time, then Jennie said to her:

"I suppose I shouldn't tell you this, but Elaine got back the other day and told me about the rumor they're spreading about you down there."

"What is it this time?"

"That you've slept around with every politician in Washington."

"Is that all?"

"And that you have a reputation here of being a very high-class whore."

Carol paused to absorb this intelligence. "Well," she said, with not much passion behind it, "that's something you've just got to expect."

"Is it really?"

"Yes."

"Something's happening to you down there, isn't it?"

"I don't know."

That night she gave a large dinner, an evening from her past, with two or three State Department people, a Senator and his wife, and old friends from television. She entertained them with amusing stories from her campaign travels, omitting for reasons all her own the savage details, the excesses which haunted her, and then she sat back and sipped wine and listened contentedly to the light sound of the familiar voices, and looked about the room with its bric-a-brac and its solid American furniture, and all this filled her with such feelings of security that she closed her eyes for a moment to savor them in repose.

When the telephone rang she went out to take it, knowing who it was.

"Regards from the third largest city in the state," he said. In the background she could hear voices and music.

"Is that an orchestra?" she asked.

"It's Junie and Tuffy Barlowe and their Peach Pickers. We're in the Last Stand Room of the Joseph Johnston Hotel. It's been an awful day until now."

At that moment, although she had not intended to until she met him there on the weekend, she told him what Jennie had reported to her.

"I know," he said. "I heard about it a long time ago."

"I can't hear you over that noise."

"I said I knew about it."

"Why didn't you tell me?"

"I expected it all along. I thought about it. It helps more than it hurts."

"What do you mean?" She was caught in a trance of enmity.

"Remember last week when that fat man asked me if *I'd* marry one, or let my children?"

"Yes."

"And I looked at his dumpy wife and asked him, 'Would *you* marry Lena Horne?' It's much the same principle."

"I don't quite understand."

"They all secretly yearn for a little glamour and wickedness, even down here."

"I see. So I'm the pawn for their hidden desires."

"Don't take it so seriously. Come on back down. I miss you."

Understanding it as she did, she was still angered by his response, and when she returned to join him again she might have reacted with no charity whatever. But the exertions drained them all now as the election approached; and although she did not fully comprehend it, her anger and reproachfulness had become altogether academic.

Finally, three days before it was over, they were at a rally in a city not far from the state capital. The school gymnasium was barely half filled, the heat was so oppressive that her blouse clung wetly to her skin, and the odors of old perspiration and the pervasive vapors not unlike mildew made her slightly dizzy. She took a deep breath and settled into a seat near the temporary stage, almost not hearing the familiar introductions from the local people, and when he began the same speech she had sat through on a dozen similar evenings, employing the same stories, the same pleas, the same punctuated cadences to draw forth applause, she became drowsy and fell asleep. Then she awakened with a start. Something was happening there in the hall before her, something intangible that pierced her heart, causing her to search for the sources of her forlorn apprehension. What could it be? She looked at him on the speakers' platform, a lean figure, deeply tanned and with short-cropped hair, seeing him now through the lulled impressions of fatigue as if she were watching him for the first time, as if he were anyone but the man who had known and loved her, but rather a stranger, an intruder on all the dramas and expectations of her existence. For the first time he had the look of age upon him. His forehead was lined with effort, his face ragged with weariness, his casual badinage long since vanished; he seemed to be pleading in an almost wretched desperation for sustenance. Then she looked into the crowd, at the languid faces, the listless movement of a hundred paper fans, the expressionless disregard, and in that instant, in this sinister room that disgusted her, she knew he was beaten.

THEY HAD RETURNED to the capital city on the eve of the election, and the hot breath of the town had suffused her from far out, as if somewhere among its bright façades lay the roots of her premonition. On the long final journey into the city she was thoughtful. Had she remained with him out of her old perpetual need for novelty and display? Or did she truly believe in him? She had labored valiantly with him, and now she felt she was approaching yet another coda, the time again for some fanciful beginning. The thought of it strangely excited her.

On the back seat of the car next to her, with the sirens of two police motorcycles blaring in front of them, he had scribbled something on the back of a campaign card and handed it to her. She looked at the writing: "*D.R.T., C.S.A.*"

"What's this?"

He laughed. "Your granddaddy, silly. Keep it for good luck."

She would recall the last night in much detail: the boisterous scene in the big hotel, the large crowds which had gradually drifted away, the tears rolling down his daughter's cheeks and how he had tried to make her laugh. Before the television cameras his campaign manager had said, "He has

taught both his friends and his enemies the elemental lessons
of civility," and then there was the candidate himself and his
concession before the scatterings of the faithful. He had
embraced her and said, "At least you won't be rolling ban-
dages with the other Senate ladies for a while."

"Oh, well."

"I'm a lawyer again."

"And you need about three days' sleep."

"Then I'd be ready to start all over."

He had stayed there for a time to take care of whatever
matters remain in defeat. Alone now on her home ground in
Georgetown, she sat quietly in the back garden of her house,
remembering those last hours in his home state; surely they
held some meaning for her. Now she savored the solitude
she had so momentarily abandoned. She had watched Jack
Winter throw all his ambitions and talents into his quest,
and she had seen what it had done to him: the fixed public
face, the gradual erosion, she suspected, of that deep private
side she admired, the terrible fatigue and the pain of loss.
She and Jennie went to a restaurant for lunch. A group of
self-regarding old Republicans sitting at a nearby table filled
her with contempt, and a more colorful cadre of elderly
Democrats unsettled her more so, and when she heard their
conversation, the same phrases of righteousness and acquisition, she wondered if there was anything new to know.

We are all bound together, she believed she was learning,
as if no one had ever before discovered it, in a great bond of
imperfection. Nothing worthwhile lasted! With all his sturdy
promise, the panegyrics of the Elaine Rossiters and all the
others, Jack Winter himself had not endured. Lovers tired of
love, of the formless monotonies of passion; to invest one's
love was to bargain in suffering, to court the worst deceits.

At last, her heart was telling her, she had come full circle. Everything led to oblivion.

All the disturbing words of Elaine Rossiter in the café in the small Southern town she somehow managed to bury away. As consciously as one retreats before some natural calamity she turned her back upon them. To start all over again? He had let her down. *He was a loser.* Out of all these despairing thoughts, whirling within her like dervishes, she resolved that somehow she must leave him.

CONGRESSMAN WINTER returned now as the classic lame duck, and as the hot season slipped away again into autumn the attentions once given him seemed to vanish overnight. The work of his office went on now by rote, but all its excitement and satisfactions had vanished also. Intent all the while to affirm that she was not deceiving herself, she clung to him briefly out of habit.

One day in late September he took her and her son to the waterfront restaurant where they had come before. The skies threatened rain; they sat at the same table by the broad windows, hearing the echoes of the boats' horns and the light splash of water on the wooden sidings.

For a moment he tried to interest her in a vote that had been taken in the House that day. He described meeting a colleague later in the men's room off the floor.

"There was old Thompson getting a shoe shine and smoking a big cigar," he said. "I'd barely exchanged five words with him since I've been here, and he leaned down and said, 'Goddamn it, Winter, I envy your position. You could vote to legalize gold and you could get away with it now. Just think what you could do about marijuana and abortion.'"

He must have felt her discomfort, for suddenly he said, with a dry chuckle: "Do you know when a man like me is deprived of something he truly wants and needs, it's a form of sickness—almost a physical sickness?"

His look of distress surprised her. Her mind dwelled for a moment on their first days together. She put her hand on his.

Her son had been exploring the wharves, and now he returned and sat down. "Do you remember that party for a tree?" he asked.

"How could I ever forget it?"

"Me neither."

"If I were you I'd sit still and not grow a day older."

"Not me!"

"Me then," Carol said.

"Why did you tell me Andy Jackson played for the Redskins?"

"I was testing you again."

"Where is he this time?"

"He's home changing political parties."

"Will you miss Washington?"

"You bet I will."

During dinner a former member of the Cabinet, a powerful figure with swarthy features much photographed in the surrounding press, now considered a certain winner in the general election for the U.S. Senate from a neighboring state, walked across to greet them. Three other men accompanying him remained discreetly removed, and from the adjoining tables people stopped to stare. The man chatted amiably with the two of them, then turned to Carol.

"I imagine you can't remember when we first met."

"Indeed I do," she replied.

"At a dance in Georgetown. In November of 1957."

"Mr. Secretary, certainly not. It was October of 1957."

"You were right off the plantation, I believe. Almost as beautiful as now, but very innocent and naive."

"Not all that naive, certainly."

"And then all those parties at the French Embassy. Remember? The whole world before us."

"Well, it seems happy now. Maybe it was then too."

"If I win this election and assuming we buy a house in Georgetown, how sound would your advice be on furnishing it?" The visitor looked assuredly at the two of them and smirked, rolling his eyes toward the sky.

"It would be absolutely expert, of course."

"In the event, then, I'll call you."

"I hope you will."

"Good luck in November," Jack Winter said.

"And you, Congressman, will you come back as a lobbyist? They all do, you know."

"No, sir, not this one."

As she was driving them later through the city, past Old Treasury and the White House and Lafayette Square, the rain finally began to fall, mists were forming among the trees on all sides, and the white exteriors of the immense buildings loomed like ghosts all about them. She looked at the familiar landmarks; everything was in its place for her.

Her son was sitting on his lap, and she saw Congressman Winter looking out the blurred windows at the statues drifting by. He was laughing to himself.

"What is it?"

"Nothing lasts in this town, does it? I guess even the really powerful find that out sooner or later."

"I could've told you that."

"No. I had to learn it myself."

"You were too impatient."

"And you? Were you ever too impatient?"

"Once upon a time long ago." She looked straight ahead, at the play of the rain on the avenue. Suddenly she remembered the man in the rally at the shopping center, the one she had jabbed with the campaign pin. "More and more I suppose I feel like waiting," she said. She wondered how she would tell him.

# 10

A few days later he was to return home again for a long
stay to re-establish his law practice. Just before he left
he asked her to drive through northern Virginia once more
and spend Saturday night in the same inn in Harper's Ferry.

As they traveled through the rolling country she remembered the pleasure of their journey there almost precisely a
year before, the splendor of it in the hues of autumn, her
own fine mood. The lanes and farms and hamlets which had
seemed so assuring to her then failed to stir her now. The
hazy outlines of the Blue Ridge as they moved westward in
silence seemed a little forbidding, as if she were entering
once again some uncharted terrain of her own existence.
Even the little boys in bright sweaters throwing footballs in
the parks of the tiny towns seemed inches taller and a year
older. This landscape which she had loved for years was a
map on her consciousness, and as with her own town by the
river whenever she returned after a long exile, she saw now
the hills and trees and byways in a strange perspective, as if

what she was seeing was not real, but blurred images caught in her imagination from a simpler time. Some churning awareness of her own transience, of the cataclysms of her spirit, made her look across at him.

Jack Winter was being kind and thoughtful. He tried for a time to talk with her. Her silence made him grow quiet in turn. Now they were in Leesburg once again, in the midst of the same Saturday noon bustle and movement, and when they drove past the courthouse green there was the Jeb Stuart Bar and Grill.

"Let's go back in," he said. "I really *could* use the practice this time."

"Please. I couldn't."

"Just a few minutes?"

"No. Please."

Soon they were in the terrain of sharp rises and falls, the orchards and farmlands, and on toward the crests of the mountains and West Virginia. By midafternoon they reached Harper's Ferry.

She stood on the porch of the old inn and looked into the darkening valley below. Her first sight of the confluence of the Potomac and the Shenandoah had exhilarated her, but now, in the chill sunlight, the whole vista, the sharp waters, the town below the bluffs, filled her with desolation.

"It's run by the federal government," she whispered to him. "Now it's only a toy."

"Carol, for God sakes, what's wrong?"

She sat down in a rocking chair. Her gaze focused on the canoes in the Shenandoah rapids. The past washed over her, the dreamy innocence of summer days of her childhood on Anderson's Ridge when she watched the boats in random procession on the river far below, and she felt the irony of where she was, of the fickleness of her years, of why she had again come so dramatically to this porch in the mountains.

> *In a Wonderland they lie,*
> *Dreaming as the days go by*
> *Dreaming as the summers die.*

From somewhere far away she heard his voice. He was asking her to marry him. She swayed back and forth in the rocking chair.

She shook her head.

"Remember all the things we feel the same about?" She had never heard him so beseeching. "You were great down there. You have courage."

"I don't."

His plea now, like all the quests seeking some enduring affirmation from her through all her days, evoked the same fear she had felt in the airplane in the thunderstorm, in the shopping centers with their miasma of faction, in all the desperation and anger she had witnessed there; they were all of a piece, the only fear she had ever run from. It went so deep in her that she believed in that moment she would rather be alone for the rest of her life than take the smallest chance of begrudging her reluctant soul.

The wind rustled in the pines. From far beneath them came the whistle of a train. She drew her coat about her and looked at him standing before her, the handsome face with the cracked noseline, the assessing eyes.

"I'm very sorry," she whispered. "It's not possible."

"Don't be a fool. Stop looking at the stars."

"Why should I change? I've tried before."

"Trust me. You'll never find anything this good."

"I can't."

"Why can't you?"

"Because it's not enough."

He leaned down and fiercely took her face in his hand. For an instant she believed he might crush her. "I knew it when I first met you," he said.

"What?"

"That you'd finally see yourself as unattainable."

"Oh?"

"I'll be back again. Things are changing down there. Does it matter that much to you?"

"No."

"Then what's wrong with being associated with a lawyer?"

"It's not that. I can't leave Washington."

"It's not Washington," he replied bitterly.

But now something was calling her, voices from far within her. "I've got to leave now," she said. She rose and stood next to him. "I'm going to take the car and go home. Please don't stop me."

At first he said nothing. He stood on the porch with his hands on his hips and gazed savagely at her for a long time.

"Very well."

He went inside and returned with her suitcase. She followed him as he walked down the steps of the porch and put it in the back seat of the car. As she slipped behind the wheel he leaned down again, his hand lightly touching her arm, and then he said, very softly: "I truly don't understand. Have I done anything to make you distrust me?"

"No."

"Then sooner or later I suppose you'll catch up with it, if you ever decide what it is."

"Yes."

But already he was coincidental. The car rolled down the grassy drive and she caught one last glimpse of him, solitary in the dying afternoon. Then she drove home, past the crests of the Blue Ridge, past the square in Leesburg, past the cemeteries and tossing meadows of Virginia, past Arlington and the Monument and the memorials, toward the Washington that awaited her.

# $\mathcal{V}$OICES OF THE $\mathcal{S}$OUTH

Erskine Caldwell, *Poor Fool*

Fred Chappell, *The Gaudy Place*

Ellen Douglas, *The Rock Cried Out*

George Garrett, *Do, Lord, Remember Me*

Willie Morris, *The Last of the Southern Girls*

Lee Smith, *The Last Day the Dogbushes Bloomed*

Elizabeth Spencer, *The Voice at the Back Door*

Peter Taylor, *The Widows of Thornton*

Robert Penn Warren, *Band of Angels*

Joan Williams, *The Morning and the Evening*